I0761949

PLAYING WITH FIRE

SOE CIRCUIT FORTUNAE BOOK 2

THOMAS WOOD

Thomas Wood

Cover Design by Olly at MoreVisual Ltd.

Visit my website at www.ThomasWoodBooks.com

Printed in the United Kingdom

First Printing: August 2020

by

BoleynBennett Publishing

The Circuit Fortunae Series

Into the Storm (Prequel)

Don't Look Back

Playing with Fire

Close Quarters

Other series by Thomas Wood

Gliders over Normandy

The Trench Raiders

Alfie Lewis Thrillers

1

"How do they come up with such rubbish?" Mike said, thumping at the glove compartment that kept dropping open as we sat there.

"What's wrong with it?" I quipped, knowing with a certainty that I had pushed the right buttons. "I quite like it."

"It's dreadful. It's underpowered, cramped and look at the paintwork on it. It's hardly appropriate is it?"

"I don't know what you mean," I said, my head leaning over the steering wheel, as I looked at the black bonnet, with a splash of red coming from the wheel arches.

He looked towards me, his eyebrows raised, eventually clocking onto the fact that it was merely an exercise in winding him up. He seemed to bite regardless.

"Johnny, we're two agents, living in Nazi-occupied

France. We're sitting in a car, at the end of a street, in broad daylight. The paintwork on this car is just the icing on the cake to a very big advertisement of who we really are."

"We haven't been found out yet," I retorted, as quickly as I could.

He seemed to slump down several inches on the padded bench that we shared in the car, his irate state doing nothing to conceal us.

"If she keeps on the way that she is, it won't be long," he muttered, his eyes now just above the dash-board. His head nodded out towards the front of the vehicle, which, following the long, sleek bonnet of the car, was pointed down *Rue des Culeveaux.*

The *Rue* ran eastwards, leading into the small village of *Langeais,* which apparently seemed stuck in the sixteenth century. Its old buildings and houses stood set in the very same stone in which they had been for at least one hundred years, the church spire pricking the skyline with pride.

It had seemed like the best place to arrange a meeting to us. It was not too far from *Restigné,* where we had been living for the last two months, but equally not too much of a journey from the city of *Tours.*

It was quiet which, although it seemed to bother Mike no end, it meant that we would be able to sniff out trouble before it had even started.

But, perhaps most importantly, the small village of *Langeais* had more than one exit out of it. We could exit to the west and make for *Restigné,* or head east into *Tours.* There were even options to head north and south if we were really pressed.

Although we must have been the first men to drive an automobile into this small commune of France, I felt quite safe. As if the war hadn't quite touched this part of Europe just yet.

"Why can't you trust her?" I asked. I spoke gently, so as not to rile him or frustrate him.

He had become something of a pessimist in the last few weeks, since we had ambushed the German convoy some weeks before. It was a dangerous place to be, one that I had to consciously avoid, particularly after we had seen Alfred's home being burnt to the ground.

He had been the one constant during our first few weeks in France, that had acted as our ballast. But now, he was gone. And, like a ballast, it seemed that Mike was beginning to wobble slightly without it.

"What, and you do?"

"I think she has proved herself."

"That's not the same thing, Johnny."

We sat in a silence once more, one that we had become so used to since we had first begun training for our new roles.

Sitting still and in a quiet is not something that comes all that naturally to a fighter pilot but, by the patience and perseverance of our instructors, we had somehow been able to come up with a pretty good impersonation.

The cab of the car started to warm up gently, as the sunlight became ever more attracted to the tin can that we sat and waited in. A dampness began to make itself known under my arms and I began rolling my shoulders to try and get some air to them. I dabbed my brow with the back of my sleeve also.

Mike did the same.

He let out a long, drawn-out sigh, as I felt his body sink further into the bench. He seemed exhausted.

His dark, brooding features were engulfed further still by the ominous bags that had started to form under his eyes. As I looked at his sulking frame, slumped into the bench, it would be quite reasonable to assume that he hadn't been to sleep in weeks.

It was strange, I thought as I sat there with him, as in the few weeks that we had since we had made our arrival known to the Germans, I had never slept better in my life. It was almost as if the long periods of waiting, after a short burst of excitement, was perfect to catch up on the rest that I would inevitably lose later on.

But, for Mike, something was niggling at the back of his mind, that must have been keeping him up into the small hours.

"Do you think we'll get to see Britain again?"

I didn't like questions like that, as it always threw me off what it was I was meant to be doing. But I knew for Mike, it was something to focus on. It would give him the drive he needed to pick himself up from the pit that he was in.

That was what I liked about him. No matter how far down the well he had been thrown, he would never succumb. He would always try and pull himself out somehow.

"I'm not sure I really want to. But, yes. We'll see this war out."

I had said what I had needed to, as I felt his shoulders stiffen as he hauled himself up slightly. He would only need another few inches and he might actually be able to see down the road.

But it was a start.

"Do you reckon this will actually result in anything?" he asked, nodding his head down the street. "You know, Alfred. Do you think we'll find out what happened?"

I shrugged. Silence again. It wasn't really worth thinking about. Not if I wanted to get any sleep that night anyway.

I was shocked to hear a familiar clink and, upon turning to face Mike, saw that he had withdrawn his pistol. It was sitting in his lap comfortably, his hands folded over it to conceal it from whoever might happen to walk past us.

No one had done in the twenty minutes or so that we had sat there, but we had both learned that we had to expect everything to happen, in order to be able to deal with it.

"I'm sure there's no need for that."

"Really?" he quizzed. "Then what was the point in you brining yours along as well then?"

He smirked, which grew into more of a grin as he watched me do the same.

I pulled the French pistol out from under my thigh, where I had kept it as we drove. Keeping it well below the windows of the old Renault, I dropped the safety lever from its upright position, before pulling the hammer back slightly.

The lever would now allow, when the trigger was squeezed, for the hammer to fall on the firing pin, thus ejecting a round. I didn't need to check the weapon again to see how many rounds I had; I had loaded it myself. Besides, to check again would merely increase the chances of someone else seeing it. I knew there were eight rounds in the magazine.

We said nothing more for a few moments, as we both embraced the stillness of the village that we were in.

"I don't like all this waiting around," I said, wiping the perspiration from my palms, resting them on the steering wheel. "I feel vulnerable."

"If you trust Suzanne then you have no need to feel like that."

I looked over at him with a chuckle, his eyes glistening with a faint hint of the happiness that I had first encountered when we had met.

His mouth dropped from his ears, just before mine. He had heard the noise first. His brain, although swamped with thoughts of home and defeatism, was clearly more alert than mine.

The shockwave of the explosion took half a

second to reach our ears, bursting the eardrums when it did. For a few seconds, it felt like I was underwater, giving off a peace that I had not enjoyed in a long time.

Mike experienced it too, as we both sat in our own little existences, waiting for the noises of the outside world to catch up with us.

My ears were slower than Mike's, as he began saying something to me that I could not quite work out. But the aggression in his face eventually got through my thick skull.

I needed to drive towards the dust cloud.

I flicked the key that had waited patiently in the ignition and the engine of the Renault spluttered into life. It seemed about as enthusiastic to drive towards the explosion as I was.

As I crunched it into first gear, the engine began to whine as we sped off towards the house. The wheels spun as they fought for grip on the gravel and I struggled with the wheel to keep it in a straight line.

It took us no longer than five seconds to get to the house, but Mike was already impatiently yanking at the door handle, swinging the door open before we had even come to a stop.

"Wait!" I shouted, before cowering slightly as I screamed out in English.

As if he was just as shocked as I was, he spun around to look at me, his eyes as hungry as ever to find out what had happened.

I let the glass from the blown-out windows tinkle

to the ground, the pitter-patter of displaced brick and mortar falling around us.

"Slowly. We need to be careful."

He didn't want to listen to my advice. But he knew that he had to.

He had always been rash and unpredictable as soon as his heart got pumping, and it had normally been me to make sure that he didn't do anything stupid.

Now was one such moment.

An explosion had gone off. That could have meant any number of things. One possibility was that someone had booby-trapped the house. Which could mean there was more to come.

A soldier could have set off a grenade in the house. Which meant that there was an enemy nearby.

All these considerations, and thousands of other variations, were swimming through my mind as we approached the building. I just had to hope that they were going through Mike's head too.

If he just followed his inhibitions, then we could both be killed.

It was strange though, as we stepped carefully over the broken brick and glistening glass, that Mike would have wanted to rush into this one.

He had not liked Suzanne Seguin, he had made that much plain. He had not trusted her any further than he could have thrown her. But there he was, wanting to get into the house as quickly as possible.

As the dust cloud settled, I found it strange that

there was still little movement in the village. We were the only ones moving.

It was as if the whole village had been evacuated, or as if they knew that something like this would occur and the safest option for them would be to stay away.

"Slowly," I began to mouth to him as we reached the door, which was surprisingly still intact. The same could not be said for the windows. Every single pane had been blasted from its housing by the explosion.

I nodded to him as he placed a palm on the door. I raised my pistol up.

He had been right. I had brought my weapon with me for one reason and one reason only.

I had known that something was going to go wrong.

Softly, he applied the pressure to the door. We stepped inside.

2

I could barely breathe as I stepped into the house. The dust that twirled around in the air clung to the insides of my cheeks, as I sucked in oxygen and threatened to lodge clumps of it right in my airway.

The air was so dense with powder and dirt that I could barely see half a yard in front of me, and had to rely on leaning on the wall to find my way around.

I crouched down low, so that I could see what might be on the floor as I walked. I wanted to minimise the chances of setting off another tripwire, or stumble over a waiting German.

As I looked behind me, I could make out the vague figure of Mike, as he too felt his way along the wall, albeit on the other side to me.

Gradually, we progressed through the hallway and swept into the living area. The furniture was scattered around the room, none on its side, but clearly disturbed all the same.

As we continued to move through the house, I found myself trying to work out where in fact the blast had actually come from. The whole of the downstairs of the house had been caked in a thick layer of grey powder, like you would have expected from a bomb.

But none of the items had been ruined. Nothing had been thrown more than a couple of inches from its normal standing place.

Which could leave only one eventuality.

The bomb had come from upstairs. Which meant that Suzanne would have to be upstairs too.

Something made me stop at the bottom of the staircase, as the dust started to filter out of the windows, allowing me to breathe a little more.

A voice had whispered in my ear, so quietly that it had felt like it was one of my own thoughts.

"What if she's set us up?"

I had no time to argue with him right now. We needed to clear the house and get gone, before any of the sedentary neighbours started to get curious as to what the noise had been.

There was a part of me that believed him though.

She had proved herself as a capable and loyal fighter. But she had fallen in with a German in order to get some of their information. And people like that could never be trusted.

When there were morals as loose as those, then money was never all that far away.

Stopping for a moment at the bottom of the stairs,

I tried to retrace my footsteps of thirty seconds ago. I pictured the back door, and where it led out to.

There was a small garden. A fence, only about hip height. Then another road that ran towards some fields.

We had been waiting in the car for perhaps twenty minutes. That was more than enough time for her to get away.

Maybe she had planted a bomb to go off after a period of time, in the hope that we would have already come in looking for her.

I didn't think it likely, but it was not impossible.

I shook off Mike's comment, opting instead to take my first step onto the stairs.

There was a creak on the first few but, the closer to the peak we got, the quieter they squeaked. It was either that or I was beginning to ignore them, as I prepared for what I may be faced with at its summit.

Electric currents of pain began shooting up through my lower legs, as I kept crouched low to avoid being seen on the stairs any sooner than I needed to be.

I had to keep in mind that it could have been a set up and that there was a platoon of weapons all ready and waiting for my head to pop up.

If that was the case, no amount of crouching would save me, but it was making me feel marginally better.

The noise of the stairs had faded into nothing. So too had the noise of everything else in the house.

There was a numbness to my ears as if they would only be able to pick up on the noises that really counted.

A weapon being made ready perhaps, or the breath of an officer giving an order. Nothing else really mattered. It all became a surplus.

I let my mouth hang open loosely, to eliminate those noises that swim around your head when everything else seems so silent. I needed to be able to hear anything that could change my fortune, as I felt increasingly vulnerable.

I was glad that I was out front though, so that I could set my own pace to proceedings. I was worried about Mike, and the level of rashness that he seemed to jump into things with. At least this way he was held back. It would teach him that getting out quickly was not all that mattered sometimes.

Getting out alive was.

We made it to the landing.

Pressing my back into the wall, I gave the area a once over with a sweeping glance. I did not glean much information whatsoever.

The dust was thicker upstairs than down, and most of it was still finding it difficult to settle on the ground. The fine powder clung to my cheeks again and stuck to my throat.

Wheezing, I pushed off the wall, to begin the task of clearing each room, one by one. Only then could we begin to discern what had happened there.

The first thing that I could make out was a small

table, strewn over the landing, as if it had almost been decapitated.

All four of its highly polished oak legs had been severed from the table, discarding its contents as far as it could.

I ignored it as much as I was able, treading on smaller items while kicking some of the larger ones out of the way.

I stopped by one of the doors, before lunging into the room, expecting to feel the pain of searing bullets the second that I did so. But none of it came.

The room was clear. Clear of Suzanne. Clear of any enemies. Clear of all the windows.

I moved to the next room.

The closer we got to the room at the far end of the house, the thicker the dust became, the more disturbed the furniture was.

As we cleared the second room and drew closer to the final one, I noticed that great clumps of wall were missing, like internal windows into the room.

There was no doubt in my mind, and I was sure Mike's was the same, that this had been the room from which the blast had originated.

It meant that we would have to be doubly careful, in case there was any kind of secondary device that had been rigged to go off the moment someone came in to help.

I scanned the doorway ahead of me, but I could not see anything. The grey mist, that was now hovering in the air defiantly, was preventing me from making any clear judgement.

Carefully, slowly, I ran my hand along the edges of the doorframe, searching for a tripwire or a concealed grenade.

Behind me, I felt Mike's arms stretching out, his pistol raised and covering my every move. If Mike saw anything that he didn't like, it would be his job to get us both out of there. I would need to trust his judgement.

It was a good job that I felt like I did. Otherwise, I would have struggled to get anything done.

As I came to the end of my search, I was grateful that I hadn't felt anything that resembled a booby trap.

But, as I turned away, my little finger got caught on something. Something thin and taught. Something that seemed very much like a tripwire.

I tapped Mike on the leg. He didn't need to know anything more; he would just need to know that I had found something. He would then stay as still as possible.

I placed my pistol on the floor and stretched myself out on my stomach.

Down at a much lower level, I was able to see underneath the blanket of powder that was levitating in the house and I could get down to business.

I could see the wire clearly, and I berated myself for not noticing it sooner. I had almost given Mike the all-clear. I had nearly killed us both.

With the light touch of a spider, I traced the wire with my finger to just inside the doorframe, where I felt a small wooden peg, driven in hard between the bare floorboards.

Lightly caressing the wire, I found that it was wrapped around the peg, only once or twice, but enough to make it as taut as it was.

It was what was on the other side of the peg that I would now have to be worried about.

As my fingers danced along the wire, I felt it. I had been expecting it, but it still filled me with such a dread that I had to stop my fingers from quivering.

There was the heavy ceramic ball, connected by a thin piece of fabric, around which the wire had been wrapped several times.

It was a rudimentary device, and one that seemed to me to have been constructed in a hurry, but it was effective.

All we would have had to have done was rush into the room, and it quite possibly could have been the last thing that we had ever done.

Without wasting any more time than I strictly needed to, I began to unfurl the wire from the peg. The obvious thing to do would be to take the wire away from the grenade, thus rendering it safe.

But the wire was wrapped tighter around the grenade, and it would take me too much time. Time which we didn't have. I needed to make this thing safe, but I also needed to be able to get out of there quickly.

I was rapidly growing in confidence as the wire loosened its grip around the peg, and I felt bold enough to begin muttering to Mike.

"Tripwire…seems like someone left it in a hurry…Must—"

I tugged ever so slightly too hard on the wire, which I was sure didn't matter too much.

But I had heard the sound of something heavy being dragged along the wooden floorboards. It had not been dragged far. But it had been far enough.

In the split second that I had between realising what the noise was, and moving, I could not believe that I had been so stupid.

The trap had been set in a hurry, but not so much of a hurry that they didn't put another grenade on the other side of the door frame.

"Move!" I screamed, launching myself to my feet and finding the nearest bit of wall to bury myself into.

Within two seconds of my realisation, the grenade exploded, reigniting the levitating dust in a more aggressive pattern, whilst simultaneously sending hot shards of metal into the door frame next to me.

The explosion continued to ring like a high-pitched squeal for a number of seconds, but I could still make out Mike's voice as he spoke.

"Well, that's one way to disable it, old fruit."

We had started to run out of options the second the first explosion had gone off, but now that a second one had boomed out through the locality, we were presented with a rapidly diminishing list.

Mike charged in; pistol raised. I followed, the burning hot sensation on my cheeks a mixture of shame and exertion.

Mike stopped, halfway across the room.

It was large, and quite clearly had been someone's study room at one time or another. I was just hoping that they no longer needed it.

The bureau that had faithfully seen many a letter written on it, was now nothing more than a splintered wreck, as was the many draws and cabinets that had littered the room.

In the far corner, a bookcase lay melancholic on its side, old well-thumbed books now lying in tatters around the room.

But it was the arm that poked from the top of it that seemed to grab both of our attention.

That and the head that it was attached to.

3

"Wait," I said, as Mike lunged towards her. "Check that there aren't any more wires first."

We both began to scan the room, like inquisitive children on some sort of treasure hunt. The only real difference being that the treasure we might find could well be the one that killed us.

As we scrabbled around on the floor, I drank the apparent absence of any kind of noise. Nothing stirred at all in the house, not even a slight dust particle. Everything seemed perfectly still, for the first time in a long time.

I began trying to reconvene all my thoughts into one piece, instead of the array of places they had been scattered, as if they too had been subjected to the blast.

The drab, old stone walls were now punctuated with large holes, great chisel-like clumps laying on the floor where they had fallen.

The glass, had there been any in there to begin with, was now completely gone. There was nothing but a peeling and splintered wooden frame, which went quite well with the state of the rest of the room.

The whole place was decimated.

Wardrobes and dressers had cracked and splintered, the bed frame buckled and bent out of shape, even the ceiling had not been immune from damage. Large flakes, almost like snow, began to drift down onto our heads, as a crack ran right the way from one side of the room to the other.

"I can't see anything."

"I guess we better chance it then. Watch the window."

I waited for him to sarcastically tell me that there wasn't one any longer, but we both knew that now wasn't the time to be cracking jokes. He did as I had said, tucking his pistol into his slacks.

"How is she looking?"

I didn't answer. I didn't really know how.

She was lying face down as I got to her, the back of her head matted with blood that was quickly beginning to brown out of impatience. Deep lacerations had penetrated the skin on the backs of her arms, almost like she had been whipped in the most barbaric of ways.

Her clothes, which had seemed so pleasant not half an hour before, were ripped and torn, singed at the corners and clinging to her flesh, which itself was beginning to brown and blacken on account of the burns.

I quickly looked around me. But I could see nothing that could claim to have given her the wounds that she had. The lacerations, singed clothes and burns would all have come from the blast, more than likely the first one that we had witnessed from outside. But what was unexplained was the deep gash in the back of her skull, where blood continued to pour like a burst river bank.

It was larger than any kind of broken wall could manage and the bruising around her neck told me that something must have struck her there also. Something long and straight. Like a plank.

But there was nothing in that room that could have inflicted that sort of injury on her, not close enough to her anyway. Something or someone had struck her across the back of her head.

"Is she alive?"

I tried to roll her over so that I could get a good look at her face. The last thing I wanted was to find that we had been caught out, and Suzanne was long gone.

The body was heavy and uncooperative, which at least filled me with some reassurance. Suzanne had seemed like the most uncooperative person that I had ever met. At least she was being consistent.

Her body slumped morosely as I moved her, I could tell that it was Suzanne. Her face was caked in a mess of blood and dusty powder, but there was no mistaking her.

Her face, still somehow retaining the innocence that had drawn me to her, was buried under a thick makeup, but her features seemed more pronounced than ever. Her petite face, with charming freckles still poking their way through the dirt, seemed quite untouched.

But, as I swept my hands around her face, I found a deep gash that ran along her jawline, so fine that it could almost have been mistaken for a paper cut, had it not been for the great valley that had opened up.

"Is she alive?" Mike repeated again, as I felt him abandon his post and waddle his way over to me.

As he crouched down next to me, I was able to garner some sort of confidence, a reassuring presence.

I felt for a pulse. I kept feeling. Every few seconds I moved my fingers around, refusing to stop until I felt what I was hoping to find.

Then, just as I was about to give up, there was something there. It was weak and erratic, as if her heart was panicking at what to do in this sort of situation. I supposed that it had never before been in this sort of scenario.

"Yes," I gasped eventually, finally letting my breath out in a sigh. "But only just."

Mike sprung to his feet, to retake his post at the glassless window.

"Look," he croaked, remorse drowning his voice. "We need to get out of here. Hastily too. She's obviously had her cover blown and she doesn't look too good neither."

"What are you saying, Mike?"

"Come on, Johnny…We need to make sure that we can get out of here. But to get her out is going to slow us up. And where are we going to find a doctor for her? She's going to need proper help and we're going to be spending a night under the stars now that she's been compromised…She won't last ten minutes overnight."

"We can't leave her."

"Why not? We've both lost people before, Johnny. We had to leave them behind."

A memory flashed across the front of my forehead with a searing pain, both physical and emotional. I had lost plenty of men under my command up in the skies over Southern England, and Mike had too.

I had even lost a dear woman as well, one that I had thought that I would spend a great deal more years with than the few we had managed.

"That was all different."

"Why?"

"There was nothing we could do for those men burning in their cockpits. There was nothing we could do for my wife. They were already dead. There's still hope here."

He chewed away at the inside of his cheek for a moment, perhaps a little too hard as his eyes began to fill up rapidly. He began to scoff and laugh, for what reason I wasn't sure. But it settled the deep-seated fear that had been festering in my gut.

"Alright, old fruit. You win. But if we get into any trouble, promise me one thing."

"What's that?"

"That you will die first."

"Deal."

We smirked at one another, as I began to manhandle the corpse that was Suzanne Seguin. There was no time to do things gently or compassionately, we simply needed to be shot of the place as soon as possible.

Mike's pistol led the way out of the room, as I dragged Suzanne by her armpits.

Mike, showing an almost inhuman strength, bundled Suzanne's legs under one arm, his pistol in the other and guided us down the stairs, setting her down with a grunt when we made it to the bottom.

He had never appeared like a particularly strong man, but he had mustered it from somewhere, and I couldn't help but wonder whether it was out of a desire to get Suzanne out of there, or to help me.

Either way, it didn't matter. We were on the move, and that was all I could focus on for the time being.

Suzanne's body squeaked and resisted as she was pulled over the back bench of the old Renault, Mike conjuring up even more strength as he dragged her from the far side of the automobile.

As he did his best to squeeze her inanimate body into the back of the car, I raced for the driver's side.

I wasted no time in forcing the car into gear, the irritating whine of the engine a welcome blessing to my ears and, within a minute of dragging Suzanne down the stairs, the three of us were on the move once more.

The car seemed intent on trying to roll us over, as we hit every bank and imbalance in the road as we sped along. My backside smashed into the bench with a thump on more than one occasion, and my heart sank as I thought about the kind of damage that I was doing to poor Suzanne.

But we needed to get away and speed was our best chance of doing so.

"Where are we going, Johnny?"

His voice was strained and panicked, which wasn't all that surprising, but I was hoping for something more soothing.

"I don't know! But as far away from this blasted place as possible!"

I could not see his face, but I could tell that his darkened, ruddy features were agreeing with me, just until we could think of something better to do.

We screeched off one side road and onto a bigger one, one that I recognised with an unencumbered relief. I pulled at the wheel and took us west. We were going back to *Restigné*.

I let the car slow naturally for a few moments, before changing down a gear and driving at a more inconspicuous speed. I hoped that not only would it make us appear like more normal travellers but help us both to get our heads together. There was a lot that we would need to talk through in the next few minutes.

"How is she doing, Mike?" I asked, realising for the first time that it had been hours since I had last had a drink of some description.

I began to turn my head to look at him, but a sweaty palm pushed me away.

"Keep quiet. Just drive."

"What's up?"

"Take this right up ahead. Don't signal."

I did as I was told, the tyres losing some of their grip on the gravel as we hared around the corner.

"Where are you taking us, Mike?" I asked, as I negotiated large dips in the road, trying to make things as comfortable as possible for all those involved.

We seemed to be heading up a dirt track of some description, not a paved road by any means. Large, imposing mountain pines sprung up all around us, robbing us of what natural light we had. We hit several holes in the road as a result, the chassis of the car groaning more than I did.

"Mike!"

I demanded, as another undulating bit of track threaten to rob us of one of our wheels.

Eventually, he spoke.

"The car. Behind us. Two men inside. It's been following us for the last couple of miles. They have to be Jerries."

I turned to look.

He was right.

There was no way that they weren't. Who would have followed us up this kind of track, apart from the gamekeeper who patrolled this land? And they never had brand new Mercedes to carry out their work in.

"What do you reckon?" I asked, my hands slipping on the steering wheel in anticipation of his response.

"This one is your choice, old fruit. But I know what I would do."

I sighed, as I tried to guess at how much road we had ahead of us, and how far we could get at speed before we burst a tyre or were sent spinning off into a grave of trees.

As smoothly as I possibly could, I flicked the gear stick into first gear, easing up so slowly on the clutch that I could barely discern any movement from it.

Then, with every ounce of energy that I could muster, I slammed my other foot into the accelerator.

4

The car lurched as it tried with all its might to put up some form of protest. The Renault *Celtaquatre* was low to the ground and rock solid, really not the kind of automobile for the sort of terrain that we were now racing along.

I felt every tiny bump and I feared that the tyres were losing air quicker than a stone in water. The car pulled violently over to one side and I did my best to fight with the wheel to keep it steady.

There were groans coming from behind me, but not from Suzanne as I had hoped. Mike was having a terrible time in the rear of the car, as he did his best to protect Suzanne's body from the undulating terrain and the awful quake of the car.

More than once his head collided with the windows around him, a sobering thud each time that threatened to shatter the glass. His dark, inch-perfect hair was now a memory, as the grease and slime that started to drip from it gave it a life of its own.

Mike's face, which had often appeared moody and forlorn to me, somehow seemed enlightened as he sat in the back of the cab. It was as if the excitement, the not knowing what was going to come next, was enthralling him.

"They're not in uniform," he croaked, in between groans and head smashes. "*Abwehr*? *Gestapo*?"

"Does it matter?" I replied, curtly. To anyone else, I would have felt rude speaking in the manner that I had done, but with Mike, I knew that he understood. We were working, there was no time for small talk.

My arms began to ache as I gripped the wheel even tighter, fighting with the car's every instinct that seemed to want to catapult us from the dirt track. My eyes burned, along with my head, as every ounce of energy was focused on making sure that we got away from the pursuing car.

The octagonal speedometer in front of me reached its plateau, refusing to go any higher than the speed we had settled at. But it wasn't going to be enough. We needed more power. A lot more.

I wanted the one thousand horsepower, V12 liquid-cooled piston engine of a Hurricane to somehow find itself under my command once more. It would make getting away from the Mercedes a lot easier if I was able to fly.

There was suddenly an incredibly strained cry like

someone had captured a fox and was trying their best to throttle the poor thing. Then it called out again.

"Johnny! Hold on, Johnny!"

It was almost as if the little Renault had suddenly been fitted with the Merlin engine that I had so desperately desired, as we lunged forward with a renewed energy and purpose.

I thought for a moment that maybe we had suddenly become considerably lighter but, quickly checking behind me, I realised that all three occupants of the automobile still remained in situ.

Just as I was about to turn around to face the dirt track and trees once more, the car lurched forward again, hopping at least a few feet before settling back down to its normal speed.

It was only then, as I watched the ugly black monster recoil slightly, that I realised what had happened.

The menacing grin of the grill of the Mercedes came in closer again, and this time I felt the crunch of metal on metal as it connected at a more destructive speed.

Still, the faithful Renault resisted the Mercedes, instead opting to carry on unperturbed.

"Johnny…" Mike's voice began to whimper, whinge even. "We're going to have to stop. They're going to get us."

"No," I resisted, gritting my teeth and pressing the pedal down firmer into the body of the car.

I knew what he said was true; the pedal was practically pressing through the floor and if anything, we would begin to slow as the whine of the engine increased.

We were going to have to admit defeat on this little battle.

Mike said nothing more, simply allowing me to reflect on things and come to my own conclusion.

"Alright, but just so that we are on the same page, we are going down with a fight. Aren't we?"

"Absolutely, old fruit."

I could tell that there was a beaming grin across his face as he said it, and the sound of his pistol being withdrawn would only accentuate that.

"Righto. In that case, you better hold on. I have a plan. Anything from Suzanne?"

"She's still out for the count."

"Make sure she doesn't fall off the bench or anything, will you? This one might hurt a little bit."

"Roger that, Red one."

I slowed the car right up, allowing the resistance of the track around us to work its magic, rather than dabbing the brakes. I changed down into first gear, positioning the car in such a way that it might look like we were about to take a turn.

But I continued straight on, waiting for the Mercedes to pull nice and close into us before I made my move.

"Hold on."

It was the only instruction I could think of giving

to Mike, but I listened to it myself as my knuckles whitened on the steering wheel.

There was nothing more to say and, for what felt like the tenth time that afternoon, I plunged my foot into the accelerator, deep and hard, as the car spluttered into life once more.

The Mercedes grew smaller in my mirrors, as we suddenly managed to break free from them for a moment. It did not, however, take them all that long to get back up to speed, and the menacing grin was threatening to punch us once again.

I did not let them have the satisfaction, as I now slammed my foot into the brake, as hard as I possibly could.

With one foot still on the brake, I began manoeuvring around so I could slam the clutch in and select the first gear once again.

My face came within half an inch of smashing into the dashboard, and I heard Mike begin to grunt as he tried his hardest not to fly through the windscreen.

The wheels skidded around on the gravel and for a moment I felt the car swerve, making for a tree at the side of the road but, just at the right moment, there was an almighty crash.

I felt the back of the car begin to crumble, and the sound of metal contorting into other metal began to scream into my ears.

Mike was showered with glass but from my view, everything was going swimmingly.

The pursuing car had sped up so much to catch up with us, that it would not have had that much time to react to my sudden braking, which had sent it flying into us.

The Mercedes came to a standstill, just as we began to move off again, at a lightning speed and with the engine working on overtime, now hollering at the top of its lungs as it did so.

"Did you really have to do that? That's not going to hold them off for long enough!"

Mike's nose was dripping blood, so too was a small gash in the hairline of his forehead. I, on the other hand, was fine apart from an increased presence of perspiration.

"Get your pistol ready!" I screamed at him as I suddenly abandoned all notions of eloquence and diction. He seemed to know what I had meant.

We had managed to gain ground on the Mercedes, around thirty or forty yards. It wasn't enough to hold them off for too long, but it would do for the purposes that I had in mind.

In an overexuberant flourish, I flicked the steering wheel round, hard, keeping my foot on the accelerator momentarily. The car began to slide along, sideways, before slowly coming to a stop.

By the time the car had stopped crunching over the gravel, Mike was already leaning out of the window, pistol up and ready.

The car now began idling, as I abandoned my post and began tearing at the cushion that I had been sat on. I yanked a small D-ring, which had a black 'X' painted neatly next to it.

'X' marks the spot had been one of Mike's little embellishments to the car.

As I opened our treasure chest, the first round was ejected from Mike's pistol, which made the sight that greeted my eyes all the more welcome.

I pulled the MP40 submachine gun from the concealed crate, the magazine already loaded and ready to fire.

I leant out of the passenger side window in the front of the car and began squeezing a few rounds towards the windscreen of the car that refused to stop coming at us.

Mike disengaged, leaving me to do all of the offensive work, while he began to tug at Suzanne's arms to get her clear of the vehicle.

The sound of bullets striking metal was all that filled my ears, that and the ear-splitting pops that occurred each time I depressed the trigger.

The windscreen of the car shattered into millions of tiny pieces, allowing me a better view of the two men coming towards us.

One of them, the passenger, had his head ducked down so low beneath the dashboard that I could only see the peak of his trilby hat.

The driver on the other hand, had the unenviable job of keeping his head above the parapet, which made him the obvious target of choice for me.

He began to swerve, trying to avoid the bullets that had recently claimed his windscreen.

He could not avoid them forever and, as he swerved over to his left, one of my rounds caught him perfectly in the neck, sending an explosion of red through the cab of the car.

The Mercedes kept coming, deviating from its path slightly as its driver slumped backwards in his seat.

The black monster was now so close that I could see the horror etched on the passenger's face as he realised what was about to happen.

Instead of standing my ground and firing off a few more rounds, to make sure that I got my other target, I laid flat on the bench of the car, gripping tightly onto anything that I could find.

The grinding sound of metal smashing into metal filled my ears again, as the two vehicles tried their best to mould into one.

The Renault spun around as crystallised glass began to prick at my skin, and I was showered in the stuff, some of it somehow finding its way into my mouth.

There was a brief moment of calm, followed by a series of coughs. Some of them were my own, as I realised that tiny specks of blood were accompanying them. I would have to worry about them later.

"Mike!" I spluttered as I staggered from the car, a headache like none I had ever experienced beginning to descend and blood starting to fill one eye.

Gunshots began to ring out, as three rounds struck the side of the stricken Renault, great clangs like a dulled gong ringing out among the trees.

Hearing no response, I fumbled around for my pistol, becoming blinder by the second. My right eye was now totally obsolete, my left beginning to succumb to a haze from the periphery.

I could make out a dark figure stumbling towards me, but everything appeared dark and everything staggered. I had no idea of determining who it was that was approaching me.

The figure came closer, but still no movement of recognition, no call of identification.

I was certain that I saw an arm reach out to me, a blackened, horrible arm.

I squeezed the trigger. And again. And again.

The figure in front of me tumbled backwards towards the ground, coming to rest at the side of the now decimated Renault.

Collapsing to my knees, I fell beside the figure, who was fighting with himself to stop the blood from slowly drowning him.

As I lay there, my world darkened once again as something else came into my hazy view.

I pulled the pistol up and squeezed the trigger. A click. It had jammed.

"It's me. It's Mike."

If I had possessed any liquid in my eyes, I would have cried. By a stroke of good fortune, I had narrowly avoided executing my very best friend.

But it was about time that I was given some good luck.

"Come on, admit it," I croaked through blood-soaked saliva.

"What?"

"That Renault isn't as bad as you were making out."

I couldn't see him, but I knew that he was grinning at the fool who had almost shot him.

5

My body felt like it was beginning to shut down, quite against my will.

I forced my eyes to stay open, despite the fact that it felt like they might simply fall out if I continued to do so. Gradually, the blood began to drain from my eye, affording me a marginal better field of view than I had possessed a few minutes' before.

However, as my vision cleared, my mind began to haze all the more. The pain inside my skull was so tremendous that it felt as though part of the bone had been crushed, or at the very least morphed in some way.

There was an almighty pressure on the front of my skull, one that threatened my brain to give up completely.

But I willed it to carry on. If only for a few minutes' more.

The pain, as I managed to stagger back onto my

own two feet, was almost unbearable and, had it not been for our most precarious situation, I imagined that I would have fallen to the ground immediately.

I could just see the beat-up Renault out of the corner of one eye, a hint of steam and smoke just wisping from under the bonnet.

Apparently my driving skills had not been quite as prestigious as I had thought. I had managed to outmanoeuvre the Germans, that much was true, but I had failed to outmanoeuvre the tree that we had ploughed into.

"I tell you what," Mike said chipperly, as he tucked his weapon away in his trousers. "I think we have done the styling on that car the world of good."

All of its windows had been decimated, with only a few shards here and there clinging to its housing in the corner. The headlights hung off at odd angles, completely dislocated from the body of the car, much like the driver's door which wanted independence itself.

Bullet holes and strike marks were all over the car and it was the first time that I realised that our pursuers really had managed to get quite a few rounds down towards us before they had met their fate.

One had even struck the pillar right by the driver's window, just inches from my face.

We had been extremely fortunate.

My legs in a far worse state than the Renault, I began to stumble my way to the Mercedes, like a new-born calf taking his first steps.

My body thumped onto the bodywork with a clang, as I tripped up on the dirt track. It was a good job that the occupant inside the Mercedes was already dead, otherwise I would have woken him up with a start already.

I fumbled around inside his jacket pockets, trying to see if he owned anything of any worth.

Despite the windowless appearance of the car, the interior stunk strongly of tobacco, and I got more than a slight waft of it as I flicked his jacket around without too much of a care.

Unsurprisingly, the man did not have anything of too much worth about his person, other than a large quantity of rolling papers, tobacco and some matches. It was a wonder that he was able to pull on his jacket under the weight of the stuff.

They were clearly planning on being in the Mercedes for a long while.

Mike grunted as he began heaving the body of the second man back towards the car.

I chuckled to myself softly as I pulled out the identity card of the passenger, the one who had been wearing the trilby, now stained in a deep scarlet.

I poked a cigarette into my mouth and lit it, as I inspected the card.

"What's so funny, old fruit?"

I flicked it towards him for his perusal.

"*Kriminalinspektor beim Geheimen Staatspolizeiamt.*"

Mike shook his head, passing it back to me.

"What does it mean?"

"He's an inspector," I said, as I lit another liberated cigarette, passing it to Mike. "At the secret state police office. Hardly a secret if their identity cards say it loud and clear."

"Gestapo?" he asked, as I tucked the card back inside the man's jacket, pulling the trilby over his eyes to avoid his eternal glare.

"Indeed."

"So, we're in it up to our necks."

"Very much so."

It was as far as our conversation went, as we sucked in the last few breaths of tobacco before we started to take our situation a lot more seriously.

"Looks like they were planning on staking out that road for quite some time," Mike said, producing a brown paper bag stuffed with sandwiches and battered apples.

"Tobacco and food wasn't all that they brought along with them," I said, beckoning Mike over to the boot of the car.

"Blimey," was all that escaped his lips for a moment as he took a look inside. "There's enough petrol there to get all the way to Berlin."

"And back again."

Six Jerry cans stacked on their sides on top of one another filled the entire boot space of the Mercedes.

Mike's quip about Berlin played on my mind a lot more than it should have done. There was plenty of fuel there for a nice long trip, and my mind began to play havoc with my emotions, as I thought of all the places that the Gestapo had been preparing to take us.

Or maybe they hadn't been planning on taking us anywhere but were instead intending to simply cremate us where we fell.

In what could only be described as a strange case of irony, it was the Germans who found their corpses doused in the petrol, not ours. The rest of the Mercedes, and the Renault too, got the same treatment, giving off a burst of heat as two cigarettes were tossed into the mix.

But only after Mike and I had taken a good few drags on them first.

The two automobiles now cooking nicely next to one another, we both silently agreed that it was definitely time that we got a move on.

The noise of the chase, followed by gunshots and soon a pillar of black smoke, was sure to draw some attention.

I found myself gazing at the licking flames, the soft crackle and pop somehow enticing me into its embrace. I watched as each column of flame danced wildly, as air was sucked into its grip and began to take hold on the rest of the car.

I had held a long fascination with flames, the flippant way in which they quivered always captivating me. But what they now made me think of, filled my stomach with bile that wanted to escape rapidly.

"What now, old fruit?" Mike interrupted.

It wasn't a question that needed too much pondering.

"I don't know."

We had no way of getting out of the wooded area that we were in and, even if we did, we had nowhere to go.

It had appeared that Suzanne had been compromised, which meant that they more than likely knew exactly where she had been staying, which just so happened to be the same place that we had been staying.

It seemed foolish now, but at the time it had been the most comforting thing to do.

We had no real contacts that we could depend on, none that we could absolutely attest had not given Suzanne up in the first place. We were in that forest, with one gravely injured woman, with no transport, no friends, no real prospects whatsoever.

"I suppose that our best hope is to move away from here. Get some distance and angles away from the crash. Then we can get our thoughts together somewhere further along the line."

I knew that, had my head been in the right place, I would have come up with something similar, but in the event, I was more than grateful that Mike had taken the lead. My brain power was significantly lacking as a result of our little scuffle.

Mike was thinking about our best chance of survival, but there was only one thing that I could think about.

"Suzanne. Where is she? Is she alright?"

His face fell slightly, as if he had been hoping that I would have forgotten about her.

He held out an arm to stop me from getting around the car too easily.

"Hold on, old fruit...She took a stray round...to the arm. She's been unconscious since we got her from the house. I think it's about time that we had a frank discussion about her."

"What do you...No, Mike. No way."

The strained expression told me that his conclusion had not been an easy one for him to come to, but that he had given it enough consideration to believe that it was the right one.

After everything that she had done for us, I found it difficult to think that we could abandon her so easily. It was true that she had not been the easiest person to operate with for quite some time, but she had helped haul us out of some pretty big pits in the same breath.

"Mike, if she had given up on us as easily as that then we would be dead men."

His cheeks reddened slightly, at the inference that I had made that he had suggested abandoning her.

"It's not giving up on her, Johnny," he said sternly. "When you see the state of her you'll realise that we won't last ten minutes with her on our backs. Especially when we have nowhere to go."

I pushed his arm out of my way, rather too forcefully, as I felt the prickliness of both of our exhausted minds beginning to press in. It had not been the first time that we had clashed over something. In fact, over the last few weeks, it was fair to say that our relationship had become strained.

Mike had developed into an incredible cynic, one who could not see the silver lining on a cloud made of silver, never mind a grey one. His attitude had become decidedly defeatist, and one that I was worried would begin to rub off on all those that we worked with.

I staggered around the burning wreckages and towards the tree that Suzanne had been propped up against.

Sure enough, her arm was leaking blood, but not as much as it perhaps should have been, which wasn't a good sign.

Her skin was pale and clammy, almost beginning to turn yellow and, despite the roaring fires to keep her warm, I could still feel that her cheeks were cold underneath the superficial layer of heat.

She was in a bad way. Such a bad way in fact that I felt it pertinent to check once more that she had a pulse.

It was there, weaker than before, but ever so slightly steadier.

I knew that Mike was right. We would probably do far more damage to ourselves in carrying her than I cared to imagine. For two fit and healthy men her bodyweight would be no trouble. But for two men who had just been involved in a hairy encounter with death and who were finding it increasingly difficult to work in unison, it would be a practical impossibility.

As I went to look away from her, I noticed a slight movement. A twitch under one of her bruised eyelids.

I stared, wondering if it was my own battered eyes that were playing tricks on me, showing me things that I wanted to see.

"Mike."

He crouched next to me, just in time to see a slight twinge in Suzanne's once pretty and full lips.

Blood dribbled from her draining lips as she began trying to speak.

"No. Don't talk Suzanne. Stay still."

But she was as defiant as ever and continued to move her lips around, like a fish struggling out of water.

Then, only just audible above the roaring flames behind us, was a voice. A weak and crackled one. She was only just decipherable.

"Harry Landes. *Allé du Bois. Charsay*. You two should go there. *Allé du Bois*."

I looked at Mike and he at me. Neither of us were really expecting anything from her mouth, so what she had said had shocked us on more than one count.

"*Charsay?*" I asked, hopefully.

"North of *Langeais*. But I wouldn't know where *Allé du Bois* is."

"She wouldn't have told us if she didn't think we could find it."

"What about her?" he asked, a twinge of conflict gripping at the back of his throat.

"We need her, Mike. We need to at least get her as close to *Charsay* as we can. Then maybe we can leave her somewhere and get this Harry Landes to come and get her?"

"If she lasts that long."

"I…heard…that."

There was an attempt at a pain-ridden, bloody grin. It filled me with a warmth, or maybe it could have been the awful, hissing flames that were threatening to remind me of something I would rather keep hidden.

6

My dreams were infiltrated by my memories once again.

It had only been a routine observation trip; just Mike, Suzanne and me. After what had happened taking out the *Generalfeldmarschall* security had been tighter than a hangman's noose.

But we needed information, not least to find out whether or not it was safe to step outside Alfred's house. Besides, with the four of us all cooped up together, the cabin fever that I was experiencing had started to feel as though it might be life-threatening. If not for me, then for Suzanne or Mike. It had taken a matter of days before they were at each other's throats.

But the routine intelligence gathering trip ended in nothing short of pure tragedy.

We had been able to see the large cloud of black smoke, that lingered over *Restigné* like a curse, for a number of miles as our legs began furiously pedalling towards what had been our safe haven.

Mike had been the first to call out in desperation, in a tone that would haunt me for the rest of my days. It was the despairing howl of a man in anguish, far worse than any animalistic cry of pain that I had heard many times in my life.

"No!" he screamed, losing balance on his bicycle and clattering to the ground, the bell ringing solemnly as it hit the floor. He scrabbled around pulling himself back to his feet, before standing shoulder to shoulder with Suzanne and me.

We could do nothing but stare.

Despite the intense burning fury of the flames, Suzanne was maliciously cold.

"We need to leave. Now."

"But, Alfred—" I whimpered, helplessly.

"But nothing. There is nothing we can do for him now."

We watched as some of the villagers tried in earnest to get to the front door of Alfred's house, but all attempts were futile. The whole building was one giant fireball, as if a thousand incendiaries had suddenly detonated. I was almost able to believe that the very bricks with which the building was made, would somehow ignite, such was the ferocity of heat that billowed out.

"How did they find him? How did they know?" Mike asked in disbelief, his eyes flooding with tears in much the same way that mine had done.

"It doesn't matter now. We can ask that question later on. We need to get to safety."

"I thought Alfred's house *was* safe."

There was a silence as we pedalled after Suzanne, the tears rolling from my eyes to my ears as I pushed myself faster and faster. There was nothing that could have been done for Alfred now.

Poor man. He had served us so well. But at least now he would be reunited with his son, and I would have to wake up.

7

The sight of two dishevelled and bruised men wandering around a small village would have been enough to arouse anyone's suspicions, which was why Mike and I had decided that only one of us should go to find Harry Landes.

Charsay was an even smaller village than *Langeais* had been and, as I staggered around the quaint Norman settlement, I found it all rather peaceful. The peace, however, was replaced by a thumping heartbeat in my burning ears, as if it was hurrying me along to sort this mess out.

My face had been briefly wiped down with a rag by Mike, my clothes straightened, and my general appearance cleaned up considerably.

There had not been a great discussion about who should go to find Harry Landes but, had our circumstances been slightly more favourable, I was certain the whole conversation would have descended into a full-blown row.

Mike had insisted that he should be the one to go into *Charsay*, on account of the fact that he looked a great deal more appealing than I did. I, on the other hand, had argued that was exactly why I should go; my bloodied and bruised face would hopefully tease out the compassion of the first villager that I could find.

Besides, if I was to find myself in the hands of the Germans, then Mike was in a much more favourable condition to get himself away from the area and carry on our work elsewhere.

The street was cobbled and chipped, the surface giving out under the duress that it must have been under for centuries. There was not that much worth noting in *Charsay*, but my eyes were not really up to the task anyway.

They continued to throb away inside my skull, like two ferocious fires that continued to ravage anything within its sight. It seemed like it was destroying every ounce of brain power that I had, for I soon found myself banging on the first front door that I could find.

I had given up; my body was slowly shutting down and it felt like I would be of no use to anyone.

But, the warm, gentle face that answered suddenly filled me with an optimism, some sense of renewed purpose. I pulled myself up to attention, instead of supporting myself on the wall of her house.

She looked me up and down, as I conjured up the energy and courage to try and speak.

"Madame..."

She held a hand up to my face and I watched, transfixed, as the hand turned into a single finger, which she pressed to her lips.

She then turned away from me, as the thumping heartbeat in my ears quickened. The sudden feeling of guilt and shame washed over me completely, as I realised how foolish I had been.

I had gone against one of the very first things that I had been taught at the finishing school in Arisaig, Scotland.

We were never to trust anyone; we were never to trust any situation and we were certainly to never trust our own instincts.

I had done all three. I had assumed that the first person that I had met would be trustworthy, purely because I felt like they should have some sort of compassion on me. I had trusted the advice given by Suzanne. We were in such a deep mess that her advice was the only light that I could see.

As I began to hastily shuffle away from the old lady's house, she re-emerged, this time pulling a woollen shawl over her bony and undernourished shoulders. Bemused I stood there, as she gripped my wrist and began leading me back down the garden path.

I chuckled to myself inwardly, wondering if she too had a similar identity card to the men that had chased us in the Mercedes. If she did, then I must have been arrested by the oldest Gestapo officer in the whole of the Reich.

She stumbled and tripped almost as much as I did as we crossed the road, her frail and weak legs almost unable to support her own bodyweight.

The shawl did little to keep her warm, as her quivering and stick-like fingers began quaking and clutching at it to prevent the chill from taking hold. Her mousy, greying hair flapped wildly in the breeze that seemed to pick up exponentially as we crossed the road, and I found myself having to slow down to avoid treading on the backs of her legs.

She walked slowly, but with purpose, her head held high and proud, as if she was taking her very own son to the house across the street.

The house that the frail, dishevelled woman led me to was nothing like her own. Her garden was well kept and tidy, the windows clean and there wasn't a single cobweb in sight.

The front gate that we had come through was shedding itself of paint, and creaked open on one hinge, the other staying firmly where it was on the gatepost, completely detached from the gate itself.

The garden was overgrown, every blade of grass reaching up to my shins at an absolute minimum. The blades themselves seemed completely disheartened, bowing in every direction and browning at the tips.

I somehow felt colder, as the wind began to pick up even more and I noticed that barely a single windowpane was intact. All the windows had some sort of defect, and I could only imagine as to how cold its interior was, now that the protection of glass was hard to come by.

The door, an ageing, shoddy looking thing, was damp, the edges of which had surrendered to the ground a long time ago. As it opened, I noticed that it barely made a sound, owing to the fact that it was only held in place in its frame on account of a chain on the inside, which had been clinked undone in order to greet the two rather unkempt figures on the other side.

For the first time, the woman spoke and, although I had not been expecting her voice to be gruff, the gentleness of it took me quite by surprise.

It was something in between a whisper and a mumble, one that was quite clear to hear, but almost didn't want to be.

"Un de vos garçons."

Her voice felt like it was riding on the waves of the wind, her very tones dipping and swirling with another gust that pricked at the hairs on the backs of my arms. Had I not felt like I was being set up in some way, I would have been quite grateful for it, as my face was still burning as furiously as if I was still stood next to the two smouldering cars.

"Un de vos garçons, Harry."

It was only at the second time around that I began to allow her words to percolate into my mind.

Harry. Harry Landes.

This was the man that I had been sent to find. I looked up, just as she spoke again, for a third time.

"One of your boys, Harry."

The man who looked me up and down, apparently deciding whether I was one of his boys or not, was a complete contradiction to the building that he inhabited.

He was crisply dressed and clean, and not a single thing about him seemed to suggest that he would have enjoyed living in the environment that he did.

Underneath his arm was a rolled-up newspaper, as if he had been expecting to fend someone off with it. But, by looking at it, I could tell what kind of a man he was. For whatever reason, he had found himself in *Charsay*, but he longed to be somewhere far grander, somewhere far more important; *Tours*, perhaps. But *Lyon* seemed more like my guess.

He had the air of a businessman about him, a successful one at that. He looked at me as if I was some sort of proposition, to be acquired or tossed on the scrapheap. For a moment, I thought I was for the latter.

Had it not been for the quiet muttering to the woman stood in front of me, I would have been quite certain that I was destined to be disposed of.

"Merci Madame Joie. Merci d'avoir recommencé."

The woman began to scurry off, after a soft pat on my shoulder, which she practically had to jump at to reach.

Merci d'avoir recommence.

Thank you for doing this again.

We stood in silence for a few seconds, waiting for Madame Joie to manoeuvre her way out of earshot, which couldn't have taken too long; if her ears were as frail as her outward appearance seemed to suggest, I doubted that she was even able to hear an air raid siren.

Harry Landes looked at me scornfully, as if he was about to produce a scathing attack that would see me blush far more embarrassed than I had ever done before.

Instead, he said nothing, stepping to one side and allowing me inside.

He tried his hardest to slam the door shut, but it barely made a noise as it sauntered back into its ill-fitting frame.

As soon as he had pulled the chain across the door, he began to bawl at me, as if somehow the latch had managed to block out the entire outside world.

"What do you think you are playing at? You could have got us both into some serious trouble there! Who are you anyway?"

I chewed over his questions, as I pondered why I had done what I had done and gone against not only my instincts but my training too.

I wanted to reply to his queries but found myself answering his question with one of my own.

"Can she be trusted?"

He looked at me confused for a moment.

"Madame Joie? Yes, of course…the poor woman

wouldn't be able to recognise her own husband if he somehow came back from the dead…besides, you're not the first that she's found."

He began to calm down, quicker than a hot fire once it is doused by icy cold water, which probably had something to do with the sub-zero temperatures that his house reached. He rubbed at his head and sighed. He had grown weary of being disturbed by Madame Joie at the door.

At long last, he began to unwind the paper that he had, until that point, kept steadily down by his hip.

As the paper rolled itself flat, he tossed it onto a dusty old table at the bottom of the stairs and kept hold of the pistol that he had concealed inside of it.

"One can never be too careful about who is invited in nowadays."

He spoke near-perfect English, so polished in fact that he seemed that he was putting it on ever so slightly.

"Now," he muttered, wandering into one of the rooms that darted off from the hallway. "Who sent you here?"

I was suddenly reminded of the urgency of the situation and how, the longer I dallied there with what appeared to be a member of a decaying Franco dynasty, the larger the chance of both Suzanne and Mike being rounded up by the pursuing Germans.

"Suzanne Seguin. She's in trouble."

I omitted the fact that I had another accomplice, just in case this man was not as trustworthy as

Suzanne had us believe. I felt like I could at least try to grapple back some of my credibility as an agent who had gone through months of training.

If we were to be captured, I didn't want everyone back at Baker Street hearing about the way in which we had simply stumbled into a French hamlet and found ourselves captured soon after. If the Germans hadn't shot me, then I would have died of pure shame.

"You don't say. People don't come to me unless they are…Where is she?"

"Do you have a car?"

"Yes."

"It's not a Renault, is it?"

8

The car journey back to Harry's house was carried out in a near-perfect silence. Mike and I kept ourselves occupied by continually staring over our shoulder, expecting to see another Mercedes bearing down on us with its menacing grin.

Suzanne drifted in and out of consciousness, spread out over the back seat of the car with her head resting on my lap. Every now and then her eyes would flicker, stare at me for a while, before closing themselves again.

Each time she did, there was a slight moment of alarm, before the recognition kicked in and she realised that she was safe. At least that was what I hoped she would think. I didn't even know if she could see me at all.

Her body was limp and cold and, as she continued to lay there quite helplessly, I could not help but think about how I could have done more, how I could have protected her more.

The whole morning had been somewhat of a blur. Mike and I were still working through our codes and ciphers for the transmission that would come later on in the evening. But now all of that would have to change.

But it was Suzanne who had shocked us all into action, bursting in from the street without warning and declaring that we had to get to *Langeais* immediately.

"My contact. He has information that he needs to share urgently. A high-value target for us. But it needs to be passed on right now."

"Now, hold on a minute," I had interjected, but the other two had already made the decision.

"How far is it?"

"Fifteen minutes, if we take the car."

Mike and I had barely had time to study the maps like we would normally have done, to take the time to work out our entry and exit points and to ensure that we knew where we were going. Nothing would arouse more suspicion, if we saw any Germans, than hesitation; even the slightest hesitation at a junction would be all that it took to alert those watching that we were not natives around these parts.

If only I had put my foot down, and insisted that we had reconnoitred the target better, to make sure that we were going to be as safe as we could be.

If only I had done that and then maybe none of us would have been in the pain that we were in as we sat in Harry's car.

I berated myself for even being so naïve as to think that the meeting had been safe. The thought that the whole thing had been a set-up had not even crossed my mind, not until it was too late anyway.

As Mike turned from the front seat next to our chauffeur, I could tell that the same things were going through his mind, only they were eating him up far more than mine. He had been the one to have encouraged Suzanne, he was the one who had shot me down for any reservations that I had.

He knew that he had become a liability, he had stopped thinking. Whether it was complacency or fear, I did not know, but the fact was that his spontaneity was meaning that we were flying incredibly close to the sun.

And that was not how we had been trained.

The fact remained, however, that the net had been increasingly getting tighter around this small pocket of France recently, to the point where I had even tried to breach the subject of trying to get to safety.

The only place where I knew that I would feel totally secure would be London. Specifically, I wanted to be back at Baker Street. That was where everything was sent, it was where everything came from. If we could get back to them and tell them what life was really like in France, then I was sure that, even if I did not save my own life, then I would at least save the lives of some other agents.

"Right. Get her out."

He was more than a little blunt as he threw his door open and began striding to the back door of the ramshackle property, pulling his sandy coloured hat onto his head as he did so.

Harry's attire was nothing short of ridiculous and, as he unlocked the door to the house and went inside, I realised that his lack of empathy was too.

He appeared at the door, looking how Howard Carter must have done before discovering the grave of Tutankhamun, his dickie bow slightly skewed, just like the slanted face that he seemed to possess.

His face seemed waxy and pointed, like all his features were pointing to some indiscernible focal point. His greying hair flapped about in the wind under the rim of his hat, which he promptly tucked away, hoping that we had not seen it.

He was tall and, as he stepped through the doorway he had to duck ever so slightly, more to avoid his precious hat from being knocked to the floor than anything else.

His hands started beckoning us over urgently, as he flicked his head around the tiny street which had seen more activity in the last few hours than it had done in the three hundred years previous.

"Aren't you going to give us a hand?" Mike asked, irritated as he struggled to breathe with the weight of Suzanne gripped firmly under his arms.

"Not in this jacket I shouldn't think." He spoke confidently and in almost a perfect rounded English, that wouldn't have been too amiss in one of the royal courts.

He was clearly an educated man, but not one who had been educated in the art of chivalry and cooperation.

I saw Mike's eyes widen as we bundled Suzanne into the house, as he took in the ragtag appearance of everything around him. The furniture and décor of the house itself wasn't in such a bad condition, when compared with its outward appearance, but everything seemed coated in a copious layer of dust, one that would take hours to clean up one day. There was a musty smell to the place, one that I had not noticed before, but now clung to me even harder as if to make up for that fact.

As we plonked Suzanne down on the old table in the kitchen, wobbling slightly after years of neglect and damp, I couldn't help but think that we were going to be responsible for her death at the hands of some gruesome infection.

"She needs a doctor," I grumbled, my voice crackling under the strain that my head seemed under.

"Yes," Harry agreed, without really offering anything else to us. I looked at Mike.

He shrugged his shoulders, before furrowing his eyebrows slightly at the inactivity, as we stood staring at the semi-conscious body of Suzanne.

"Well?" I said, irritated.

"Well, what?" Harry said, his head turning slightly to inspect Suzanne's wounds.

"A doctor."

"Yes, I agree."

"Well, do you know one that we could summon?"

It was then that I realised that this man was not trying his hardest to hinder us, nor was he angry at us for suddenly descending upon his home. It was at the same time that I came to the conclusion that Suzanne had trusted this man, not because he was a fierce patriot or shared a mutual disdain for the Germans, but because he was clueless. He seemed to have no perception of the outside world at all.

"Yes. Should I get him?"

"I would have thought so, don't you?" Mike's head nudged towards the table, where the blood was now slowly drowning the dust and soaking itself into the fibres of the table.

He quickly scarpered out, his brightly polished brown leather shoes clapping along the floorboards as he went. Within a matter of moments, his head was peering back around the door frame.

"I won't be long. Half an hour at most."

He disappeared again, drawing out a sigh of relief from both Mike and me.

We said nothing. Until Mike spoke.

"What do you make of all that then, old fruit?"

I couldn't think of anything else to say to him,

other than give him a wry smile, which seemed to be a sufficient answer at the time. In truth, I did not really know what it was he was asking, as so much had happened over the last few hours that I felt like I needed a couple more days to process it all.

He pulled out a carton of cigarettes and proceeded to light two of them before passing one to me.

I took a drag.

"Are these the German cigarettes?"

"Yeah," he breathed after whistling out a mouthful of smoke.

"Then you better get rid of them," I said, indicating the carton that was in his hand.

"Why?" he queried, his eyebrows coming together like window shutters.

"If anyone caught you with them, Mike…"

He swung his arms around, as if he was in the middle of a PT session.

"There's nobody here, Johnny. We're absolutely fine. Suzanne said so."

"What, you trust her now? It's taken her to be shot and almost killed by the Germans for you to finally put your faith in her?"

He shrugged, dismissively.

"And we're not fine, Mike. You know since Alfred died that the net has been closing in pretty quickly around us recently. You saw it today. Those Germans would have searched Alfred's place, so they could have found anything."

"I didn't leave anything there, Johnny."

"How can you be so sure?"

"What are you trying to say?"

Both the cigarettes glowed away in between our fingers, as we did not have a need for them any longer. As my fingers grew warmer as the tip got closer to its end, I felt my whole head beginning to glow like the cigarette.

I was becoming infuriated with the way in which Mike was insisting on carrying himself. There was something not right with him, something that was making him less likely to think things through, less likely to consider the risks.

And I was beginning to think that I was going to get killed.

"Those Germans. The *Gestapo*. How did they know that we would use that road?"

"Are you accusing me?!"

I knew I had overstepped the mark. Deep within my heart, I was convinced that Mike wasn't the sort and, even if he had been, we barely left each other's sides. There was something else that had gone wrong. But I couldn't tell what it was.

Mike had the decency in him to not mention anything again, instead opting to work his way through the German cigarettes, instead of throwing them away. He didn't offer me anymore.

The doctor that Harry ushered through the door seemed just as eccentric as he did, carrying an over-sized bag that must have been larger than the man's torso. He immediately set to work, with murmurs and grunts as he disapprovingly assessed Suzanne's situation.

He looked at us suspiciously but, crucially, he asked us no questions.

Before too long, he was ushering us away, out of his workspace so he could see the light. We were only too happy to oblige. All three of us.

"Thank you, Harry," Mike grunted, offering him the last of the *Gestapo's* finest cigarettes. He turned it down. Mike still refused to offer it to me.

"You are welcome."

"You said that I wasn't the first?"

"*Pardon?*"

"Out there. Earlier on. You said I wasn't the first that the old lady had brought to you."

"*Non.*"

"Suzanne has brought you others before?"

"Yes. She has. You could probably say that the trouble always finds her. But, then again, she does not help herself."

"What makes you say that?" I asked, rather forcefully, as I felt the hairs on the back of my neck stand to attention, as if ready for a fight.

"She craves it. She always has. She has always followed the trouble. But now, it follows her. Literally," he said, with a smirk.

I felt my hands tense as I resisted the urge to make them into fists, as if somehow, I was offended by what he had said of Suzanne. It was fair enough, I reasoned, as the poor woman was now lying on a kitchen table having all her bullet wounds stitched up.

"You're telling us," Mike quipped. "The woman's brought nothing but trouble to us since we met her."

9

Over the next few days that we spent in Harry's house, my unease grew without ceasing. I felt as though that the net had been closing in for some time now, and that by staying in one solitary place, we were merely inviting the Germans to come and find us.

The fact that I barely knew where we were, and did not really know Harry all that well, did nothing to contribute to setting my mind at rest. In fact, the inability to walk around the small village and get to know my bearings caused me to be overcome by a sense of ongoing nausea and discomfort.

For three days no one really said a word, apart from the occasional offer of a drink or a cigarette, which were both beginning to run out.

Mike and I knew that it was only a matter of time before we would have to move. We were no good to anyone in Harry's house, we were barely any use to ourselves as we sat there staring into space, and wondering what may lay in store for us next.

I tried to distract myself frequently by ensuring that Suzanne had everything that she required to aid her recovery. The doctor that had visited us had done a marvellous job in patching her up and now the only indication that she had been wounded, was the eternal cleanliness of her skin that seemed so wax-like that it didn't seem real.

She spent the first two days asleep, before awaking on the third day after our little run-in with the *Gestapo*.

For a while, there was nothing that Mike or I could really say to her, it was simply our job to ensure that the security of her little network remained intact. And, since we had met her, we had done nothing of the sort. We had fallen far short of the mark that was expected of us.

Mike and I kept vigil over her for the best part of the week, each day becoming more and more unsettled in Harry's house. I wasn't even sure if she really knew that we were there, but it seemed to comfort all of us to know that we were still together. That was one thing that we hadn't failed in just yet.

"*Michel. Jean.*"

It had been quite some time since I had last been addressed in my French alias, and for a moment I had almost forgotten that I was no longer who I had been the year before.

She tried her hardest to look each of us in the eye, but it seemed that the pain that she had experienced was still eating her up more than we knew. As she faintly opened her eyelids, I realised how much I had missed their presence, the eyes that seemed so disinteresting but somehow commanding my deepest attention. It was a dangerous feeling to have, and one that I was sure had led a lot of men to their demise.

Despite her appearance, frail and weak, the athleticism that she had once possessed was still quite visible, as well as somehow the female innocence that came with the young woman. She still did not seem the kind of woman who was capable of sneaking around after curfew, or being involved in an assassination attempt.

"I have been thinking… I have been trying to think. And I think it would be best if we returned to my home."

Instead of looking to one another, like we would normally have done, Mike and I simply decided in unison, the first time that we had done anything cohesively in a number of days.

"No, Suzanne. It is not safe. The Germans obviously know who you are and where you are getting your information from. We cannot go back to your home, not until all of this is over anyway."

"*Jean,*" she whispered, gripping my arm with her clammy sweat-ridden palm. "I need to go home. *We* need to go home. We cannot do anything while we're here. We are too far away from where everything is happening.

"Besides, I fear that it will not take too long for the Germans to begin searching around *Charsay*."

I struggled to process anything that she had said, my eyes instead resting on the hand that was now tightly gripped around my lower arm. She had never done anything like that before, and it made it difficult for me to try to see things objectively.

I realised that I was quite enjoying the contact.

"It has taken them a week already."

Mike stood tall in the room, not physically, but because he seemed so certain of what it was we were meant to do.

"Exactly," her hand suddenly relinquished its grip on my forearm. "They would have had time to interview any witnesses by now. If anything, they'll have an even better idea of where we are than they did a few hours after the blast."

Mike shot up from his chair and began pacing around with his hands on his sides, sighing and muttering. Suzanne opened her mystical and captivating eyes and locked them straight onto mine. I almost wished that she hadn't done it. In that moment I knew that she had already decided that she was going home.

We had but one choice; either we went with her, or she would simply go alone.

"Mike, I think it would be best if we went back. We haven't exactly been in the fight here, have we?"

He shot round to look at me with a disapproving glare.

"I knew you would side with her. Honestly, I did. But I would have thought that you would have tried to think it through a little bit more than you have done. Try thinking for yourself for a change."

"And what do you mean by that?"

He barely hesitated as he spat out his accusation at me.

"You're thinking too much with your heart. Use your brain. This isn't a game that we are playing, Johnny. We will die if we make the wrong move, don't you understand that?"

"Of course I do. But we are also here to do a job, Mike. And what good are we doing here? There's a group of resistors here, that need our guidance. They are all sitting on their hands while they wait for us to walk through the door again. Our job is to carry out surveillance, equip these fighters, and disrupt the Germans. How much of that have we done since we have been here?"

For a second, I thought that Mike was stepping over towards me to smack me straight on the nose, an eventuality that I really did not enjoy the thought of. My bruises that I had sustained all over my body the week before, had come up nicely, a wealth of blues and greens all over me. And the addition of another one on the bridge of my nose was not a welcome thought.

But he hesitated, as he turned to face the figure who entered the room. I did not know how long he had been there, or how much he had heard of our little conversation, all I knew was that Harry had appeared in Suzanne's room.

He looked as ridiculous as ever, his hat tucked under his arm, a checked tie a glaring mustard colour, set against a beige suit that made him look even more like a Victorian explorer than he had done when I first met him.

In his hand he carried a brown leather suitcase, one that looked almost as if it had been cut from the same sheet as his shoes. He brushed off some of the dust from the top of it, and inexplicably gave it a little blow to get rid of some of the dirt that we could not see.

He looked up at us, through his half-moon spectacles that made him look more like a lawyer than any kind of resistance worker. Had it not been that we were trying to be as inconspicuous as possible, he would have made the perfect agent. No one would suspect that he was capable of organising any kind of resistance.

"Ah, Suzanne. So good to see that you are awake. I have news from those around *Tours*. They are all in good spirits and are looking forward to having the three of you with them again. They are in great need of your help. It seems that the net has not only been cast around you three, but around most of the circuit."

I felt like looking at Mike, but instead, I was drawn to Suzanne, who was already knowingly looking at the two of us. She knew that we now had to head back.

Mike knew it too.

"Harry, when you next see them, tell them that we will be back."

"Of course, Suzanne."

"And I would also like you to come with us."

"You're joking? Can't we at least discuss things first?" Mike spat, looking at me for some sort of backup.

I suddenly felt quite cold towards Mike, as if I barely knew him and didn't trust him in the slightest.

"How do we know we can trust him?"

"Mike," I said, "He helped us when we needed it. And now we've been here for a week and we're still alive."

He unfolded his arms and let them dangle down by his side, as he let out a great sigh that almost became a moan. His hands were placed on his hips again, as he barged past Harry who still stood in the doorway.

"Getting some fresh air."

As he skulked out of the house, an uneasy silence descended on the three remaining occupants in the room.

I began to mourn the loss of my friend, the one that had seemed so jovial and happy in his former life. I thought back to the time that we were out on dispersal, the endless waiting for the Germans to fly over and begin taunting us from the air.

It was hours that others would spend reading books and writing letters, but for Mike, it was a time spent thinking up a new way to have some fun, a novel idea to put a smile on everyone's faces, despite the fact that our number was waning every single day.

Now, the dark moody features of his face that seemed to sink back even further into his head in the last few weeks, were a pure reflection of how dark his heart had become. It was almost like the man that I had known, was dead.

I walked over to the window, resting my head on the glass that seemed so flimsy, as I watched him skulk around in the backyard smoking his way through yet another packet of cigarettes.

I barely flinched as Suzanne spoke, hardly even recognising the fact that she had spoken.

"Harry, would you fetch me a glass of water?"

As far as I knew, there was no audible answer, apart from the sound of retreating footsteps as the brown leather shoes clipped away and down the stairs.

I ran my finger along the window pane as she spoke, collecting a nice grouping of dust on my index finger.

"He'll come around. I'm sure of it. I know for a fact that he wants to be back in the action. That's why we'll be living in *Tours.*"

I turned to face her, folding my aching arms as I did so.

"*Tours?* Why *Tours?*"

I couldn't understand why we would be heading

back to the nearest city that we could find, especially when two Gestapo inspectors had recently been murdered in cold blood.

"It is where everything is happening. It is where everything will happen. We need to be there, to guide those who need us."

She propped herself up in her bed, grimacing and grunting as she did so but beckoning closer at the same time. She lowered her voice, to something close to a whisper.

"Besides, there's something about Mike, something that I cannot trust. And I think *Tours* is the place to be to get to the bottom of it."

I furrowed my brow, hoping that would be all it took to get an answer from her. But she was having none of it.

"What do you mean?"

"You and Mike. You haven't exactly been the best of friends lately, have you?"

"What's that got to do with anything?"

"Do you trust him still?"

"Of course."

"Well, what would you say to me if I said I thought that I could no longer trust him?"

"I would say that you're a bit of a damned fool."

"Well then, I suppose I am a fool."

10

It was always a risky situation while we were transmitting to London. The wireless set that we had was pretty heavy and burdensome, making it incredibly difficult to pack up in a hurry, which was what so often happened, while transmitting.

It was not unheard of for us to be forced into packing up the set, midway through one of London's responses, which meant that sometimes we went days without any proper communication or any orders.

We had an incredibly small window to send our message, which also included the tiresome process of security checks and confirmations. It was frustrating, although we knew it to be vital to our survival.

On one such night, shortly after Suzanne had told me about her distrust of Mike, we found ourselves in a pretty favourable position. There was a good chance that the Germans had been trying to locate us ever since we switched the set on, however, this was one rare occasion where we had not heard one of their radio finding trucks sweeping the nearby area.

It meant that we had managed a full conversation with London for once, being able to send a full report to them, and for them to send intelligence and orders back to us. As Mike signed off, with his obligatory '*Fortunae, out,*' he flashed me a grin.

The journey back to the safe house in *Tours* was also fraught with danger, particularly as we had to transmit under the cover of darkness, which meant being out after the curfew had come into effect. If one was to be spotted by a German patrol, or even a sympathetic Frenchman, the chances were that we would be arrested before the night was out.

It meant that ducking into darkened doorways and throwing oneself in amongst a host of thorns was not atypical, but it also meant that a discussion of what had been transmitted would have to wait until we were safely behind four walls.

I was pleased with the way in which the transmission had gone and felt relieved to have had some sort of contact with London, however brief it had been.

Despite my relief and comfort at the thought of those working tirelessly in Baker Street, my mind seemed to be elsewhere.

Suzanne had said that she could no longer trust Mike, and I could not help but wonder what it was that had made her come to that conclusion. But, then again, she had always snuck out, and had ways of gathering intelligence that neither Mike nor I could compare to. It was this thought, as I mulled over the orders that we had received from London, that maybe what she had said had an element of truth to it.

Mike had seemed particularly keen to get to *Langeais*, as if he had wanted Suzanne to be in that building as soon as possible. He had also made no secret of the fact that he did not like her that much, and in my tired state, I found myself in between two adversaries, as they bitterly interlocked horns against one another.

I stopped, changing the large suitcase, that contained the wireless set, from one hand to the other, as my arm grew weary and painful. At the same time, I rubbed my hand over my dry face, picking out individual hairs that were trying to grow out around my chin.

I was beginning to become fearful and concerned for myself. I had started to distrust everyone. It seemed as though even my best friend, my longest accomplice, was not above suspicion anymore, and that was a very dangerous game to be involved in. Everyone knew at the finishing school in Arisaig, in amongst the Highlands, that there are only two things that got an agent killed; complacency and paranoia.

And there was a very fine balance between the two, a balance that I was struggling to maintain.

Without warning, I suddenly felt something smash into my stomach which, without being able to tense my muscles, managed to find its way almost to my spine. The wind was knocked out of me, and as I struggled for breath, a hand was placed on my shoulder forcing me backwards.

I suddenly realised that I was face to face with Mike, his warm breath beginning to make my eyes water almost immediately.

He put a finger to his lips before pointing backwards with his thumb, as we managed to hide in an alleyway between two houses.

My chest ached tremendously as I tried to get my breath back, by which time the trundling grumble of an engine had already started to shake the ground around us. Mike turned around, to inspect what it was sweeping towards us, his body having a faint shiver to it. Whether out of fear or excitement, I did not know.

Both of us stood as still as we could, as I tried to make sense of the situation now that my mind was beginning to catch up.

I watched as two large trucks, their headlights tapered and focusing solely on the ground, began to light a small patch of road ahead of them. As they passed, I made out the laughs and guffaws of men who felt safe in the land that they occupied. After the orders that we had received that night, I could only hope that in the next few days their complacency would be eradicated.

They passed us without much trouble or hassle, and I finally felt able to breathe again properly. Together, we both let out a sigh of relief, as I realised that the trucks were heading in the very same direction that we had just come from. Unfortunately for them, if they were following a wireless transmission signal, they were already too late.

We staggered back down the street, turning onto *Rue de l'Église*, the streets that we had come to call home in the last day or so. Even in the dark, the tall imposing Gothic spire of the local church captivated my attention. It seemed to loom larger than anything else that I'd ever seen before, and I thought about how wonderful it must have been up there, to be able to look down on the surrounding area in the knowledge that it was almost impossible for anybody else to know that you were there.

I felt my pace consciously quicken at the thought of who might have been up there that night.

We snuck in through the door to number thirty-one, without knocking or having to pass along any passwords to get in. Those sorts of things cost you precious seconds, seconds in which your life might be snatched away from you without warning.

The house was in a much better condition than Harry's had been, with all the windows intact and fairly strong, and with a noticeable absence of any dust anywhere. There was no occupant to the house, and so I wondered how clean it must have been when someone was there day to day to maintain it, if this was the state it got into while unoccupied.

It made a pleasant change to being in the dust-ridden hovel that Harry called home.

Somehow, both Mike and I had become rather breathless as we found ourselves on the safe side of the front door, and spent a few seconds breathing deeply to try and rid ourselves of the cold sweat that accompanied us in our little escapade in the night-time air.

It was just enough time for Suzanne, who was sitting at the table, to quickly pile away the pieces of paper that she had strewn about. She hastily stacked them on top of one another, before leaning on them to guard them from our view.

"So?"

"We managed a full transmission. We've received orders. And passed on the information that we wanted to," Mike said, his voice crackled and faint.

"And the orders?"

"Nothing we can do about them tonight. I think it's best to discuss them tomorrow, when we've all had a full night's rest."

Mike agreed with me, but Suzanne seemed hesitant, she wanted to know everything now and act on it immediately.

Mike trudged up the stairs to bed, with me following a minute or two later, Suzanne still sitting at the table, making sure that whatever it was that she had hidden remained so.

As I hoisted myself up the bannister to my own bed, a hand, not so clammy and weak as before, gripped my wrist. I looked down towards Suzanne, her eyes wide as if she had been caught in some sort of terror.

"Those papers," she said. "They're nothing to worry about. They are just a bit... Personal."

"It doesn't matter to me, Suzanne. Just be careful about how it looks to everyone else."

She nodded gently, satisfied at my reply.

I, on the other hand, had been far from satisfied by what she had said. The papers, in the two or three seconds that I had to see them, looked far from personal to me. Suzanne had seemed to have forgotten that I'd spent hours looking at, and studying, maps of various areas, countries and continents.

I knew a map of Europe when I saw one. The fact that she possessed such a map was not so much of a concern to me, but the reason behind why she had lied to me about their purpose was of great worry.

It seemed like the continuing saga of distrust and dishonesty had stepped up another level. Mike did not trust Suzanne. Suzanne did not trust Mike. And it seemed that both had secrets that they wanted to remain hidden.

"Good night, Suzanne."

She hesitated for a moment, still keeping a grip on my wrist and refusing to let me go. I looked into her charming eyes for as long as I dared before having to revert my gaze.

"*Jean,*" she said with a dose of melancholy to her demeanour. For a second or two, I thought she was going to reveal something to me, something that had been on her heart for a very long time, that had been burning with a passion that she could no longer subdue.

It was almost a desire of mine for her to say what I was imagining. But what came out was far from that.

"I know that you and Mike have been together for a long time. You've seen a lot together. But I hope that does not cloud your judgement when it comes to questioning what he's doing."

"What do you mean?"

Her eyes filled with tears, as if what she was about to say was of no pleasure to her but was actually a source of great trouble and tumult. I urged her to tell me what it was she had to say, placing my free hand over hers and giving it a slight shake.

"Who received the transmission tonight?" she asked, fearfully.

"Why does that matter?"

"It matters tremendously, *Jean.* Tremendously."

I had excelled at learning the Morse code alphabet up in the Highlands, while at the finishing school. The little dits and dahs fascinated me, the way in which two people could speak using noise other than the sound of their own voices.

It had not taken me long to learn Morse code, but my proficiency in being able to receive it, at speed, meant that it was always Mike who would receive whatever news London sent us.

"Mike did, tonight," I did not want her to think that I was any less of an agent because I could not keep up with the beeps that shot through my head quicker than a bullet. "Why?"

She sighed, having a great deal of trouble in maintaining eye contact with me as she spoke.

"I do not wish to say too much right now. But all I can say is that whatever orders you receive tonight, we must be exceedingly careful when we act upon them."

"Suzanne, what is it that you are not telling me?"

"Please be assured that I do not take any pleasure from what I am saying to you, after all, it is the lives of my friends at risk as much as your own. But I do not trust *Michel.* Do not go to sleep tonight, and you will know what I mean."

She suddenly relinquished her grip on my arm, and immediately I found myself desiring to have that physical contact back with her once again. There was no romantic element to it, but having been isolated from much human contact, apart from a very select few, it was only natural to want something that resembled something of a friendship, of hope.

She disappeared into the darkness of the house, as I was left on the stairs completely bemused about what to do.

I was tired, I had been up for many hours, but I was troubled by what Suzanne had said. I knew that I would have to wait up all night just to find out what it was that she could not tell me.

11

"So?"

"So, what?"

"What Suzanne said to me. Is it true? Do I have a reason to not put my trust in you?" He stared at me solemnly for what felt like an eternity, as if he was trying his hardest to use his gaze to correct my thoughts, to make me believe that he wasn't who Suzanne thought he was. I stared at his face for as long as I could bear, his dark, wavy, hair, which was slicked back as far away from his forehead as he could possibly get it, seeming to sparkle in the darkness of his bedroom.

He had a naturally small forehead, which he was particularly conscious about, especially when he supposed that the mark of high intelligence was a much larger forehead than he possessed. He tried his hardest to pull himself upright, pushing his shoulders as far back as possible, attempting to bring himself up to my height.

He fell far short, as he always would do unless he was in possession of some stilts, but it seemed to be making him feel a lot better in doing so.

Without much warning, the features of his face, that indicated such a serious and forlorn man, were suddenly shattered. The smile that I'd longed for, the one that I had not seen in a long time, suddenly broke out over his face.

It was as if we were back at the dispersal hut in North Weald, trying to rid ourselves of the possibility that we would be scrambled at any second. No one liked to think of it, especially when the sun was so bright and glorious, as it meant that for some of us, it would be the last sortie that we would see.

I thought of all the men that I had first started out with, which felt like so many years ago, their faces slowly disappearing, often one by one but sometimes by two or three, to become nothing more than smudge marks on the squadron chalkboard.

In those few moments where he was smiling, it was almost as if every problem that we had, every qualm and disagreement that we had voiced over the last few weeks, had vanished, and that nothing really mattered any more. Not even this war was of any real consequence, just so long as we had each other for friendship.

But it was all wishful thinking. The conversation

that played itself out in my mind had never happened. All I was doing was trying to remain positive, and trying to kid myself that Suzanne's concerns were merely misgivings. But I knew that they weren't, she wasn't the kind of woman to get that sort of thing wrong.

She had her reasons for distrusting Mike.

Forced back into the real world by my pessimism and frustration, I watched Mike, this time for real as he walked away from me.

I had been tired, so very tired, but what Suzanne had said to me, about waiting up in the night, had played on my mind to such an extent that every time I put my head on the pillow, a new, fanciful dream popped into my imagination. I wondered what on earth it was that had rattled Suzanne so much that she felt like she had to come to me to express her concern.

I had not wanted to hear it, while at the same time I was almost relieved that it had happened. I did not want to hear Mike get up in the middle of the night, but equally, it felt like it meant that I could trust Suzanne to a greater extent. What she had said, no matter how harmful it had been to hear, had been true; Mike was preparing to leave the house in the middle of the night.

I looked at my wristwatch. It was three thirty-two in the morning.

I barely moved a muscle, as I heard him manoeuvring around in his bedroom, presumably pulling on clothes and finding his shoes in the darkness.

He clearly waited until he thought that all the

other occupants of the house had gone to sleep, before trying his hardest to sneak out without so much as a squeaking floorboard.

I thought to myself how quiet he was being, and felt quite proud that we had received such good training in order for us to be able to tiptoe around in such a way that others could barely hear what was going on. But then the thought crossed my mind, that it was not a result of our training that made him so good at sneaking around, but practice. He had clearly done this before. Suzanne had heard as much, and it worried me about how often he had been doing it beforehand.

I sat up slowly in my bed, trying to mask any noise as nothing more than a rummaging around in my sleep. I rolled my neck around in the joint, its crunches and cracks something that brought me great relief. It had been nothing to do with the bed that my neck ached so much, but a lasting effect of sitting in the cockpit of a Hurricane and scanning the skies endlessly for the fearful 109s that would creep up on you and riddle you with bullets.

It was something that I both craved for but did not miss. I longed to be back in the seat of the cockpit, cramped in its small confines, but up in the freedom of the sky, with one slight twist of the paddle sending you into a steep dive, before being able to level out with such a hit of adrenaline and ecstasy that it could send you quite mad.

I loved being up in the air, where down below it

could be so grey and overcast, but one short burst through the clouds and you would be in a pure brilliant blue. I longed for that freedom, where I could race along at three hundred miles an hour and invert myself for no apparent reason.

But, as I too prepared to leave the house, I realised that I'd forgotten the fear that I experienced sitting in the cockpit.

I could no longer remember what it was like to have a 109 on your tail and the paralytic feeling of doom and destruction that came with it.

I would never forget the first time that happened, as I lined up my gunsight with a *Heinkel* preparing to drop its load on RAF Manston. The dorsal gunner was slow to react, by which time I was safely hidden from his fire by his own tail fin. The bomber, despite my presence, flew straight, and it did not take me long to match its speed and altitude.

Pitching the nose of the hurricane up ever so slightly, to allow for the trajectory of the rounds, I squeezed off a two-second burst of .303.

Almost instantly a trail of white vapour suddenly sprouted from the port side engine, and I could almost sense the panic within the *Heinkel* as they realised they might not make it home.

I had a strange sense of joy in my stomach, which was quickly cut short, as a voice cracked away within my ears.

"Hello Red One. You have a fighter on your tail. Break contact."

They were the words that everyone dreaded to hear, and as I dived I could do nothing but watch, as wisps of smoke began to skirt along the surface of my wings.

Somehow, I managed to avoid the grasp of death that day, and made it home with nothing more than a few bumps and scrapes on my beloved Hurricane. It had been a hairy experience, one that made me ever grateful for the cool air that I breathed when I had managed to take my mask off.

The night air in *Tours*, was biting, but fresh, and gave me the same sense of relief and renewed purpose as I sucked it into my lungs. It felt like the first time that I had fresh air in a very long time, but all the while, there was a crushing weight on my chest that refused to leave.

The blackout had always concerned me, even if I had a weapon on me, it still made me feel uneasy. It was only when one was out and about that you realised just how much you depend on the artificial lighting of a street lamp, or the light of the moon. There is something rather eerie about a residential street that is consumed by darkness. It almost seems darker than the rest of the world, on account of all the shadows and dark crevices that spring up as a result.

It was the kind of people that you could find out in the blackout that filled me with more of a dread than anything else. There were stories aplenty of murder, robbery and assault, none of which I particularly fancied on that night.

But, as I continued to follow Mike in the darkness, I realised that if I found out that he was any one of those kinds of criminals, then it was the best possible outcome from what I could see.

I followed him at such a distance that it was almost impossible to see him, but close enough that if he was to suddenly duck down a side alley or change course, that I would be able to catch up without really losing him for more than a few seconds. All the while, I knew that it was Mike that I was following, as his stocky frame almost waddled, rather than walked. He had long had some sort of ankle injury, sustained at St John's College whilst playing rugby for the first fifteen.

I had never been much of a rugby player, and even if I had, I would have been reluctant to have joined in what I saw as a rather brutal and ungentlemanly game. Mike was always quick to correct me whenever I voiced that assumption.

The longer that I followed Mike, the sweatier my armpits and the more irate my heart became. The more that Mike kept walking, the more I became agitated to find out what it was he was doing out in *Tours* in the middle of the night.

Whatever it was, I knew that it would not be an admirable or desirable activity in which he undertook.

With my head swimming with ideas of crime, black market activity and, at worst, treachery, I kept my gaze fixed on the man that I had thought was my best friend.

Without much warning, Mike began to turn on his heel, forcing me to throw myself at the nearest building that I could find to afford me some sort of cover within its darkened shadows.

From where I was hiding I did not think that he could see me, but I could see him almost as clear as day.

His face looked shifty, worried, as if he had been finally found out about the deepest darkest secret in his life.

He looked left and right, up and down the street, to check that he had not been followed by a German soldier, or worse, one of his own friends.

Without knocking, without even reaching for a key, he turned the door handle on one of the houses and disappeared inside.

All of a sudden, I felt quite alone. Not just physically, but emotionally. There was something sinister about watching your only friend disappear into a house after he had snuck out in the middle of the night, hiding something from everyone that he knew.

A chill swept over my body, as a cloud covered up what moonlight was around that night, and I quickly realised that I would not be able to hang around for much longer, now that I was stationary.

Feeling as empty as I ever had done before in my life, and as quickly as Mike had disappeared into that house, I turned on my heel and made my way back to the safe house, feeling like my sense of security had never been lower.

As I wandered back I realised one thing that I frequently found hard to admit over the last few months, but nonetheless found myself doing anyway.

Suzanne Seguin had been right all along.

It turned out that I could not trust Mike at all.

12

I crawled along on my stomach and I found myself smiling at the thought of having a forked tongue and slits for eyes. Maybe I would feast on a rat or two while I was down at that level.

All of a sudden, I got a face full of leather, with a nice coating of sopping wet mud to go with it. I was annoyed with myself, not least because I would now have to carry the dirt around with me, but also because my simple following act had failed.

Mike turned around, also on his stomach, to look at me.

It was the second time that I had been following him in as many days. But, this time, he knew that I was there.

He lifted up an arm awkwardly and tried to shrug.

"Sorry," I mouthed, spitting out the dirt as I did so.

My whole stomach was coated in the mud, so I

decided not to become too hung up on the fact that my mouth was now joining in with the rest. The mud was thick and gloopy, as if it had been deliberately whisked and folded in order to make it as dough-like as possible.

It was cold too, so cold in fact that it was impossible not to think about it. It caused such a chill in the middle of my bones that it felt like my blood would soon go the same way, and I became frustrated with myself that I had not yanked another pullover on before we had left.

I had to keep reminding myself, however, that the more that I was wearing, the more laborious it would have been to get to my main weapon, which could have cost me precious few seconds.

There was little about my person, as Mike turned away from me once more and began to pull himself through the mud. Apart from the small haversack, strapped tightly to my back, I did not have much else to offer.

But it was undoubtedly the most important item that we had as a group that night and, if I was able to do my job properly, then none of the conventional weapons; the rifles, pistols and submachine guns, would need to be used.

For, inside my canvas haversack, there were two packages, each one not much bigger than a chocolate bar but nowhere near as gratifying. It was hoped, by every person that had set off, that these two blocks could do a lot more damage than a squadron of RAF bombers ever could.

If we could do that, then maybe the air raid sirens would stop, but the destruction would most definitely continue.

The two packages were Clam mines, small, but highly concentrated explosives with just enough TNT in them to give the Germans a jolly good headache. They had, so Mike had told me, been developed by the same chap who had made the Limpet mine, a fully submersible, magnetic mine that could take down a ship the size of the Titanic in a matter of seconds.

The Clams, however, were smaller, more specialised but it was hoped that they would have just as serious consequences.

Within the next few minutes, it was hoped that I would be able to get the Clams ready for their big show and well on their way to hopefully confusing both the Germans, and the RAF.

I was taking a certain pleasure from the fact that Bomber Command might one day soon look at some aerial photographs of the area, and begin scratching their heads as to how it came to pass that such destruction had occurred without their presence.

There was always a fierce rivalry between us fighter pilots and our heavier brothers in Bomber Command. It was a friendly one, as we enjoyed the feeling of protecting each other, but everyone always relished the chance to get one up on the others. And this was the prime opportunity to do just that.

We did not have too much more distance to cover, which was just as well, as I wasn't sure that my arms could continue to bear the weight of the rest of my body for much longer. I could walk for hours, days even, but as soon as I was required to pull myself along, I was fortunate if I was to last more than a few minutes.

We paused for a few seconds, just inside the tree-line, but now only a few hundred yards away from our target.

Despite being so close to where we wanted to be, I could see nothing of what it was that we were there for. The night seemed so dark, so barren of any source of light, that it seemed to me that not even Mother Nature had wanted us out that night.

There was a chill to the air, the kind that reinvigorates rather than debilitates. Having said that, the tips of my fingers were beginning to numb ever so slightly and, while everyone else took sips of water, I struggled with the buckles on the satchel strapped to my back.

But, ever the good agent, I persevered, pulling the chocolate bar-shaped explosive charge from within the canvas enclosure.

As I turned it over in my palm, I thought it was highly peculiar how such a small device could do so much damage. We had heard stories of similar mines bringing down several ships in one night, with the claim of one instructor still ringing in my ears.

"The entire fleet of the German Navy could be sunk in a weekend. All it would take would be some very carefully placed explosives."

I thought of a gaping, sucking hole in the side of a steely-grey ship, as the sorry vessel slowly sunk to the bottom of the ocean.

But there would be none of that tonight, not unless we had got very lost indeed. We were inland, almost as far inland into France as it was possible to go, and there wasn't a floating vessel in sight.

It was difficult not to think of the glory and ecstasy that would come with a successful operation. I could just imagine the brown file that landed on some of the most influential desks in the country, with images of how successful we had been.

I pushed it to one side, frustrated with myself that I was thinking of it almost as an absolute certainty. We had been trained to be confident, even to the point of picturing ourselves as the victors in each situation, but we had also been warned against the dangers of complacency.

Our enemies might have left gaps in their security, gaps that we were only too happy to exploit, but they were by no means fools. And we would do well to remember that, as we hid just inside the treeline.

"Pass one here," Mike breathed, in keeping with the wind.

The breeze that passed over me was peaceful and calming, but all the same chilling and uncomfortable. I wondered if Mike had felt the same.

"Are you alright, old fruit?"

His question was kind and caring, but all it did was fill me with rage.

Since I had followed him the night before, I had tried to keep my distance from him, to try and make myself as objective as I could. The bottom line was the one that had been drilled into us in the Highlands, that if he was now siding with the enemy, I would have to kill him. Regardless if he had once been my best friend or not.

It was difficult for me to begin preparing the groundwork of such an eventuality.

One of the most pressing concerns of mine would be how I was going to do it, as I had a plethora of ways stored in the back of my mind. Captain Fairbairn had been a terrifying man, who had trained the Shanghai Police in brutal methods of brawling, which he called 'Gutter Fighting'.

He had pressed home that the objective of such a fight was not merely to restrain your opponent or to be able to get away, but to end the fight as quickly as possible, by any means.

Fairbairn showed us how to win a fight, with a swift and powerful kick to the groin, or a powerful chop to the neck which, if done correctly, could kill a man if we had wanted to.

We had not spent very long with Fairbairn, as we were rapidly moved on to something else, but along with his handbook, he had left a lasting impression on everyone.

"Barbaric," one fellow had said. "Totally barbaric."

"Brilliant," said another.

Many of us had agreed with both men.

But, as I thought of chokeholds and vice-like grips, I couldn't imagine myself doing it to Mike. There was some sort of mental block.

He was still my friend after all, and we had been through so much together that I despised the thought that it would all have to be cut short simply because he had his head turned by the Germans.

I tried to think of ways around it, including using his contacts to our own advantage. Maybe there was a chance that I could persuade him what he had done was terribly wrong.

"Yeah. I'm fine," I replied.

"Let's get to work then."

I nodded, without really looking at him.

He passed me a small bag, which had two vital pieces of equipment in them. They had been carried separately as, with them in place, it made the Clams ten times more vulnerable and, if there was one thing that I did not particularly want for anyone, it was to be picking me out of bits of trees that I had managed to disperse myself into.

I twiddled the pencil-like object in my hand, marvelling at it. It was a very well machined piece of equipment, and I wondered if its creator had known what tremendous work it was doing out in the field.

The 'L' Delay would act as our fuse for the

evening. Everything would hinge upon it. If it failed, the Clams would be about as deadly as a slap on the wrist.

Moving away from Mike, so that what little light that existed was not shadowed by his movements, I slotted the time pencil into a small incision that was made at one end of the Clam.

It fitted rather snugly, the fuse sticking out of the top by an inch or two, ready to do its duty.

Now, all that was necessary was a gradual removal of the safety pin at the top of the pencil.

This would then initiate the slow, mechanical stretching of a piece of lead inside the pencil, to the point where it would, just like me, be able to bear the tension no longer. The striker would then slam down onto the percussion cap, thus giving the Germans one almighty headache.

And, as it always was with this kind of operation, we were to be as far away from the detonation site as possible when the thing went up. Preferably, we would be in a brand new safehouse, where a pleasant, warm bed would be awaiting us. We could never stay in the same house again after we had pulled off such an act.

I did everything that I dared to, save pulling the pin on the lead delay pencil, so that I could at least feel confident that my weapons were ready to go into battle.

I balled my hand into a fist and stretched them out again, trying to ignore the tremor that was trying its best to remind me that I was a coward.

Mike looked over at me, his face unconcerned. I hid my hand as best as I could, so that I didn't worry him, but his face seemed so at peace that I didn't think anything would shake him at that moment in time.

It struck me as odd for a few seconds. He was so calm, so tranquil. There was something wrong with him. Something that made me think we were about to get a bad piece of news. My stomach churned awfully.

13

The chill that seemed to burst through the centre of the earth began to bite away at my insides, consuming my every thought. I tried with all my might to get some sort of feeling into my extremities, wriggling and waving my toes around inside my boots and clenching my hands as tight as I dared.

But nothing seemed to work, not to the extent that I needed them to, anyway.

There was a great deal riding on this operation, and it wasn't just the thoughts of the Bomber Boys in the mess gearing up to have a crack at what we couldn't achieve.

The message from London had been clear, there was more than bragging rights on offer tonight. It had been a most unusual break from protocol to receive that kind of a message and, as the message was received, Mike's eyes had bulged at the weight of responsibility that had been thrust upon our shoulders.

We couldn't be certain what it was that was hinged on our success, but it hadn't stopped us from trying to guess.

"Do you reckon they're preparing for an invasion, old fruit?"

"They've been preparing for that since Dunkirk."

"What about maybe sending us some help?"

"Could be. Or maybe someone wants to give us the chop."

"Hmm."

Mike hadn't liked the idea of that. He was still enjoying his time in France, as was I, but there was something going deeper for him, further than just kicking the Germans in the groin and causing them great discomfort.

A thought popped into my mind, and not for the first time. He was somehow gaining something from all of this. Profiting somehow.

I had heard of stories of men being paid off by the Germans, or others who sold resistance supplies to anyone that would buy them. But Mike didn't seem to have any more money than I did at his disposal, and nor was there any resources being pinched from anyone our side of the fence. Not that I knew of anyway.

I had no choice but to cut away from it all, to trust Mike. I would merely have to rely on the hope that when it came down to the wire, the memories that I would be able to hark upon as we stared down the barrel of death would be enough for him to come to his senses.

But that, according to Captain Fairbairn, was a romantic view, one that very rarely happened in the thick of a fight. Fights were won, and lost, on primal instincts alone, not human emotions.

The more I thought about how all this was going to end, the colder my body became, a cool sweat just beginning to drip from my brow.

I wiped away at it, as I sighed from the exertion of pulling my body around the floor. It was a sentiment that I knew to be shared by every person with us that night.

We were few in number, but that did not mean that our ambitions or capabilities were low. Quite the contrary was true, in fact.

The five figures that now advanced towards the target were all highly trained, or at least had an admirable amount of experience to warrant a place on the team. Mike and I had trained for months to be there. So too had two of the three Frenchmen on our team, albeit in a completely different country and under different circumstances.

Harry Landes, on the other hand, seemed to be the odd one out in our little team. He had no experience of being in amongst a battle, next to no knowledge of any weapons or explosives and, it came to pass, no awareness when it came to sneaking about during curfew.

Harry, still dressed in a most ridiculous manner, having made quite the fuss about surrendering his tie and jacket, seemed to have no desire to keep his voice down as he spoke at the top of his range the whole way to our target.

The closer we got to our target, and therefore closer to the enemy, the more frustrated we all grew.

"If you don't keep your mouth shut, I will shut it for you. Got it?"

He looked at Mike for a second, his mouth hanging open, a concoction of the fact that he had been mid-way through a sentence but also out of shock. It appeared no one had spoken to him in that tone before.

It had the desired effect. Whether it was out of nerves or a genuine bravado that Harry had been gassing away, it stopped pretty abruptly after Mike's succinct outburst.

"Here we go then. Just over this knoll and we'll be there," Harry mumbled quietly, his eyes darting towards Mike even while he was doing the job that he was meant to do. He was acting as our expert local guide, despite the fact that we all knew exactly where the train station was.

As we crouched and squatted our way over the top of the grassy hill, the midnight dew just seeping into the fibres of our clothes, I impatiently imagined the sight that was to meet our eyes.

During the day, the train station was a hustling hub of activity, where every man and his dog would come to be able to get to work, or as far from their troubles as was possible. The latter was getting harder by the day, as the Germans' vice-like grip continued to press down on the throat of every Frenchman, and a few Englishmen alike.

The residents of *Tours* could only really use the trains for work nowadays, and even then, the chances of getting a pass were slim. It seemed like the only ones that could travel the railway lines unhindered were the Germans and their mistresses.

But now, after dark, the station would be in a semi-darkness, with the odd flash of a torchlight as it swept its way around the railyard.

The train line itself ran right the way through the station, with a small brick-built hut that stood in the centre of the platform.

It was what was contained in the sidings that would be of our particular attention that night.

It was Mike who had spotted them at first and, being unable to risk having a second look, a series of local men, handpicked by Suzanne, had followed his footsteps to check that what he was seeing was not a mirage.

He had seen flatbed railway carts, the kind that would soon be loaded with armoured vehicles and heavy weaponry and transported to wherever they would be needed next.

Mike had seen them beginning to load up the day

before, but only with a handful of antiaircraft guns. But it was from one of Suzanne's loyal followers, a railway worker by the name of Étienne, who had delivered us with the golden nugget that we had all been hoping for.

Tanks had been loaded on, as well as two six-inch artillery pieces that looked far more menacing than the armoured vehicles. If we could somehow manage to derail the sidecars, complete with their loads, then there was a chance that we would be able to hold up the entire regiment. We finally had the prospect to really inconvenience the Germans far more than we ever had done before.

But, best of all, Étienne had heard of something that none of the others could have garnered from their brief strides past the station.

The regiment of armour was preparing to move out in the morning, and they needed to take supplies.

At the very end of the line of flatbeds and carriages was a large, steel cylinder. It was filled with fuel for the vehicles. That petrol tanker alone would have been enough to justify our presence, but it would be able to assist us in our attempt to throw everything in the station towards the gods.

"What's the time?" Mike's voice breathed into my ear.

"Coming up to one-thirty. Not long to go now. Two minutes at the most."

We were waiting for the long hand to hit the six

on my watch face. Everything needed to be done to the second.

Étienne had worked on the railway for the last five years, but crucially had been employed by the Germans ever since the occupation. His quiet persistence and observation, the seriousness of which even he hadn't realised, was all about to pay off.

The guards were due to change at one-thirty exactly. In all the time that Étienne had worked there, he had not known them to be late in changing once. Which was good for us, it meant that they were predictable.

As I lay just the other side of the knoll, I thought of one of the last times that I had adopted a similar position.

There was a hut, just through a copse at the edge of a woodland, surrounded by a low fence, which was irritatingly guarded by a length of barbed wire around its top. There was no way over it, not if one did not want to rip their trousers in a most embarrassing fashion.

The only way in was to slide through one of the gaps, designed to let the guards and occupants in and out when they needed passage. But getting in was easier said than done, especially when there were always at least three pairs of eyes trained on each clearing.

That hut had been in some remote country estate in Scotland, where I had felt quite safe. But the lessons that it had taught me remained with me even while I was lying in the grass near *Tours,* almost a thousand miles apart.

No one wanted to be out on stag for four hours at a time, especially in the middle of the night. But that's where the Germans' belief in their superiority lead to a great chasm in their security.

Their men were exposed to the chill of the night, just as we were, but were expected to fight off the call of their beds, as well as the boredom of pacing up and down, and remain as vigilant as though they had been told the enemy was crouching at his door.

But it was impossible, even for the battle-hardened German who had no experience of any kind of defeat.

It was why we were waiting for the end of their shift. In the few minutes leading up to the end of their time on patrol, they would be at their weakest; thinking of a warm cup of coffee, or the sumptuous rest of their pillows.

We were close enough now to hear a few calls from men who were desperate to be relieved. They were in high spirits. I couldn't blame them; they were about to get their heads down after all.

Normally, I would have felt guilty that I was about to prevent them from getting to bed or cutting their lives short. But there was to be none of that.

This was to be a quiet-as-a-mouse situation. We wanted no one to know that we had been there.

The fuses were set for eight hours which, according to Étienne, would mean that the convoy would be well on their way to their destination. If we were to have any good fortune, the Germans would struggle to even know where the charges had been attached to the rail carts.

"Okay," I gasped, almost taken by surprise despite the fact that I had been staring at my watch face for the last ninety seconds. "It's time."

There was no rush of air or bellowing of lungs like you would normally expect for an attack as important as this one. But war was changing, and we were at the tip of the spear.

We lifted ourselves from our positions and slowly waddled our way towards the station.

The guards would be changing, and by moving as slowly as possible, we made it incredibly difficult to be seen.

We had been trained to make no sudden movements; no arm signals to one another, no sudden dropping to the floor when a rifle was raised, not even a sudden jump if you triggered a mine.

But, as we continued to advance on our target, it became apparent that some sudden movement was going to be necessary.

One of us was going to have to be the one to make the decision. It might as well have been me.

I grabbed Mike's sleeve, hauling him to the floor. I felt, rather than heard, the ground all around me rustle as the others voluntarily did the same.

I felt my nostrils flare with anger and fury as I

stared at him, water gushing to my eyes as I tried my utmost to keep some semblance of composure.

Mike's face was not one that mirrored my own. While anger simmered inside my stomach, it seemed only disappointment bubbled in his.

But the same question was on both of our lips.

Where were the trains?

14

I felt as though I was slowly drowning in my own thoughts as we began our retreat back to our starting point. Whatever had happened, there was one thing that was clear in my mind. Our evening out, which had taken days to prepare, had ended in total failure.

We had simply been too slow to react. If we had been able to rustle up a few more explosives, a few more men and ideas, then we could have gone the night before, when the flatbed carriages were all still in position.

The bounty might not have been quite so plentiful, but the thought that we had failed as a result of our greed was one that I could not shake.

My body, awash with aches and pains that I had accrued on our approach, began to protest at the situation and, for a few moments, I even interpreted its calls as ones wishing to return, to place the explosives somewhere else.

At least that way we might have the Germans scared that we didn't care what we hit.

But then, as the pains began to float to my head, I realised that it was unlikely the trains would have simply disappeared, and how it had all conveniently moved on by the time we had got there.

As I pulled myself back over the grassy knoll that we had perched behind not half an hour before, my thoughts became all the more sinister, seditious.

In our planning, we had remained so tight-lipped that we had barely breathed a word to each other about exactly what we were going to do.

We wanted to go in under the ethos of dying to plan would mean we would have to plan to die. Spontaneity was what was going to get us through, it meant that we would adapt to the situation easier, otherwise, we could have been so focused on our plan that we could end up flat on our faces.

But, even still, there were a number of people who knew about the target. Mike, Suzanne, Harry and I had been at the head of the table, with several other locals reporting back to us on what they saw.

We had asked at least three men to go to the station and report on the busyness of the sidings that were less than half a mile away. It wouldn't have taken a genius to work out what our thinking was.

I berated myself, for allowing that many people, people we barely knew, into our thoughts. It was plain to see that we had been betrayed.

Or was it? My mind was so tempestuous that I did

not know what to think any longer. I played with the idea that maybe the regiment had been called up at a moment's notice, to shore up some other defences elsewhere.

Or maybe they had simply finished loading up earlier than expected.

I needed to push all these kind of thoughts from my head. They could wait until later. But, even then, they would be too soon. Everyone knew that paranoia was an agent's biggest killer.

Let that get the better of you and you're no more help than a small child with a pea shooter.

Thankfully though, courtesy of the Germans, there was something at hand to distract me from my neurotic musings.

A flash of light sparkled in my eyes, so bright that it was as if I had looked into the sun in the middle of the day.

But it was approaching one o'clock in the morning. The sun was nowhere to be seen.

It took my brain longer than it should have done to process that the source of the light was, in fact, from a flashlight.

It danced around on the top of the knoll for a few seconds, and I slid down the bank with as much decorum as a worm, desperately trying to get out of the beam of light.

I knew that it had been too late though. The pillar of white had splashed straight across my face.

I knew that the German guard who was clutching

the torch in his sweaty palm would have seen me as clear as anything. He would have seen the beads of perspiration on my brow, the creases that enveloped the entirety of my face and, I was sure of it, that he would have been able to see the agonising thoughts that poured forth from my mind.

To my right, I caught the whisper of a voice, harsh enough to be recognisable as a word that you wouldn't want your mother to hear.

It lifted my spirits, only for a second, as I entertained the idea that maybe I hadn't been the only timid, frustrated face to have been caught in the light.

Whoever it was on the other end of the torch though couldn't have been the brightest fellow. He did not call out to any of his compatriots, or rush back to get some help. Instead, he kept coming towards us, his light shining off to the right as he searched for any more movement along the knoll.

I chanced a quick look over the parapet.

Behind the man, the dimmed lights of the train station continued to strain away into the night, locked in a battle with the all-consuming darkness that would only be ended by the rising sun.

His face was silhouetted against the light, so that all I could make out was the vague outline of his coal scuttle helmet, that always looked far too big for its occupant's head. I was yet to see one that looked as though it sat comfortably on a man.

I couldn't tell for certain, but the way the man held himself I made a wary guess that he was an older gentleman. His shoulders were hunched over and lopsided, perhaps under the weight of the rifle slung over one of them.

He walked slowly, but not out of choice, it seemed as though every step he took towards us caused him immeasurable pain.

Despite his underwhelming and lacklustre appearance, there was no denying that the man was brave. No one would have ever caught me approaching a bank of grass in the middle of the night after my flashlight had just caught someone in its glare.

But, then again, maybe he hadn't seen us.

Either way, there was no way that we would be able to risk it. The poor man was dead as soon as he had flicked his lamp on.

As the light beam got bigger, I pushed everything from my mind. I became solely focused on the man behind the lamp.

I didn't feel sorry for him, not really. There was an element of remorse, but it was more because my hand had been forced and I would need to do away with him, rather than try and get away without being seen.

It was all too far gone for that.

But, as he reached the top of the mound, I realised that maybe he hadn't seen us after all.

His rifle was still resting on his lopsided shoulders, and he was bouncing around on his toes as if he was stood on hot coals.

Then, there was the noise of buttons being undone, followed by the sweet stench of urine as it came cascading down the other side of the mound, onto the three men below.

It was warm, but not warm enough to make me feel comfortable. In fact, it had the opposite effect.

I closed my eyes and waited for the man to finish, which seemed to take longer than any I had ever had. The man must have been holding it in for ages. I almost felt sorry for him.

My remorse and sorrow towards the man suddenly surged, as I watched a pair of clumsy and cracked hands reach out from the darkness and clamp themselves firmly around the calves of the man, just above his boots.

He was suddenly yanked violently backwards, his knees appearing to lock out and almost pop from their natural positions.

The man, with nothing more than an exasperated grunt, hit the floor face first. A nice cracking sound accompanied his fall as his nose gave in to the force.

The steaming urine from his own bladder would be one of the last things he would see.

A boot, dirtied and battered from the constant crawling through the grass, was pressed down into the back of his neck so that he couldn't move while the rifle was stolen from his possession.

To his credit, the man obeyed every silent command and barely moved a muscle as he felt a pair of hands running over him, searching for anything that could be of any use. His passivity continued, even after the hands had stopped rummaging, and as the first blow of the rifle butt came down on the back of his head.

His skull seemed to put up even less of a fight than he had done, as it quickly disintegrated, leaving a sticky mess of blood over the rifle.

The polished oak stock came down thrice more, until there was nothing more of the man's head other than a beaten pulp and random clumps of matter.

The whole time the man hadn't uttered a word. Not even a grimace towards his compatriots had been grumbled.

The rifle, itself battered from the fight it had just found itself in, was discarded on the ground as if nothing had happened, almost like it had simply fallen from the man's shoulder.

"Come on then. We ought to get a move on."

Harry and I sat, open-mouthed, as we stared at the beaten mess that Mike had just created. He spoke with such a coolness that I thought that maybe it hadn't been him that had just pulverised the man's head.

But it couldn't have been anyone else. The blood that dripped from his hands and face was enough to tell me that.

"Why did you do that?"

"He saw us."

"No. No, he didn't. You didn't need to do that."

"I didn't see you trying to stop me."

I tried to look into his eyes, which seemed nothing more than two black beads of darkness now, like a rat.

I tried to search his soul, in an attempt to draw out some sort of memory from his past that would restore him to his former self. But there was nothing there. He seemed like he had disappeared altogether.

There was something hiding in him though, something that seemed to supersede all of his emotions and judgements. But, without clambering into his head alongside him, I doubted that I would ever really know.

But I was sure of one thing. I needed to get rid of Mike, and soon. He was rapidly forgetting everything that he had been trained in. And he was becoming a liability.

We began to retreat back to the treeline, safe in the knowledge now that there wasn't a single German following us.

My limbs felt heavy and cumbersome as we trudged back. Normally, I would have some sort of elation or adrenaline to drive me on, to make my body think that it was fine, but I had nothing. All I had was the pain in my limbs and the emptiness in the pit of my stomach.

I had never felt so deflated, so dejected. But there was something that did make me want to carry on, a sense of duty perhaps. I needed to know what it was that was making Mike behave in the way that he had done these past few days.

Things were beginning to tenuously link themselves together in my mind, but I forced them from becoming anything too sinister. I did not want to do anything that I would not be able to remedy further down the line. Not yet anyway.

Once again, as I had done so many other times before, I erased everything from my mind.

I would take things one step at a time. All that I could focus on now, was making it back to that tree-line. I would take things from there.

15

By the time that I had reached the treeline, every bone in my body ached as if I had just climbed the tallest mountain known to man. But none of that pain was in any way comparable to the pain that was now excruciatingly searing through my head.

I knew that the situation was bleak, that we had just wasted a lot of time and effort in observing the movement of the troops, gathering intelligence and stockpiling explosives. And now, we had no chance of using them for the foreseeable future.

What was worse, was that Mike had unnecessarily killed a German sentry, which would put the entire local garrison on alert. There was no way that we would be able to pass that one off as an accident, no one trips and smashes their skull into a thousand pieces in a moment of misfortune.

I looked at the weary and disappointed faces that met us just inside the treeline, each man armed with some kind of weapon, that they had been only too glad to have received earlier on in the evening. Each one of them had their own reason for resisting the Germans, but they all were united in the same courage and bravery that I was finding it difficult to conjure up.

They had been expecting an almighty explosion at some point in the not too distant future, but as they saw us returning with satchels full and hearts empty, they knew that their moment of triumphant resistance would have to wait for now.

Once inside the comforting embrace of the trees, a few branches swaying in the breeze and hitting each other with a slight crack, the men slowly allowed themselves to speak. They were mere mutterings at first, but the longer we let them go unchecked, the more energetic and powerful the voices became.

One or two of them rushed up to both Harry and to Mike, to make their protestations known to the two men. Some of them were already hoisting their weapons from their shoulders and holding them up as if they were preparing to defend themselves.

Others milled around in small groups of two or three, waving their arms around in a terrific windmill-like fashion, as they vented to one another about their frustrations and annoyances. Something had really got their goat.

I could understand their frustration, I was feeling it just as much as they were. I also acknowledged silently that this was their homeland, and the prospect of denting the apparent invincibility of the occupying forces was not one that should be abandoned on the technicality of a missing target.

To them, there was no missing target. Any man that breathed a word of German in this country was an enemy worthy of being subdued.

Their voices continued to crawl upwards in volume, until a smattering of birds suddenly launched themselves from the treetops in a fright. As their scatty wings slowly subsided into the enveloping silence of the trees, the men around me, about ten in number, began to continue their tirades with a renewed vigour.

My heart began to race as I thought that, at any moment, we would be surrounded by a German platoon that had managed to sneak up on us and catch us unaware.

And that was the last thing that we needed right now.

My head throbbed as my mind quickened, searching for some sort of solution to the most surreal of situations. The thought even crossed my mind fleetingly that I should agree to their demands and launch some sort of pathetic assault on the train station, however futile the whole thing seemed.

Although, seeing the passion and fervour that hid behind their eyes, I would have happily led those men on a march to Gestapo headquarters in Berlin, confident in the knowledge that they would somehow find a way through.

They were fired up. But the train station in and of

itself was not a target that would have the Bomber Command boys kneeling at golden statues of us. These chaps would have to wait.

"What's going on with them? Have they had too much to drink?" I asked Mike as he managed to break away from the mob intent on the destruction of someone.

Mike and I had refrained from the wine that was passed around the men shortly before we had left, despite the fact that I missed the taste of the sweet liquid as it passed over my lips. The French resistors were more than happy to let the bottle pass us by, it meant more for them after all.

"No, I don't think so," Mike replied, as he reached a clammy hand to his forehead to peel off a layer of sweat. We had worked hard in crawling to and from the station, but there was more perspiration resting on Mike's head than on my own.

It was only then that I had remembered what he had done. At the thought of the German's skull, cracked and smashed with bits of splintered bone, I unconsciously stepped away from him slightly, just in case he happened to be in the mood of cracking more than one head that evening.

It was a far cry from how we had been a few years' before, studying together at St John's College, Cambridge and getting in a right state together. Mike had been sensitive and mild-mannered, but could be aggressive when he needed to be, but only in moderation, and mainly when he was on a sports field.

He had a brilliant mind, reading the history of art and architecture and excelling in every element of academia that the college could throw at him. But it was that very same mind that had become perverted, twisted, into the one that now stood beside me.

It had been a gradual process, but one that I struggled to comprehend. He had a hatred of the Germans now, that wasn't just a gentlemanly rivalry that it had been when we had been flying Hurricanes together, but a deep-rooted, passionate one, that I found hard to be heard over.

I thought back to the death of one of the fellows in our Squadron; Teddy Higgins. I had not seen the man go down, I had not even been in the cockpit of my kite that day, but Mike had. And he had blamed himself for his death, a result of his parachute neglecting to open.

But I failed to see how that could have turned Mike into the cold-hearted killer that he had become. It was the luck of the draw. That was how war went, and I thought that he could accept that. But clearly, he was finding it difficult.

Harry, still dressed in all his finery that seemed so out of place in a situation such as this, coolly stepped over to the most vocal of the group, with the air of a diplomat around him. He was a curious figure, standing there in the dark, shirt still pressed within an inch of its life, as he spoke to them like a union worker to his disgruntled comrades.

He spoke forcefully, but calmly and, one by one,

like a well-respected schoolteacher, his subordinates slowly wound themselves down, so that their grievances were nothing more than mutterings once more.

I inched towards Harry, who gave me a sense of confidence that I did not feel that I got from anyone else. Despite everything, he seemed as though he was in control, not just of the situation, but of himself. The same could not be said for me, my heart was beating faster than the winner of the Grand National.

It seemed as though he had done all of this before; the sneaking around, the sudden crushing disappointment, followed by the pacifying of his fellow resistors who seemed incandescent with rage.

I took a few moments to simply watch him, the contours of his face moulding and contorting depending on who it was he was speaking to. His face moved around in the dark so much that I thought at any moment he would simply turn into another person altogether, as if there was already one waiting beneath his skin and dying to get out.

But nothing came.

I went and stood next to him.

"Thank you, Harry. What did you say to them?" I asked, rather sheepishly at the thought that, despite all the training I had received, calming a group of Frenchmen down had not been a lesson on offer.

"Nothing much. I just listened to them for a while. I let them vent. We Frenchmen are good at doing that. We love a good moan."

"But why were they so animated?"

Harry cleared his throat and looked to the floor, for the first time that night coming across as slightly vulnerable, ashamed even. He shivered slightly, as the chill of the night began to bite into the greatcoat of excitement that had been enshrouding us all for the last few moments.

"Maybe that is not a question for me, my friend. I think you should ask your compatriot about what it was they were saying."

"Mike?" I asked, knowing full well that he was the only compatriot on the team.

Harry remained silent, apart from giving me an answer with a knowing glare. Mike's head was already dipped low by the time that I had got to him.

"What did you say to those Frenchies that got them all riled up like that?" I asked, my words jabbing at his very soul.

"Look…Those trains were meant to be there, alright? I didn't know that they would react in the way that they did." He continued with his mitigation for as long as I would allow him to.

Everyone else had fallen silent, observing the two lonely figures, quite apart from the group, as they sounded out their disagreement together.

"What did you say to them, Mike?" I asked, more forcefully, the impact of the words hitting home greater than an enemy round.

"Earlier on…before we left…I…I…I promised them a fight this evening. I thought we would need them. I said that they would taste some blood."

"You did what?!" My throat ripped as I strained to keep my voice down but also allow the anger to surge to my throat. Every inch of my body was suddenly consumed by perspiration, my skin reddening with fury at his words.

Within seconds, I found Mike pinned up against a tree, my fingernails digging into folds of flesh that had inadvertently been caught in my grip. I held him by the lapels of his jacket, which creaked and ripped as it tried to break free.

A torrent of words suddenly poured from my mouth, as I almost completely lost control. A fist connected with his cheekbone, as he went limp in my grasp. I had seen red completely, so much so that a picture of Mike's skull, cracked and splintered, lay in my hands, after I had given him the same good news with a rifle as he had done to the German sentry.

It was only after the fourth blow to the trunk of his body, his spittle and saliva all over my face, that anyone did anything to help either of us.

It was Harry who managed to restrain me to the best of his ability, two of his men holding Mike up in pain so that we were still at eye level.

"Why would you tell them such a thing? Risk everything, after everything we've been taught. Why would you kill that man? He hadn't even seen us."

His eyes were now overcome with tears, as he realised that this was not the sort of fury that would simply pass away.

Harry's grip on me loosened, as if he wanted me

to have another go at Mike. It was then that I realised that he had allowed me to strike Mike, he could have easily stopped any of it coming to blows. But, maybe he didn't want to get that jacket of his any dirtier than it already was.

There was no need for me to lunge at Mike anymore, the physical pain I had inflicted was already enough for him. But it didn't mean I was finished with him, I had one parting blow.

"It wouldn't surprise me if you had something to do with those carriages disappearing."

16

I began to hate myself for it, the more time that I gave to the thought, the more I became utterly convinced that Mike had something to do with the disappearance of the carriages.

However, there was a bone somewhere in my body, smaller and weaker than all the others at that time, that told me that Mike's involvement could not possibly have been as bad as I was thinking.

Mike had been the one to see the trains first, which led me to believe that he had also been the last one to have seen them too. Mike had always had a mysterious and slightly devious streak within him, and the thought of him paying off some of the other resistors, simply for them to say that they had seen the train, was not one that I could shake off. There was even a chance that money was not even necessary.

The local resistors made no secret of the fact that

they wanted a fight, and so it was not unreasonable to believe that Mike, himself frustrated with the lack of progress that we had been making, had in some way been embroiled in a plot to get us into a skirmish with the Germans.

"I really think you should take more time to consider this, my friend. You work hard. You are tired. Sometimes that makes a man's judgements ever so slightly warped."

"I know him, Harry," I whispered, leaning over the golden oak table, "I know him. There is something going on with him. Something eating him up. And it wouldn't surprise me if it was to do with those trains."

Harry sighed, bringing his hands to rest on the table in front of us, as he leaned into me and whispered urgently in my face.

"You must be careful. If you focus entirely on what you *think* he has done, you can put yourself in great danger. After all, you must remember that no one died the other night."

"Not this time they didn't." I leaned back in my chair, letting my entire body slump with exhaustion. My face felt heavy with grease and grime, the huge golf balls under my eyes making it difficult to even blink, never mind sleep.

The prospect of sleep was one that I could not entertain, not during night hours anyway, as I was constantly on guard waiting for Mike to make a move once again. I had resolved with myself that the next time I heard him leave, I was to catch up, and confront him. There was no other way to get to the bottom of this than to attack it head-on.

I looked Harry up and down, as he surveyed the latest news in the newspaper spread out across the table, his pointed and waxy nose directing his eyes towards the print, his spectacles hanging tantalisingly close to falling from his face completely.

He had a new suit on, one that I had not seen before, but one that looked remarkably British in tailoring. It was almost khaki in colour, and had more pockets dotted around it than a snooker table.

His hat, the one that he always wore, was by his side as always, and I supposed that he had the small revolver resting underneath it, always ready for action.

Everything about him, his posture, his demeanour, even the way he read a newspaper, screamed that he was a gentleman of the most decent kind. How he had become embroiled in the ungentlemanly warfare that we advocated was beyond me. However, I was glad that he was there.

Over the last few days, I had needed someone to speak to, to get things off my chest, and to get a different perspective on the rather blinkered war that I was fighting. Harry had been the one who had allowed me to speak, the only one who seemed to have shared in any kind of suspicion of Mike. But, as he had so often reminded me, he was suspicious of everyone. After all, the very same men who had fought to keep his country free in the last war, were now the very same men who had surrendered their nation to their oppressors.

I watched as his beady little eyes, as dark as a rat's, scanned the words printed on the page before him. They twitched so violently that I was convinced he was not taking any of them in and was merely using it as an excuse not to talk to me any longer.

"All I'm asking, Harry," I rasped, reaching for the mug of tepid tea laid out before me, "is that you keep an open mind. I don't think Mike—"

"Enough. That's enough. You have got to stop doing this. You have been sent here to do a job. And all you are doing is fighting your friend. Do you not see how that will prevent us from fighting back? You must stop, we are all on the same side after all."

He rustled up his paper without much order and flung it under his arm as he stormed from the room, leaving his trusty hat behind. He really was furious; I had never seen him abandon that hat before.

I bit my tongue as he walked away, wanting desperately to protest, to argue how I was not so sure that we were all on the same side. But I refrained, conscious of the fact that I had already lost Mike as a friend, and I did not want to tip Harry over the edge.

I looked around me sheepishly, hoping that no one else would really have taken notice of Harry's outburst. But I knew full well that everyone in the room would have heard every single one of his words.

Fortunately for me, the only person who happened to be in the room at the time was Suzanne, the bruises on her face now ballooning and turning a deep purple in colour, each one looking as if a handful of blueberries had been pressed into her skin.

She did nothing to acknowledge my look, except to sit there and carefully consider what was going on around her. She had started to change from the woman that I had first met, the one who had an opinion on everything, and was not afraid to voice it at every given opportunity.

Now, she was a thinker, more because her mobility was restricted and so she had no other weapon with which to fight. But she was also an observer, silently taking in every bit of intelligence that she could gather on every single person in the house, building up a profile and garnering evidence that she could use against anyone of us from every possible source.

I had found a new respect for her, in her relative silence, in that I desired to be just like her. As with Harry, I looked her up and down, hoping to find some sort of support in her pleasant, but battered, facial features.

I noticed something in her hand, and it flashed white just long enough for me to catch sight of it, as she screwed it up into her palm and stuffed it away inside a pocket somewhere.

The parts of her face that were not blue with

bruising suddenly flashed scarlet, as she tried to hide the fact that she too was now keeping something from me.

Before I could enquire as to what it was that was playing on her mind, she was already speaking as she manoeuvred her way around the room to take Harry's place, across the table from me.

She had a stern look in her eyes, the very same eyes that looked so cold, until one just looked deeper. For a brief second, she looked almost like a mother figure, who was lovingly approaching her foolish offspring, ready to reprimand them for yet another misadventure.

But, as she drew closer to me, something changed her mind, something which told her she would need to change her approach.

"Look, I know that I told you about Mike and how we should keep an eye on him." She looked nervously to the bottom of the staircase, aware that Mike could arise from his bed at any moment. "But, for what it's worth, I don't believe that he was involved in what happened the other night."

I paused, waiting for her to fill the void of silence, but her eyes stubbornly refused. She wanted me to say my piece.

"It's not just the fact that the trains were gone," I croaked pathetically. "But it was the way he killed that sentry. There was no need for it. He could have compromised everyone there. And that body isn't going to go away by itself."

I closed my eyes, the picture of a crushed skull lying before me smashing into my chest as I sat there in the comfort of the kitchen. It was that picture, coupled with the one of Mike holding a rifle butt high above his head, that refused to shake from my memory while I stared at Suzanne.

"My father used to believe that there was honour to war, a gamesmanship if you like. Everyone, in his world, would follow the rules. But there are none, anymore. We all broke them, long ago."

"There's fighting a war without rules, and then there's common human morality," I retorted. I rose to my feet and began pacing around the room, the cramp that had been knocking at the door for the last couple of days, finally beginning to sink its teeth into all the muscles that it could find.

My body was fighting the tiredness, hard. But the cloudiness that was enshrouding my mind was beginning to cloud my rationality. I could feel my temper wearing thin by the minute.

"What you need," Suzanne said, spinning around in a chair to follow my movement. "Is something else to focus on. I can see it is killing you both to be cooped up in here. This was not why you were sent to this country after all."

I nodded, trying to shake away the cobwebs that were beginning to obscure my sound thinking. I sat down next to her, pulling my chair in as close as I could get to her, so that she needn't raise her voice quite so much. I was aware that her chest had been crushed greatly in the blast, which made breathing, as well as speaking, more difficult than it was for me. I pulled my body in towards hers, until I felt the moist warmth of her breath on my flushing cheek. Suzanne continued.

"What happened to me… What happened to the trains the other night… I… I think, maybe," she jumped, suddenly, as a figure appeared in the room that we had not been expecting.

Mike's stocky, rugby player frame, had inexplicably managed to glide down the stairs and into the room without either of us noticing.

He noticed the slightly sheepish look on both of our faces, as we were caught embarrassingly close to one another. Instinctively, we both recoiled slightly, leaning back in our chairs so that we did not come across as suspicious as we had looked.

"What's going on?" Mike demanded as he strode into the room.

"N-Nothing," I tremored, as if the headmaster had just caught me stealing apples from a local farmer.

Suzanne, as commanding as ever, seemed unfazed as she spoke.

"What happened with the trains," she began, "and what happened to me… I think they are somehow… Related. I think there is something connected to all of our misfortune recently. If we can sort it then we can get back to normal."

"And how do you propose that we do that?" Mike asked, his speech as pointed as a bayonet.

Suzanne was unperturbed, and deflected Mike's aggressive questioning with a simple command.

"Sit down. I have an idea about how to sort it. But I don't think you two are going to like it."

17

"No. No, absolutely not. You must all think of me as some stark raving loony if you think I would agree to that. You've got more of a chance of getting that Bavarian to sue for peace than to get me to agree to that idea."

"I think he'll warm to the idea," Mike said, trying to alleviate some of the tension that I had managed to smash down on everyone like a sledgehammer. The look on Suzanne's face told me that she had been expecting every element of my reaction entirely. At least I knew that it meant I wasn't being completely unreasonable.

I shot a look towards Mike, the smirk that had crept up the corner of his clammy cheek quickly falling away. His wasn't the only skin that appeared greasy and slimy. All of ours did. Harry had assured us that he knew someone who could get us a proper bar of soap, on the black market, but until that promise came up trumps, we had to make do with an amalgamation of fats that Suzanne had resourcefully conjured up.

The smell that clung to the walls of the room that we found ourselves in was almost unbearable, the only thing able to combat it was the plumes of smoke that dwindled in the air from everyone's fingers. Until recently, Suzanne had never smoked, but now she had no choice. It was either that or smell the perspiration on one another for every minute of every day.

"Well, I for one think it is a splendid idea. It's not like we're getting any luckier, is it? And it would be better to be able to confront it, head-on, before it begins nipping away at our heels too much."

A scoff passed over my cracked and sore lips, "I thought you would say something like that."

"What do you mean by that, old fruit?" He cut the last couple of words short, as if they had snuck up on him and leapt out without his say so. The last thing that either of us seemed to want at the moment was to appear like we were friends, that would be a sign of weakness.

"You want a distraction. You want something that you can do without giving any of the consequences a second thought."

I stopped short of calling him an all-out traitor, but in my heart, I thought that the reason that he needed a distraction was to be able to continue giving up our secrets, betraying us behind our backs.

He said nothing, settling instead with an icy glare

that, had I only just met him, would have filled me with the most overwhelming fear that I could imagine. But, in the event, nothing seemed to pass over me other than a slight chill to the backs of my hands.

I turned away from him, caring little for the fact that it might appear that I was the weaker link in the chain. Instead, my eyes fell on Harry Landes, the peculiar Frenchman acting in his normal, peculiar way.

He seemed disconnected from what was being said, but nonetheless present and subtly taking everything in. He was trying his hardest to avoid being sucked in, finding the whole thing as mightily awkward as the rest of us. But, behind the glazed look in his eyes, I could see the brainpower working in overdrive as he considered everything, quietly, as he tried to come up with some sort of a solution.

"I do not think it is such a big ask," Suzanne's quaint voice peered into the void of silence, her soft tones making her English sound like another language. "All I am asking to do is to meet my contact. It is how I always gathered information before, that is all. He can help us; I am sure of it."

"Your contact will already be dead, Suzanne. The sooner that you face up to that fact, the better."

"You cannot know this."

"I do know it. Look what happened to you the last time you tried to meet him." My arms waved around, trying to point her attention to the scabs that had formed up her arms and the bruises that still glowed under the surface of her skin.

"The poor man was in all likelihood set up himself. He probably had no other choice but to meet you. I doubt he knew that you were about to get blown up."

"That is not what happened."

"Oh, yeah? Then how can you be so sure? You're asking all of us to put our lives in his hands, and you don't even know which side he is working on. For all you know he could be back with his Fatherland."

"No, he's not."

"Why not?"

"Because he is not like that."

"Why would a man lead you into a trap like that then?"

"Why would you care so much about what happened anyway?" she exploded, rising from her chair with a wince to her face.

"Because I don't want to see you come to any harm! It was awful for me…" My face blushed red almost immediately, as the tears that threatened to roll down my greasy cheeks made a similar move in Suzanne's eyes.

I felt like I had said too much, as a lightning bolt of pain ripped across my chest as I collapsed into a chair nearby. I had been sapped of all my energy.

"Yes, well this is all very…touching," Mike's words were long and drawn-out, like a barrister who was carefully making his closing statement in court. His darkened eyes scanned each occupant in the room, making sure that he had total command over our attention.

"But sitting on our hands and telling one another of our affections is going to get us nowhere. We've been holed up in these awful houses for the last few weeks now. The Germans are getting closer to us, and if we don't do anything soon, we'll be about as much use to this country as a car with no fuel."

He looked the three other people in the room up and down. He didn't leave enough room for any one of us to speak, it seemed that he had not made himself quite clear.

"We need to make a decision," he affirmed, giving us each a nudge in the direction that he wanted. I felt his words gently prod me in the back, as if he was directing a criticism towards me for being the indecisive one.

There was a moment before I spoke where all the eyes seemed to be upon me, the stagnant air freezing as the cigarette smoke twirled and danced no longer. Everything hung quite still, as if patiently waiting for me to speak, so that everyone was able to breathe once more.

My stomach churned around and tied itself in several knots as I began to deliberate over the proposition before me. It was not a decision that I had wanted to make, nor was it one that I thought should have even been put forward.

However, it was true that the net was beginning to

tighten on us and, to continue being any use to the brass back in Baker Street, then we were going to have to sort this problem out, one way or another.

I just had to hope that my gut instincts were wrong, and that I would see the next episode of my life out relatively unscathed.

"Alright. Let's go with Suzanne's plan."

Mike almost burst into tears at the news, forcibly suppressing a wide grin from bursting across his face.

"Great. We should get the wheels in motion at once."

"But there's one condition to it all," I announced, cutting his celebrations short.

"What's that, old fruit?" he queried, the sentiments surrounding the nickname genuinely returning for a moment or two.

"No one else knows about this. No one else joins us. It is to be us four in this room and us alone. I do not want a repeat of what happened by the train station."

My eyes darted over to Mike viciously, as I imagined him tracking down a few of the more vocal resistors who could be persuaded to have a pop at the Germans.

"It will be safer that way."

I knew deep down, that it wouldn't have made an iota of difference if the rest of the resistors were there or not. In fact, we probably would have been safer with their guns behind us.

But in truth, I did not want those men to die

needlessly, for some silly little plan that had been proposed, negotiated and agreed to within the space of half an hour.

We began to make moves to prepare ourselves for the outing that we were about to embark upon. There was a feeling within me that knew that nothing was going to go to plan, and it wasn't even hiding itself in the pit of my stomach this time.

My hands, that had sweated for what felt like months on end without ceasing, perspired even more, as my palms slipped over the small, and frankly inadequate weapon, that I would have about my person once we left.

I knew, just as all the others did, that if we had to use these weapons, then we may as well have saved them purely for personal use. The way in which that we had to execute the plan, meant that if Suzanne's contact had in fact seen the light of his Fatherland, then the entire German army stationed in France would be there to greet us. There wasn't much stopping power in a *Modéle* 1892 revolver's .3 inch round.

"Are you okay?" Suzanne's shoulder bumped into my arm as she drew up next to me. I took a slight step away from her, in case the unnatural closeness was to draw anyone's attention.

"Do you trust him?"

"Who?"

"Adolf…your friend, the German."

Her eyes, for once, appeared interesting, as the dull colour began to brighten as she spoke.

"Yes, I trust him. And his name is Martin. Not Adolf," she said sternly, clearly offended that I would make such an insinuation.

"And he trusts you?"

"Yes."

"How did you get his trust?"

She shuffled around for a moment, clearly deciding that now was the time to end the rather abrupt conversation. She turned away from me.

"I'm sorry," I muttered under my breath, so the others did not hear what was coming to pass between us. "Sorry," I repeated again, as I won her attention once more.

"That map," I grumbled, my voice even lower as I changed the subject. She looked up swiftly, her eyes now as piercing as a bayonet through my heart. "Where did you get it? Why do you have it?"

"It does not matter, *Jean.*"

"Were you planning a little holiday?" I scoffed, as I watched her lips purse together even tighter. Whatever it was the map had been to her, it wasn't a topic of conversation that she wanted to particularly engage in.

I suddenly realised that I was scared, not of what the map might represent in Suzanne's secrets, but that I could lose her affections if I was not careful. With a sudden bolt through my heart, I realised that I was becoming sentimental about her. I felt as though I needed her more than I needed Mike.

She turned away again, her eyes returning to their unremarkable state, her lips still tightly clamped shut.

I gripped her arm, no longer caring what Harry or Mike may have made of it. They did not seem to care all that much.

"I care about you, Suzanne. If the wrong person finds you with that map, then you could be in a whole heap of trouble."

"Trouble? What on earth do you call all this?" She replied, waving her arms around the room, bringing herself to the attention to the two other men who were preparing their weapons.

I sighed as I released her arm, Mike's icy stare chilling my bones as Suzanne walked away.

She was right. I had been in trouble ever since the war had started back in '39. And I wouldn't be out of it until the war was over, or I was dead.

18

We sat with our backs to the church, on an aging, moss-coated bench that seemed like it was going to snap and splinter at any second. Neither Suzanne nor I dared to move much more than an inch, in fear that we would soon find ourselves sitting uncomfortably on the damp grass beneath.

The churchyard was small, with the boundary wall nothing more than fifteen yards from where we sat. Nevertheless, the place was inhabited by what appeared like hundreds of headstones, each one telling a different story of someone long departed.

Some grave markers stood tall and proud, while others, like their aged occupants, stood crooked and hunched over, falling towards the ground in slow motion.

The church was raised up in a higher patch of ground so that the bench we sat on could look down upon the graves as if we were in the heavenly realms.

There was an odd irony to it all, but I couldn't tell where from.

What was best of all, however, was the field of view of the entire churchyard. The small waist-high gate tapped gently against a wooden post in the breeze, leading out to a small road that led the faithful to the house of prayer.

It was quiet enough and, as Mike and Harry wandered around the local vicinity, I became gradually more comfortable that we were alone.

"Why here?" I asked her, as I scanned each headstone for a figure that I knew not to be there.

She replied with silence, just staring out over the graves that I always avoided walking over, no matter where in the world I was. There was a pause of two or three minutes, where it felt like the whole world had ceased in its madness and had taken time to stop, to think.

For a minute or two, it felt as though my very heart had ceased to beat. I was quite calm.

"Because," she declared, proudly, "it helps me to reflect. I have always liked them."

"Do you know of anyone here?"

"I know them all really. I have spent many hours here since my husband died."

"He is buried here?" I asked, my tongue growing large in my mouth, wary that I had voiced something I shouldn't.

"No. But it helps me feel closer to him."

She stopped for a few minutes more, as she pulled

her coat around her tighter, and tensed her muscles. The bench creaked under the strain that she had suddenly forced it into.

My mind wandered, interrupted only by her quaint voice once more.

"They are quite funny, aren't they?"

"What are?"

"Cemeteries."

"I've always been scared of death."

"It's funny how there are thousands of them in this country. Some are built for the rich, some for the accomplished. Others are made for the poor and destitute. And yet, every single person in those graves are the same really. Just a body. In the ground."

A chill swept over my body, making me repeat Suzanne's movements of the few minutes previous. I huddled my limbs in towards the centre of my body, in the hope that the sense of dark macabre that had descended over our conversation would somehow be shielded from me.

There was a moment, as I sat there, that I felt comforted at the thought that I would end up like every man who had gone before me. Just a body. In the ground.

But, as Suzanne sat in a moment of contemplation, my comfort began to wane considerably.

"Are you alright, *old fruit*?" she asked, trying to put on as manly a voice as possible. I scoffed, turning my head away as I longed for the days when Mike was first trying to get that name to stick to me.

"Yes. I'm fine. These kinds of places get me thinking. Differently to you."

"Of the dead?"

"Some dead. Some living. Others I don't know about either way," I shrugged.

"Friends of yours?"

"And yours…Alfred."

She turned away from me abruptly and, had it not been the case that we were waiting for someone, I was sure that she would have run as far away from me as she possibly could. I could tell by the way that she held herself, her hands still clutching around the outsides of her coat, that she had been rattled considerably.

"I do not wish to talk about him," she said, an artificial sniff thrown in for good measure.

I did not feel the urge to force anything out of her and so sat in a moment of peaceful reflection, with just one other person on my mind.

Alfred had been a loyal soul, a faithful friend in the short time that I had known him. He had been the one to have hoisted me out of a prickly situation, that would have otherwise seen both Mike and I in the confines of a Gestapo cell, quicker than we could have ever imagined.

I owed my life to him and a lot of other things besides.

The longer I reminisced about the quiet solidarity he had shown to both Mike and me, as well as

Suzanne, the more I wanted to press her, to force her to talk about him.

"But he was your father in law, Suzanne. You cannot just forget about him."

She swung around as if she was about to deliver the best right hook that any boxer could ever give. My jaw clenched as I waited for the blow. Instead, all I received was an icy cold stare, that seemed like it could even chill the heat of the sun's core.

Her mouth twitched irritably, as if she wanted to say something desperately, but she knew not what to say, nor how to say it.

Instead, her eyes widened, before narrowing, like she had seen something protruding from my face that was alien to her.

But then, in what was a great relief for me, she turned away, to face back out over the headstones and towards the lane that fed the church.

It was only after my body began to return to a reasonable temperature that my ears began to tune into the noise. At first it was warped, the sound amplified so much that it sounded almost fabricated.

But, as the vehicle drew closer, I realised that it was the growl of a small car. The noise grew, before plateauing in an irritating whine, as the sheen of its black bonnet reflected its darkness towards us.

Together, we traced its path as it failed to slow down as it passed the church. Either the person drove past so often that they saw no reason to, or they cared so little for the dead that they kept their foot down on the accelerator.

The car kept on going, before stopping some way up the lane.

"It's not him," she said, breathing a sigh of relief.

"No."

As we spoke, a movement caught my attention in the corner of my eye. It wasn't fast, but equally not slow enough to avoid my notice.

With an incredible amount of fear and trepidation my head, with equal amounts of resistance and opposition, began to turn towards the movement, as I expected to be met with a group of well-armed Germans.

What I saw however was not the hard-nosed, scar-infested face that I had been expecting. Instead, there was a cheesy grin, attached to sunken eyes and flaring nose.

I rubbed my eyes as I made a conscious effort not to empty my bowels all over the bench. Mike was standing at the opposite end of the churchyard, Harry on his shoulder, as they both nodded towards us in acknowledgement.

Every bone in my body wanted to leap from the bench and lunge at his stupid little face, the grin so unbearable that I thought I would scream at him from the other side of the churchyard.

But my silent scream never came, instead, just a crackled whimper limped feebly from the back of my throat. Sounding like a wounded animal, I voiced my relief that we hadn't been caught out by the Germans.

I looked at my wristwatch.

"Thirteen more minutes."

"You're very precise."

"We were taught to be. Two minutes hanging around outside a rendezvous point could be the difference between winning the war and losing it."

"Do you really believe that?"

"Absolutely."

She chuckled and I suddenly felt very warm towards her. I enjoyed seeing her smile, I enjoyed her being happy. There was a desire rooted within me that wanted to entertain her more, to see her charming smile again.

But quickly, the smile drained from her face, just like the rosy hue that had tinted her skin as she had smirked.

I watched as the sadness that had suddenly gripped her sucked at every ounce of energy that she possessed. The deeper the feeling became, the plainer it was for me to see that this was no fleeting moment of sadness.

It was an utter despair, that had brewed for a long time, one that had eaten her up inside to the point where she was nothing but a shell.

The streaming tears that began to rush down her face gave some colour back to her cheeks, as they fell like a schoolboy's marbles onto her lap.

"These places," she sniffled, this time a genuine

attempt at trying to keep her composure. "These places, they always remind me of him."

Gauging her difference in reaction since I had mentioned Alfred, I could only guess that she was talking about someone else. Someone that meant a great deal more to her than her father-in-law.

And I imagined that these kinds of places had made Alfred think of the very same person whenever he frequented them. Distracted, there was a brief moment where I pondered whether Suzanne and Alfred had visited this churchyard together.

"Your husband?"

"Yes," she trembled, through the cupped palm that settled over her mouth.

I felt a pang of guilt shoot through my heart like a branding iron, as I found myself rather pleased that she was in this predicament. For the first time since I had met her, we found ourselves in a situation that leant itself to the idea that she needed me.

Ever since I had arrived in France, it had been me that had needed her; for her local expertise, her connections with other resistors and her safehouses. But now, as we sat on the bench in the churchyard, both Mike and Harry warily watching what was unfolding on the other side of the yard to them, she couldn't rely on herself any longer.

"I feel scared, all of the time and I wonder if he was as scared as I am right now. You know...When he was shot down."

She looked at me, with eyes the size of footballs, both of them filled with more water than the *Seine*.

"If I know anything about being a flyboy, Suzanne, it's that those who get shot down are the bravest men that I have ever known. Fear is only felt by the ones that get left behind."

She tried her hardest to blink away the tears, with a soft smile that told me that she appreciated my efforts, but they were not quite enough.

"I started all this to keep my mind off things, you know. As a way to get back at the men who killed him. But now, all I can think is, if he was still here, whether he would be proud of me or not. Or would he be downright disgusted?"

Without thinking of how it looked to Mike or Harry, or anyone else who happened to be within the near vicinity, I gripped her hand, settling our sweaty clutches in her lap.

I looked deep into her eyes, trying to see past the copious tears and sadness, and into the very depths of her mind.

Keeping a tight grip on her hand, I whispered, unconfidently at first but growing in my sincerity.

"Of course, he would be proud, Suzanne. He is proud of what you are doing."

To my astonishment, I felt her hand turn and grip mine in return.

19

Our hands rested themselves in each other's company for what felt like an age, as I could not tear my glare away from the now conjoined skin. But somehow, I could tell, that our exchange was not quite over.

In anticipation I looked up, locking on to her eyes once again. They were still as plain as always but, the more that I looked into them, the more that I discovered. The longer that I spent admiring their beauty, the more vibrant and exciting they became. I marvelled at her as her eyes glinted sweetly and I finally began to take notice of the true beauty that she possessed.

She seemed to see right into my heart as I stared at her, as her words cut through me like a sword.

"How can you forget them all?" she asked, curiously, verging on prying.

My mind was suddenly awash with all the faces that I had once known, who had either perished at the hands of a German bomb or bullet or were now nothing more than memories who existed in a past life.

My wife, in her wedding dress, standing at my shoulder at the altar of the church, stood next to me once again, her perfect and unblemished face a complete contrast to the one that had been buried in a pile of bricks.

She lingered for some moments, until I was brought back to my senses by the unusual movement in the palm of my hand. The clammy, sweaty grip that had clasped together some moments ago, was still maintaining itself.

I looked around, hoping earnestly that neither Mike nor Harry had moved around to get a closer look at what it was we were doing. But Mike was still stood where he had been, this time with Harry nowhere to be seen.

"I lost my only child," I blurted, somehow managing to fight back the urge to blub and weep into her shoulder.

It had been the first time that I had audibly acknowledged such a loss, after many months of denial and attempting to comfort myself.

The bereavement had smashed into my chest like a cricket bat, taking me to places that I never knew existed. At one point, I had found myself lying in a stream in Cornwall, a police officer and landlady staring down curiously at me.

But, even then, I had not told anyone what had

happened. It had only been because of Mike that my Commanding Officer had found out, that and the fact that I had apparently forgotten how to fly a plane overnight.

I felt like every muscle in my body had suddenly become unserviceable, until I felt my fingers curl up in a weak fist. I was so surprised that I looked down.

Wrapped around my pathetic fist was another hand, more elegant and smoother than my own, that gently encompassed my knuckle and gave it a firm squeeze. I felt the blood quickly rush back into it as she let go, the colour returning from the pale white to its warm scarlet.

Briefly, I felt as I had done when I had first met my wife, the cosy, friendly feeling of security that we could both give to each other. There was an instant connection, one that went past the physical touch of each other's hands.

Every happy memory that I had ever shared with her came gushing back to me, as did the feeling of overwhelming grief when I looked up to see the face of another woman.

Nevertheless, there was a familiarity in Suzanne's eyes, as we continued to sit on the churchyard bench, that gave me an element of comfort. She had made me realise that I hadn't erased my wife from my memory, she was very much still there, front and centre.

"I haven't forgotten them. Any of them," I said, my voice growing in strength as the tears retreated.

"It's just that there are bigger things now. More important things."

She gave my hand another tight squeeze, one that I was able to reciprocate, but it was not the elongated, drawn-out embrace that I had hoped for.

From over Suzanne's left shoulder, a figure had appeared warily, one that I did not altogether recognise.

It was a man, that much was evident, and a soldier too by the way that his shoulders were squared, and his head held high. He moved slowly, as if he had by some misfortune found himself stood in the middle of a minefield, and he was carefully selecting his route out of it.

He, like I had, avoided the grassy knolls and undulating ground of the deceased, instead choosing to walk in amongst the headstones where he could be sure he was not tempting fate in some way.

As he came closer, I realised that his eyes were locked onto the back of Suzanne's head, refusing to look away, even to scheme his way through the churchyard.

His face was briefly lit up by the sunlight as it bounced through the leafy cover of a large oak tree, and I had a brief glimpse at him.

He was looking around warily, obviously not expecting the company that Suzanne had brought with her. His eyes narrowed as he squinted and squirmed through the pouring sunlight, but his face remained a muggy mess, the paleness of his complexion screaming of apprehension and terror.

I thought for a moment that his level of worry and fear was matched only by my own.

"Is that him?" I asked slowly, so that Suzanne would take note of the sudden change in my tone. Briskly, she flicked her head around, her neck resounding with an audible crack.

She did not need long to look at him and, within a second or two, her eyes were back staring at mine.

"Yes. That's him."

I nodded; my lips pursed tight as I prepared to leave her.

"Alright then. Remember, exactly as we planned. Do not deviate. Otherwise we'll have to leave you."

"I know, *Jean*. Go."

With little other thought than keeping a firm gaze on the man who had now stopped short of the bench, I arose, staggering down the bank of grass and towards the headstone where Mike stood.

An onslaught of reluctance washed over me as I turned my back on her, as I realised that I not only wanted her to survive, I wanted to be alongside her when she did. But, I knew that in a second, everything could change and as my glare was fixed on Mike, I prayed vehemently that she would still be sitting on that bench when I got to him.

"What was all that about?" he asked, as I noticed a figure emerge from the church, at the opposite end from where the soldier had come.

He peered around the corner, his hands crossed over in front of his chest, inquisitive at the flurry of visitors that he had in his churchyard.

The verger was small, his frayed cassock surely older than he was, a hand-me-down from some long-deceased guardian of the building. His neck was crooked and slightly deformed, that gave him the appearance of someone who was always in total submission, his head bowed, his eyes peering upwards.

"Watch out. We've got a visitor. Looks like he wants to talk to you, Mike."

"If he ever gets here," Mike scoffed, as the man struggled to pick his feet up much higher than the blades of grass, his ancient garment brushing through the vegetation. The man didn't seem able to walk, only shuffling, each footstep taking longer and longer than the last.

"Forget him," Mike announced. "He could be a distraction. We'll deal with him when he gets here."

In unison, we turned to ignore the verger, whose presence was so humble, so quiet, that he totally faded from my consciousness almost immediately.

I watched the two occupants of the bench sat opposite one another, as I imagined Suzanne's voice forcefully taking control of the conversation. I could imagine her directing all the questions, to the point where she would cut him short if he went off task. That was what she had always done to me anyway.

But the way that she sat, her shoulders sunk so low that her arms almost dragged on the floor, was all that

I needed to know that she wasn't alright. I knew that Mike had sensed it too.

We had not seen eye to eye, but we still knew one another's instincts, to the point that we could tell the other what they were going to think in the next five minutes. But it was easy to guess what Mike was thinking, as I could not conceive of any other possible alternative.

I did not like the German soldier's body language, his slate grey uniform as sullen and morbid as his face seemed to be.

But, more importantly to me, I did not like Suzanne's body language. It was submissive, respectful even, and that was not the natural state of such a woman as her.

"It's just nerves," Mike muttered, as he shuffled on the spot beside me.

"If it's just nerves," I asked, my stare unwavering, "then why have you got your hand on your weapon."

I felt him breathe out sharply, a smirk lingering in the corner of his mouth.

"Just in case it's not nerves."

In a rare moment of solidarity with Mike, I felt around in my pocket for the revolver that was settled in there. I fumbled for the safety, sliding it downwards so that I was ready to go to battle.

"We need to move," I muttered, as Mike nodded his head in what I could only assume was agreement. "Get to that verger. Get him back inside the church. Then cover Suzanne's back."

"Roger that."

He moved swiftly, somehow managing to remain completely calm to the point that I wondered whether he was actually invested in all of this or not.

As he approached the elderly verger, I saw a broad smile sweep over his face, as he called out to the man who was on his way to greet us. Whatever he was, it felt great to know that he was on my side for now.

I stood where I was, helplessly, before ordering my legs into action.

Forgetting what Mike was doing with the verger, I returned my gaze to the two occupants on the bench, before quickly scanning the area to see if I could spot Harry. But he was nowhere to be seen.

Instead of entertaining myself with the idea of the traitorous little rodent having scarpered, I tried to read Suzanne's facial expression as I stumbled towards her.

There was nothing on her face to give anything away. It was as if she had been immortalised in stone. She sat stock-still, as the German began talking to her, a low growl rather than a soft whisper that I had expected.

I tripped on one of the corner pieces of a century-old grave and I somehow managed to regain my composure to the point where I was back on my feet.

It was strange, I thought, as the sun flashed in my eyes, that it had been able to do so given the excessive amount of cover the leafy branches had afforded me earlier.

But, as I stood still, a blinding glint dashed across my eyes once again, blinding me to the point where I could no longer see the German, I could no longer see Suzanne.

It was in that moment that I knew exactly what it was.

I threw myself behind a headstone, just as a sniper's round took a huge chunk out of the top of the masonry.

I was covered instantly in splinters of stone and dirt, as I frantically began pulling out my meagre revolver in search of some sort of response.

Then, there was a cry, a yelp. It could have only come from one person.

"Suzanne!"

20

I squeezed my limbs as tightly into my centre mass as I could possibly manage, frightfully wary that just an inch of flesh poking out from the side of the gravestone would be all that it took for the sniper to thrust a round into me.

My muscles almost began quivering the tighter that I squeezed, a current of terror shooting through them as another round whipped closely over the top of my shivering body.

There was nothing that I could do, apart from stay there, as I knew that the second that I moved so much as an inch, my head would immediately be in the crosshairs.

I realised, as the spittle quickly dried out from my mouth and the perspiration increased on my palms, that I could take little comfort from the sounds that were around me.

The rounds that were throwing themselves around

the churchyard were nothing new to me, I had been under fire many times after all. But it was the silence in between the pops and bangs, the ones that seemed to linger until my ears bled with anticipation, that were truly sickening.

It meant that no one else was firing back, nothing to make the sniper keep his head down or fear any sort of repercussions. For all I knew, everyone else was already dead.

As the sound of the silence increased, the thumping of my heart was the only thing that I was able to take any sort of reassurance from. As long as that kept beating, I thought to myself through laboured breaths, then I was still in the fight, the sniper had not won yet.

As if the sharpshooter had been able to read my mind, there was a showering of dust and large chunks of granite, as a round shattered through the remnants of the old 19th Century grave marker. It was only after the explosion of the headstone, and the coating of dust that I received, that I heard the gunshot resound out over the churchyard, the ancient walls quaking slightly at the sudden eruption of violence.

The silence became awash with thoughts for everyone else that had been with me in the churchyard; for Mike and Harry, but most importantly of all to me at that moment, Suzanne. There was something rooted within my core that wanted her to be unhurt. The thought of seeing her in the state that she had been, after we had been chased by the

Gestapo, was one that I would never want to see her in again.

I had even had dreams that her face would have been less of a mess had she in fact been killed.

The likelihood of her lying dead in the churchyard seemed to increase as the seconds ticked by, as the gunshots began to focus in on me more and the return of fire continued to be noticeably absent.

As I pondered my next move, I slowly came to the realisation that I only really had one option. The sharpshooter already knew that I was still alive, else he would not have been wasting his precious rounds on me. Also, judging by the fact that he was slowly chipping away at the grave of a man that could now only be read as '*Alain*', he knew full well where I was hiding.

Trembling like a leaf as it flickers down a gusty alleyway, I drew in a deep breath, composing myself for what I was about to do.

We had seemed miles apart for weeks, but he was the only one that I knew I could really trust to be alive. We had both learned how to become slimy serpents in that regard.

"*Michel?*" I called, my voice weak and temperamental. I felt like a child as I shook, hoping that the man that I had called out for would somehow come and rescue me, and that all this time that he had failed to look for me had been some sort of mistake.

The fact of the matter was, however, that I did not know what else to do. The longer that I sat in the damp grasp of *Alain's* grave, the faster all of my chances of getting out seemed to wane.

As the silence began to stab into my ears again, I tried to think through some other options that I may have.

I looked at my wristwatch. It was three forty-seven. Too many hours to sit tight until nightfall. The sharpshooter was using a rifle, a loud one at that, and it wouldn't be too long before the area was swarming with soldiers and police officers wanting to know what was going on.

My other option was to try and move, and pray that I did not get hit, in the hope that the sharp-shooter would waste a few more precious rounds of his in the process. As I lay there, it seemed that waiting for the sniper to run out of rounds was my only option. At least it was, until I heard a voice, calling out to me from the perceived darkness.

"*Jean? Jean Pelletier?*"

For a moment I thought that maybe we had already been surrounded by officials, as it had been so long that I had heard my assumed surname that I thought only an arresting officer would use it. But then, as he continued, I realised that it could have only been one man.

"Johnny?"

I was so shocked that he had managed to reply, that I nearly poked my head over the top of the shat-tered headstone, just as another round punched through the air, incandescent that I was not only alive, but calling out to a friend.

I pressed my face into the dirt, contorting my body in such a way that I felt my muscles begin to stretch so far that I thought they might give way at any moment.

Momentarily, I had been uplifted by the feeling that I was no longer alone, I had an ally who I knew was alive, and one that I knew would fight beside me if that's what the situation dictated. But the elation was fleeting, as I quickly realised that it would only take one more, well-placed, round, to render my cover completely useless.

I was going to have to make some sort of decision within the next fifteen seconds, or risk having my head smashed to pieces by the sharpshooter that seemed so intent on ending my life.

"*Michel!*" I rasped, the back of my throat tearing at all the vessels with a furnace of burning pain. "Can you see Suzanne? Is she still alive?"

Again, there was a silence, in which time I managed to convince myself that I had imagined Mike's response, and that I was totally alone.

But, as I began to lose all hope, there was a series of shots, three in quick succession. My body flinched with each one, my muscles tensing to prevent the impact of the headstone biting away at my skin. But the pain did not come.

The gunshots had been directed at something else in the churchyard, someone else.

Then, amidst a flurry of coughs and splutters, Mike spoke.

"I think that maybe you should be more concerned about the man with the rifle, *Jean.*" There was a weak chuckle, that sounded as if he was trying to reassure himself more than me. His voice was strained, which was no surprise, but there was a melancholy to it that screamed that he felt as though he could have avoided all of this.

There was a tinge to it that made me wary of the fact that I could not see him, and that at any moment he could simply leave me in the churchyard, to suffer my fate at the hands of the sharpshooter.

"*Michel*, I am serious. Can you see her?"

This time there was no laughter, no gunshots, just a fearful, petrified voice.

"Yes. I can see her. They are both under the bench."

"Alive?"

"Yes. She is anyway. The girl is alive, *Jean.*"

With a weight suddenly lifted from my shoulders, the clouds parting from my vision, my mind suddenly clicked into overdrive and began haring over thickets and through brambles that had, just seconds before, seemed totally impassable.

"Mike," I called, hoping that the desperation I heard in my own voice had been noticeable to him too.

"Yeah?"

"I'm going to need your help."

"I need yours," he croaked, again laced with a slight chuckle.

"Where are you?"

I could hear from his voice that he was somewhere over to my left and further forward, which meant he was closer to the church building than I was. I also assumed, seeing as he had been able to see Suzanne and the German under the bench, that he was a tougher target for the sharpshooter than I was.

Even so, he would still be in danger if he was to go through with what I had in mind.

"I'm about fifteen yards from the bank that leads up to the church door. Twenty-five from the bench."

"Can you see where the shooter is?"

"In the bell tower."

"Do you reckon you could make it to the church if you made a dash for it?"

The bell tower was the perfect place for a sharpshooter, as it gives a fantastic panoramic field of fire right the way around the church building. The one thing that any sniper would struggle with, however, would be if his targets managed to make it to the church wall. If that happened, then the angle with which he would have to fire would be nigh on impossible, without exposing himself terribly.

"Yeah, I reckon I could. Not sure about the old man though."

"What old man?"

"The verger. He's behind the gravestone next to me. I think he's wet himself."

"Mike," I bellowed, as another round came crashing from the bell tower and thumping into the tree around the same area that I supposed Mike was hiding. "I'm going to make a dash for it. If you can get some rounds down towards that tower, I'll be much obliged."

"I'll give it my everything, old fruit."

I began to writhe around on the floor like a deranged worm, attempting to pull myself into a position that would afford me a better springboard when my Olympic final came around.

I realised that the thumping heart, the dry mouth and the perspiring palms had all vanished, and now all that remained was a fierce determination to at least make it to that church wall.

If I was to die later in the day, that would be almost fine with me, just as long as I made it through the next ten or fifteen seconds.

A sharp exhale of breath signified that I was ready.

"Ready, Mike?"

"Hey, *Jean?*"

"What?"

"If you don't make it, do you want to be in the grave under the tree or one out in the sunshine?"

"I'll take the one right next to yours, *Michel.*"

He chuckled, as I counted down for the two of us, preparing to run as fast as I had ever done before.

My knees almost buckled, as they stretched out for the first time in what felt like hours, just as a cloud of dust erupted over my former hiding place. The sniper had fired at the very second that I had emerged from the other side, which afforded me a precious half a second as he began to pull the bolt back on his weapon.

I kept my head down as I felt Mike step out from his hiding place and begin emptying rounds from his pistol towards the bell tower of the church. They were token rounds, almost guaranteed not to hurt the sharpshooter, but it might just have given him something to think about on top of everything else.

As I barrelled past Mike, feeling his stocky frame falling in behind me as he expended all of his rounds, I watched as the verger emerged from his hiding place, taking his chances with the two other men who flew past him.

I hit the wall of the church with a thud, just as a round caught the verger in his shoulder, a spurt of red mist bursting through his cassock.

The old man fell to the ground and began to bellow out in agony, clutching at the hole that had been ripped open in his flesh.

We stood, dumbfounded, waiting for more gunfire to finish the old man off. But, nothing came. Just silence.

21

I felt my back desperately squeezing into the wall of the church, praying earnestly that it would suddenly open up and envelop me. I wanted to be as far away from the scene as I possibly could.

There seemed like there was nothing that I could do to comfort myself, nor the man who lay dying right in front of me.

As I watched the colour slowly drain from his face, his limbs flapping around as they debated whether to try and crawl to safety or stop the flow of blood, I hoped that he had lived a good life. I hoped that he had achieved everything that he had wanted to, said everything that was needed, because he was surely about to die.

There was a defiance in his eyes, as he looked at me, that screamed how he thought he could still make it through. I screwed my face up, wincing, as the man began trying to speak, blood-specked spittle spraying out onto his own face as he did so.

He was begging for his life, but not in the way that one might expect. There was an aggression to it, almost triumphant, that he wanted revenge on the man that had done this to him.

As he continued to flap and roll around, staining the grass around him a deep, romantic red, I felt the body beside me suddenly try to make a lunge towards him. Instinctively, my arm flew out, thumping into the determined midriff.

I felt the power behind the body, which forced me round to pin him back into the wall, exposing myself for a brief half-second.

"No, Mike. We can't."

His eyes weren't full of tears as I had expected, but instead remorseful of the fact that we had been here more than once. Together, we had seen men shot down over the blue skies of Kent and we had instigated the murder of several Germans.

The tightening knot in my stomach told me that I felt much the same way as him. We had been around so much death and suffering, that to stop one from the fate that we had sealed for others, would be a mighty weight from our shoulders.

But to do so would put us both at risk.

"But we have to do *something,*" he breathed.

"I agree," I replied, his eyes looking up from the half-dead verger with surprise. "We do need to do something."

"I don't think we're on the same page here, are we?" There was a sad smile to his question, as if he knew that I wanted to leave the verger exactly where he was. There were bigger things than the verger's life in play now, that was all.

"On any other day, Mike, I would have helped him."

"Of course, you would, old fruit."

His guard was down, a far cry from the man who had needlessly battered a German soldier to death outside a railway station.

But there was no time to consider any of that now, we had to get a move on.

"Get to Suzanne and the German. Get them back here if you can. That way you'll be safe from the sniper. If the German won't come with you, kill him."

"I think we should bring him back with us."

"Why?"

"He's useful. He knows things. We can question him about who managed to stitch Suzanne up, who moved those trains and then…"

"And then, what?"

"And then we kill him," the sadistic smile that I had seen so often before, the one that seemed to forget the overwhelming guilt of seeing someone dead returned to his face, stronger than ever. As he began to imagine the ways he would torture the man, the colour seemed to return to his cheeks.

I tried to muster up the courage to show my disapproval.

"I'm going to go after our friend in the bell tower."

"And what will you do with him?"

"Kill him," was the only reply on my lips.

"See," he remarked, as he began to turn towards the bench where Suzanne quivered, "You're just as bad as me."

He chuckled again, pulling his pistol up to his face as he began to edge along the stone wall.

"Stay safe, old fruit," he called, as his face disappeared behind the rocky exterior of the church.

I turned away from him knowing, quite possibly, that it could be the last time that either of us saw the other alive ever again. I tried to push the thought from my head that I was hoping it would be me who saw his body, and not the other way around.

My footsteps bellowed off the cold, damp walls of the church, dripping in secrecy and silence for hundreds of years. There seemed little point in trying to conceal where I was. If the sniper had half a brain cell then he would have known that we would eventually come after him, baying for the blood that had threatened to take ours.

There was a quietness to the church, a stillness that only came with a place so holy and sacred. It was a reverence and tranquillity that allowed me to begin reflecting myself, the temptation passing me by to hide myself in a pew and kneel on my burning knees.

I stared at the ornate lectern at the front of the church, a simple swan adorning it proudly, wings outstretched, realising that the very same swan had been overseeing my last visit to a house of prayer.

My wife's casket, nothing more than a bland wooden box, had been stood next to it on that occasion. My wife and child tucked up safely within its confines, forever peaceful, but forever absent from my life.

I stopped dead in my tracks as I reached the staircase, hidden behind a heavy scarlet curtain, as I looked back at all the faces that had stared upon me then with expectation.

The voices were low and muttered, but I had heard them all, the ones asking how I would cope with such a loss, how could such a man carry on without his wife and new-born son. Then there were the others, the angry voices, the ones that demanded to know when I would be fighting again, to kill the very Germans that had released the bombs on my hometown.

I became angry at every single one of them, my blood rising to the surface of my face as I wiped them away from my mind. Not one of them had cared to ask me how I was, every single one trying to second guess how I would respond.

I took a great amount of pleasure from the fact that not one of them would have guessed that I would have been where I was right then. I was taking the fight to the enemy, not for my country, not for right or wrong, but for myself.

As my feet stepped onto the damp surface of the

narrow staircase, I wiped anything that resembled a distraction from my conscious mind. I knew that it would always be there, but I was determined not to let it get in the way of the job that had to be done.

The stairs grew less forgiving the higher that I climbed, my large, unwieldy feet more than twice the width of the stairs in some places. It entertained me to think of how small the feet of the men who had built this grand old building had been a couple of hundred years before.

A small pinprick of light grew as I ascended, to the point where I knew that I must have been near the summit.

Cautiously, I poked my head above the winding staircase, to look over the landing that led to a small wooden shutter, one of its slats carefully removed from its place.

The barrel of a gun was still there, resting gently on the sill and peering down into the churchyard below. But, there was no man attached to it as I had been expecting.

I suddenly remembered that, during the last war, a group of Aussies had developed a contraption that helped a rifle fire of its own accord, in order to fool the Turks into thinking that there was more than one man in a section of a trench.

At the thought, I lunged up the final stairs, only to find my body forced into the solid wall opposite me.

A hand pushed itself up to my head and thumped my skull into the stone as hard as possible, as I cursed the man who had decided not to adorn this part of the church in fancy, heavy, colourful cloth.

As the force knocked the air from my lungs, so too it knocked the only weapon I had on my possession. As the revolver clattered to the floor with a sobering cry, I realised that I was going to have to do this with just my hands.

"Fighting dirty is the only way to win," had been the motto of the old Scotsman who had taught me his craft.

It was all that went through my mind, as the blood pulsated from my head.

I growled at the man, as my thumbs found their way up towards his eyes, pressing down as hard as I possibly could.

The man screamed, his knee instinctively jerking and connecting with my groin. I doubled over in pain, as a fist smashed into my forehead forcing me back up again.

My vision was a haze of murky shadows and bloody mists, but I still tried to lunge for the tallest, and darkest, shadow that I could make out.

Bringing my arm outwards, my palm raised to the heavens as if some sort of offering, I flicked my hand towards him, hoping that I would connect with something vital, just between the knuckle of my little finger and my wrist.

As I felt the skin to skin contact, I brought my full body weight in behind the blow, forcing an almighty pressure on to the man's Adam's apple. I hit him with such a force that it felt as though my hand would be eternally conjoined to his skin, and I felt the Adam's apple bob and retreat as it rebounded around inside his neck.

Almost instantly, the man slumped to the floor, his limbs making no provisions for his skull as it smashed into the ground with a sickening crack.

Blood gushed from the man's nose, his ears following suit quite soon after.

I left him for a moment, retrieving my revolver from the ground and placing it carefully back in my grasp. It was only then that I approached the man, kneeling down to feel for a pulse.

There was one, but it was so weak that I did not think he would be too much bother to me.

I was impressed with what the old Scot police officer had taught me, a smirk on my face at the thought of the capabilities of fighting dirty. I would have a scotch in his honour just as soon as I could.

I started to rummage around inside the man's jacket, looking for anything that may have been remotely useful to us. But, inevitably, I found nothing other than another revolver that looked even older than my own, and a carton of cigarettes, that I duly took.

As I began to check around me for anything else that could be of use to me, I realised something strange about the man.

I had been fully intending to fight a German soldier, dressed in a German uniform and firing a

German weapon. But that could not have been further from the truth.

This man was fighting in civilian clothes, a mixture of a farm labourer's and some kind of butcher's. What was more, the man must have been in his late forties.

As I looked at his face, the wrinkles and laughter lines evident even in his unconscious state, I came to the conclusion that this man must have been a civilian. He had to have been a soldier once, at some time, but now he was nothing more than an average man.

My time in the company of the unconscious man was coming to an end, and I knew that the inevitable was coming.

'Best just get it out of the way,' I thought to myself, with disgust.

I raised the revolver, so it was level with my eye line, and began to take up some pressure on the trigger. I felt it snag on the firing mechanism, ready to end the man's life as willingly as he had been to end my own.

But my hand quivered, denying me the ability to take a clear shot at the inanimate man that lay at my feet.

I tried to tell my finger to squeeze just an ounce more pressure onto the curled steel, but still, it refused.

There was a sudden bang, that shocked me to my core and caused me to flinch as I had never done before.

Warily, as I opened my eyes, I realised that it hadn't been the revolver, it was still shivering at the ends of my arms, trying to locate a target from amongst the tremors.

The clang that I had heard was distinctly metal on metal. It was a car door. It meant that we had company.

22

By the time that I'd made it to the bottom of the stairs, almost pulling the thick velvet curtain from its hanging point, the gunshots were already in full flow. I had become so accustomed to the lung shaking snaps of revolvers and rifles that I barely even flinched as a round glanced off the church wall, the ricochet missing the edge of my nose by a fraction.

The air was thick and heavy with deadly darts and men's curses, as the small scuffle escalated into a desperate fight for life.

As the tracer from a submachinegun flitted its way towards me, I could not help but think of all the times that I had engaged the Germans 30,000 feet up in the air, just a flick of the control column from dancing away from the devastating rounds.

But now, as I stood in the relative safety of the church porch, my feet would not dance in the same way that the Hurricane had done.

The Germans had already begun to make good ground, the inferior calibre of weapons and lack of manpower on our part, quite quickly becoming evident.

As my sweaty grasp struggled to keep a grip on my revolver, I began to truly wonder how much of a difference I could really make. I did not have that many rounds, I did not have all that much courage either, and for a split second, I thought that maybe Mike and Suzanne would be better off without me.

In that same second, my feet began to shuffle as if to run off in the other direction, completely abandoning my only friends. After all, I was certain that they had not yet seen me, and they may well have died not knowing that I had survived the altercation with the sniper.

But then, my heart both sinking and fluttering in equal measure, I caught eyes with Suzanne, her face not giving away an iota of fear nor confidence. All I could see was her face, as a fact, and not as a subject of interpretation.

"Where's Harry?"

I shocked myself with my sudden break of cover, as my voice screeched off the walls of the church as more rounds thudded into the ancient brickwork.

The absence of the Frenchman had taken me less than five seconds to work out, his eccentric frame and meagre firepower noticeably not a part of the fight.

I surveyed the scene, watching in awe at how Suzanne was still managing to fight, even though all she had to cover herself were a few planks of wood, cobbled together to form a bench. To my right, Mike was crouched behind a new gravestone, as he tried his best to pick off as many of the Germans as he could.

The verger, who had been so graceful as he swept across the graveyard towards us, now lay quite still, his eyes glazed and his tongue beginning to dry in the sporadic sunlight.

I brought my revolver up to my eye, ready to try and hit the portly soldier who was trying with great difficulty to conquer the churchyard wall. But, as my finger began to take up the pressure on the trigger, the figure slumped backwards over the wall, a faint red cloud of dust hanging in the air for a second afterwards.

I traced the path of the round, and to my surprise, I found that it had, in fact, come from a German weapon. I was both wary and elated at the idea of the German informer turning against his own people, utterly petrified at the fact that this man could kill his own countrymen in cold blood. It made me fear what he might do to us if we were to make it out alive.

But then, granted with the gift of a little more thought, I wondered what choice the German really had. We were, I surmised, his best and only hope of survival now. We all knew that the Germans' net was closing in on us, but the fact that this man was now firing upon his own compatriots, led me to believe that he was genuine. He had been trying to help us all along.

I felt a burning affinity to the man, as he threw himself behind the nearest headstone, a maelstrom of rounds following his path as he did so.

My gaze had been on my own side for too long, and it was not too much later that I realised that quite soon we would be in hand to hand combat with the Germans, and I had already had my fair share of that.

I discharged my weapon three times, as a small, young German made a dash for a grand old grave that stood at the centre of the churchyard. In the space of two short seconds, I had reduced the arsenal behind me by half. I now had just three rounds to fend for myself. And in my heart, I knew that only two would be directed towards the Germans.

The gunfire in the churchyard slowed as, one by one, every combatant realised that every round was a waste. There was nothing left to do, other than wait and welcome the net that was slowly tightening around my neck.

"Suzanne! Get back to *Jean.* We can regroup! Get away together!"

Mike's face was ablaze with optimism and fervour, as his eyes were awash with visions of glory and praise.

I watched in anticipation of what Suzanne was going to choose to do.

For a moment, she just stood, staring. She knew as well as all of us that the game was up. But the funny thing about knowing you are defeated, is that it somehow makes you infinitely more courageous.

The Germans were either feeling merciful, or all were caught completely off guard, as each one of them failed to fire any rounds at the attractive young woman running away.

Mike lunged from the cover of his headstone, making it to me, dragging my head back around the corner of the stone wall, just as a few rounds nicked into the structure of the church.

"Now what?" Suzanne asked.

"We could run?"

"Where?"

"Does it matter?"

I quickly grew tired of the dialogue between them, especially as I saw no fewer than three enemy soldiers emerge from their cover and skulk towards us.

"Shush. Listen."

At first, I thought that I had imagined it, and that I'd spoken far too instinctively. But, with great relief, I heard the chug of an engine, as it screamed towards us.

"Germans?"

"No…" Mike replied. "The engine is too high pitched. It sounds like a car. It sounds like a… Renault."

As he uttered the last syllable, he caught sight of a black bonnet as it screeched up to the perimeter wall not ten yards away from where we stood.

"Harry!" Suzanne screamed, as my heart sunk at

the thought that the man had returned. For some reason, I had wanted to try and get out of this sticky situation by using the intuition that the three of us possessed.

"Get in!" He screamed at us, as I chanced one last look towards the graveyard.

As my head peered around the corner, I came face-to-face with a German. Our eyes were less than an inch from each other's, and I could see the individual hairs from his nostrils, flaying as he sucked air in desperately.

The revolver, which was struggling around my hip, instinctively bucked upwards as two rounds sunk into the man's flesh. I did not even have to aim at all, I was so close that I was guaranteed to hit him.

The man immediately collapsed, and I realised that the second round must have travelled through his body and hit the man who was standing directly behind him, for he too staggered for a moment, before finding his height and levelling his weapon at me.

He was a little farther away than the first German had been, but I was still guaranteed a kill at this range. Before his index finger could find the trigger, I squeezed.

All six of my rounds had been expended. I must have miscounted, as a soft clink of an empty chamber echoed louder than any gunshot had ever done before.

The German was young and had until that

moment been quite fearful, but even he knew there was no need to be fearful when you stood in front of a man who had an empty weapon. A leer began to spread across his face, one so grotesque and boastful, that I thought it almost impossible for such a face to exist.

Full of confidence and arrogance, the young man took a step towards me, to make an even bigger mess of my insides than he would do from the distance he was at. It was the last move that the young man would ever make.

As if he held an even deeper contempt for me than was usual for two adversaries, he spat a mouthful of blood towards my face. I could not see the entry wound, but I knew straight away that a round had entered the back of his neck.

His eyes widened, as he staggered around trying to find the culprit who had just cowardly shot him from behind. He did not make it all that far before he collapsed on top of the other German that I had dispatched earlier on.

From behind the young German, another figure revealed himself, still crouching behind one of the gravestones, but this time firing in the opposite direction as he had done before.

"Make Suzanne safe," he called out in such fragmented English that it was almost impossible to decipher.

I tried my hardest to give him a slight nod, to give him some sort of comfort and the last thing that he would see in this mortal realm. It was the least I could do for him, especially as I could not bring myself to watch as his compatriots emptied their weapons into his pitiful body.

It was all over in a flash, and I was surprised to see that Suzanne and Mike were still standing beside me, albeit sheltered from the horrors of what had just happened. They each looked at me in utter disbelief, staring at the bits of bloodied saliva that had sprayed over my face.

"Get a move on then! Get in the car!"

They did not need telling twice, the kind of courage to make a man stand his ground, completely sapped from both of them over the last few weeks.

By the time that I had made it to the car, Harry was already depressing the accelerator, the car beginning to move off as I cracked my head on the side of the chassis. Had it not been for Mike and Suzanne, I may well have rebounded off the car itself, and been left behind.

As the headache began to swell in the side of my head, I allowed myself time to breathe, trying to curtail the overwhelming sense of nausea and strangulation that was coming over me.

I knew, as we bumped and crashed our way through the orchard, that there was little chance of the Germans being able to get after us so soon, but it did not stop me from staring out of the rear window to ensure that we were not being followed.

"Is everyone alright?" screamed Harry, the ecstasy

of driving at such high speed reflected in his monstrous tone.

"Did you see what happened to Martin?" Her eyes already holding far more tears than I had seen before. It was strange, I thought to myself, seeing her in such a vulnerable state. I had known her as such a vicious and courageous fighter, that I had almost forgotten that she was still human, that she was still capable of feeling some sort of emotion.

She knew the answer before I even opened my mouth, but she still maintained the eye contact that told me that she needed to hear it out loud to begin to believe it.

"He didn't make it, Suzanne. But he saved us. He helped us to get away."

23

We sat around in Harry's house; the dust so abundant that I felt every single mite slip down my throat and begin to clutch at my lungs. The longer that we sat there in the silence, the more difficult I found it to breathe, particularly as the vision of our German informant having his life ripped from him began to replay itself over and over in my mind.

Every now and then, someone would shuffle, and I took each chance to reset my mind, in the hope that the deep distress that I was caught up in was not shown on my face. I had never really been scared of anything before, but the thought of others picturing me as some sort of a coward, one who was running scared, was something that terrified me no end.

It grew so dark in the dining room, not one of us rising from our chairs for some hours, that I found it almost impossible to discern who it was that was sitting directly opposite me. As the sun began to fade away beneath the horizon, the facial features that I had grown so used to over the last few weeks, slowly began to erase themselves, until there was nothing more than a dark mass sitting in front of me.

There was a reluctance, in the pit of my stomach, that I did not want to bring up the events of the day. I wanted to bury them in the darkest pit of my memory, never to be dredged up again. The guilt that was so prominent in my heart, was exacerbated by the thought that we had betrayed the other fighters, who would have been prepared to stand alongside us in our moment of need. But we had neglected to utilise them, and I was fearful of what that would have meant for our relationship were they to find out what we had done.

If the shoe was on the other foot, and I had found out that they had undertaken an operation without our assistance, I would question how much they trusted us.

I thought it would be far too difficult to explain to them that it was not out of a lack of trust that we had left them out, but out of genuine concern for their welfare. There was nothing that I wanted less than to see these young men dead in their own backyard.

I started to find myself welcoming the creeping darkness, as if it gave me somewhere to hide, the feeling of wanting to tuck myself in some unlit corner for the rest of my days being the one emotion that I was certain of.

"So, are we going to talk about what

happened?" Mike said again, a hint of annoyance and frustration quite clear in his voice. I knew him well, so I was sure that it was a frustration that everyone else was so reluctant to talk that was beginning to grind on him. But, then again, I had almost convinced myself over the last few days that I did not know him at all. So the tone to his voice may have been one that was in complete contradiction to my interpretation.

In the darkness, I tried to search his face, his brooding features accentuated by the darkness that he was engulfed in. It seemed to suit him rather well.

There was another half an hour or so of quiet, as each one of us began to consider what they might say to the other.

In the end, Suzanne, who was still visibly traumatised by the loss of her German friend, spoke first, her voice uncharacteristically quaint and somewhat shy.

"I-I don't know what happened. He told me that he would come alone."

"Funny that," Mike started. "Wasn't it the Germans who promised not to invade Czechoslovakia? Unlike them to go back on their word, isn't it?"

"Mike," I interjected, shooting him the dirtiest look I could muster in the blackness.

"What? It's true, I don't know why we have trusted him. He was a Kraut after all."

Had Suzanne had the energy, I was certain that she would have lunged at Mike from across the table.

But she was tired, she could offer up no sort of resistance, other than a futile sob.

"What is it to you anyway? Didn't think that you would be crying over one of the men who could have killed your husband."

I could tell in the darkness that the fury was beginning to take hold in Suzanne's stomach, some sort of mutual connection between us. But I knew, however much he deserved it, a violent rebuke of Mike would do none of us any favours right now. We needed to talk, I needed to do it in the most civil way possible.

"I think it would be best all-round if we were to focus on what happened, rather than pointing the finger at one another."

I saw his shadow shuffle around in his seat, clearly frustrated with the way in which he had not got the answer to what he deemed as the most pressing question. But still, he was the next one to speak, through gritted teeth.

"Did he-did he say anything? The Kraut I mean."

Suzanne composed herself in between sobs just enough to reply to him.

"His name is Martin."

"*Was* Martin. He's dead, remember," Mike mumbled, not allowing Suzanne to forget what had happened for a single second. He needn't have bothered, his authority was well and truly stamped on the situation, and Suzanne was having a tough time trying to forget what happened to her German friend.

"Did he say anything, Suzanne?" I asked as gently

as possible, leaning towards her place at the table and placing a sympathetic hand on top of hers. I hoped desperately that neither Mike nor Harry could see what was going on in the darkness.

She waited a moment, in which time nobody said a word, in anticipation of some great revelation that had happened minutes before Martin's death. But when she finally did speak, it was a crushing disappointment to us all.

"No. He said nothing. Nothing of any use anyway."

Her voice trailed off into another series of sobs and weeps, as her steely exterior began to melt away even further.

But there had been something in the back of her throat, something that had caught her out and tripped her up as she tried to tell us what had happened. In that moment, I became convinced that she was hiding something from the rest of us, that Martin had, in fact, said something of great value.

The other two men who sat around the table had not seemed to have sensed it, as they pressed her no further on the matter, instead turning to other hypotheses about what might have given us away. Ideas of not following anti-surveillance protocol, to the notion that a traitor was in our midst, were floated between us.

I stayed as quiet as I possibly could, while trying to maintain an air of intrigue and involvement, all the while considering the young woman who sat across the table from me.

Suzanne's sobs slowly rescinded, eaten up by the all-encompassing darkness that enshrouded us all, but I could tell that the tears were still rolling for many minutes after the audible cries had stopped.

Both Mike and Harry grew tired of sitting in the darkness, and soon retired to bed, a prospect that I both longed for and yet found myself trying to resist.

I do not know how long we both sat there in the darkness for, but all the while I kept my one tough and calloused hand on top of hers, in some sort of meagre attempt to comfort her in her sorrow.

Eventually, I mustered up enough courage to speak, and quiz her about the one thing that I really wanted from her.

"I know he said something. The way that you were sitting on the bench told me that. The others might not have noticed it, but I somehow seem able to read your face even in the darkness."

She rose and began to walk into the remaining chairs and table, while she looked for a match, eventually lighting the underpowered paraffin lamp that sat in the middle of the table.

It was the first time that I'd seen her face in hours, and the deep heavy bags that dragged her eyes, reddened from all the crying, somehow made her look prettier than ever. It was a thought that fleetingly crossed my mind, and one that I quickly chased from my consciousness before I got too side-tracked.

"What did he say?" I repeated, as if this time, now that we could see one another would make some sort of difference to her response.

"Not much. But enough."

I had not expected her to give me some sort of a rousing speech, but I was hoping for far more than her weak and pathetic voice had given me. It was the kind of response that would have resulted in frustration had I got it from any other person, but because it was her, there was something that just demanded a compassion for her.

"What did he say?" I repeated again.

She looked up at me, as if to ask why what she had said before had not been enough.

"He told me to be careful. He knew something. You know it too. I told you before, *Jean.* He cannot be trusted. *Michel,* he cannot be trusted."

The patience that I thought was unceasing for her was finally beginning to crack. She had never been one to mince her words, but right now she seemed to be talking in a riddle of the most ridiculous order.

I opted to say nothing at all, except to keep my eyes on her, in the hope that she would understand that she had not given me what it was that I wanted. It was an easy enough task, the long hours that I spent looking at her, had become ones of pleasure and enjoyment to me.

"You did follow him before?"

I was not sure how she had managed to turn the

tables on my interrogation of her, but I felt utterly compelled to answer right away.

"Yes."

"And?"

"Nothing."

"Are you sure?"

I nodded, unable to bring myself to admit to her that I had my reservations over Mike and that I had seen him entering a building in the middle of the night. I wondered whether it was out of the guilt that I had brought him with me, or whether I was merely ashamed at the fact that I had not had the guts to confront him.

There were a few moments more silence before Suzanne spoke again.

"Martin was a good man," she said, the tears beginning to fall once more. "He was trying to help us."

As the small paraffin fuelled flame flickered across the room, I was able to watch for the first time as she dabbed at the rolling tears with her handkerchief.

It was as she did that, that I noticed something odd about the small piece of cloth that she was using. I had seen it before. It had belonged to a man that I knew once.

"Where did you get that?" I asked, gripping her wrist to prevent her from hiding it once more. I fed its threads through my fingers, bringing the embroidery close up to my eye.

Even in the lacklustre light of the lamp, I could

see two letters, and a bright red stitch work of the most professional kind.

A.S.

"It's Alfred's," I announced, as if she needed telling. "Where did you get it?"

It seemed impossible to me that the lone article that had survived the inferno of Alfred's house had been his handkerchief, and I continued to question Suzanne with my stare as to how she came about it. Realising that she was unlikely to get away lightly, she spoke.

"It's a long story. But, not tonight. Not now."

24

By the time that the sun was beginning to come up, the four of us were far more willing to talk, or at least be somewhat more civil to one another.

I had barely slept all night, so much so that the bags that dragged at my eyes were beginning to develop a heartbeat of their own. My mouth was furred and rancid, and I was sure that I could see a toxic, green cloud expelled from my jaw each time I exhaled. It was just as well that we were all in the same state. As such, we kept our distance as best we could.

"So, how do we go on?" Mike's question was the obvious one, but not so obvious that any of us had used the night apart to think up some sort of an answer. The truth was that not one of us knew how to proceed, as every avenue seemed to end up with us dead in a ditch or worse, in a Gestapo cell. It was a thought that not one of us could bear.

As I, like the others, looked around the room in search of a remedy to our predicament, I could not help but look into the eyes of my companions, and realise that I was in a far worse situation than I had thought the night previous.

I longed to be back in the Highlands, where all of this had appeared to be so distant and game-like. There had been more than a dose of naivety as we had trained, listening to how living in such a hostile environment, and so close together, could become such a breeding ground for distrust and betrayal.

There was a fine line, I had been told, between the paranoia that someone had betrayed you, and yourself becoming the betrayer.

But it was so difficult to step back and see that, as I sat in the kitchen with the other three.

Suzanne, her beautiful rose skin beginning to return to its fullest colour, had been all too quick to inform me that Mike had started to waiver, and that I could no longer trust him. I was sure that she at least had a point, having followed him once already to find out where it was he was sneaking, after dark.

His visits had been infrequent recently, on account of the fact that none of us really went to sleep anymore. He couldn't guarantee his safe passage when three pairs of ears were all pressed up against various doors, waiting for the rumble of a German troop truck or roaring motorcycle.

But there was still that barrier to me, the one that I had laid the foundations for back at RAF North

Weald, when Mike and I would spend hours delighting in telling each other of our lives before the war and our exploits in the sky. Mike had been the one to accompany me when my wife and child had been killed. He had been there as I changed from a fighter pilot to a resourceful agent.

He had always been there, alongside me. It did not seem plausible that he could have turned away from me so easily.

But things had changed drastically in the last few weeks. Two months ago, I had never set foot in France, and now I was trying to integrate myself so much that I would appear like a native.

But the more I thought about trying to fit in, the more I felt like I was beginning to stick out. It felt as though that every pair of eyes in the village had been upon me for the last couple of months, each pupil narrowing with suspicion each time they laid eyes on me, even Suzanne's.

I had not completely let go of the idea that she too was not to be entirely trusted. She also was hiding something from me, something that clearly meant so much to her that she would simply refuse to answer my questions.

I had seen the handkerchief, I had taken note of the map that she had somewhere on her possession, but the exhaustions sat so heavy in my mind that I could not, for the life of me, work out what it was that it all added up to. Maybe none of it did, which was why my mind was slowly beginning to close down, succumbing to the irrational suspicion that everyone was out to get me.

I looked to the window, to try to catch a glimpse of the blue sky above, in the hope that I might see a bird or two dancing through the cool air, without a care in the world. It had always helped to calm me down, to reset my thoughts. But what I saw appeared far better than that.

A lone figure stood over the sink, his hands outstretched on either side and the trunk of his body leaning towards the window. He stared up and down the road, as if expecting a letter from the postman or the milkman to suddenly turn up with his goods.

Harry's face seemed like the kindest one in the room, the only one capable of being honest and trustworthy. I found myself thinking that he was even more dependable and reliant than my own thoughts. I did not know if such a phenomenon was even possible but, at that moment, it seemed like the only eventuality.

Harry had been the one that had managed to drag us to safety, on more than one occasion now, but I questioned how much longer it could go on for. It was only a matter of time before Harry, or we, managed to get ourselves killed.

The car that Harry had driven had now been seen by a platoon of German soldiers and, if they possessed even half a brain cell, that would be where all their efforts would be directed, if they wanted to track us down.

The black Renault had belonged to a neighbour of Harry's, a couple of streets away. It was the best that he could muster but it put us in great peril. If the inspectors managed to narrow their search down to the small village of *Charsay*, then I could not imagine that it would take them all that long to discover who Harry was. Which, by extension, would mean that they would discover who we were.

I could not imagine that the Germans would take too kindly to us, as we had now given them the slip on far too many an occasion, having caused death, destruction and general havoc for the last eight weeks or so. Their fuse must have been wearing very thin indeed.

I was shocked to hear a voice and I forced myself to look away from the curious and quite odd figure of Harry for a moment.

"Might I make a suggestion. Specifically, for you both, *Michel* and *Jean.*"

"I'll be glad to hear it," Mike muttered, his voice almost as exhausted as my body felt.

Suzanne sat up in her chair, clearing her throat. I knew what she was about to say, and I knew that Mike was not going to like it one bit.

"I think, for what it's worth, that maybe you… That maybe your time in *Tours* is coming to an end. I think it might be safer all round if you were to move on elsewhere."

My intuition had been right, for Mike spun around on his heel as he shot up, the weak chair cracking into the solid wall behind him. A cloud of dust erupted from behind his head, the particles dancing gaily in the beam of sunlight that streamed in through the awkward window.

"Absolutely not! We have barely even started to cover half the things that we were sent here to achieve. We are still of immense help here, no one can doubt that!"

"I never said I doubted how helpful you could be. But the Germans are tightening their grip. And they have seen the two of you now, you will be their number one targets."

"Then so be it," Mike announced defiantly, his chest puffing outwards as if Suzanne had been insulting his masculinity.

Mike continued to pontificate and lay out his reasoning for being mightily offended, as if he was in the court case of his life and the need for mitigation was life-threatening. I, on the other hand, sat quietly in contemplation, as I always did, mulling everything over and worrying myself just as much as Mike was.

I realised, quite early on, that I was hurt, my pride dented with a hammer blow to my chest. I had thought that, over the last few days in particular, that Suzanne and I had grown closer, and that somehow that meant that she should have protected me, backed me up in some way and advocated for us to continue the fight.

She had always been the one to argue that we should continue to take the fight to the Germans, and yet here she was in what appeared to be a complete surrender.

"We still have plenty of men to carry on the work. We are all natives, after all, we have not had the training you two have had. It would be a waste to lose you two here."

I knew, however much I tried to bury it, that she was right. I was allowing my personal feelings to get in the way of the larger picture, the one where we would help in booting the Germans from this country and back into their own.

I could still not get over the slight feeling of betrayal on Suzanne's part, however.

As I stared at Mike, his stumpy legs taking large strides around the room in an attempt to assert his dominance, I could not for the life of me understand why he could not see the need to leave.

There was something that had flicked in him the moment that Suzanne had voiced her opinion, causing him to erupt like a furious volcano, his ears flushing a deep red as he wound himself up even more.

I looked across to Suzanne, to try and read her face and get a better opinion of the whole situation, but I found her already looking at me.

Her freckles seemed to be accentuated as she began to perspire at the thought that she had made a grave error of judgement. Gently, one eyebrow flicked towards her hairline, almost as if it had disobeyed a direct order.

She was itching to know what I thought on the matter, and whether Mike was acting for the two of us. But I did not get a chance to acknowledge her look. Mike had already seen it.

"You're in on it, aren't you? You knew she was going to say this."

"Mike I—"

He did not allow me to finish, as he was already dragging me up from my chair, and lifting me towards the kitchen wall, the table and chair squawking as they ground on the floor.

"You told her to say this, didn't you? It was you; I know it was you!"

His eyes bubbled with a fury almost as much as his mouth was spitting hatred towards me, as I tried to force him off with a shove.

"Of course, I didn't. What do you take me for?"

"I don't know anymore."

"What's that supposed to mean?" I asked, pulling his shoulder round so that he was facing me once more.

We stood there, like a pair of bulls weighing up the option of charging into a full fight or not.

"Look," Harry interjected, trying to get a shoulder in between the two of us, his sharp, striped suit almost hilarious in between the two reddened faces around him. "You two obviously cannot trust each other fully at the moment, for whatever reason," he shot me a vicious glance. "But maybe it would be best if you contact your folks in London. It seems like a mightily large decision to be making without at least informing them."

Harry stepped away, happy that his suggestion had poured at least a few droplets of water onto the roaring fire. His tone of voice was upbeat, almost unnecessarily so, but I could not work out whether it was because he was pleased that we had finally got our emotions out into the open, or whether he was simply pleased that he was finally in charge.

Whatever it was, it unsettled me no end.

25

I felt as though I was in a rusty old tin can, my ears filled with the sound of falling raindrops clanging off the sides and back onto my face. The shine of an empty tin can though was all but gone, instead replaced with a damp, drooling sky as I huddled to the wall of a building.

I pushed myself into it further, despite the fact that more moisture was able to seep through to my skin that way, as it offered up some sort of protection, a feeling of anonymity and discretion.

It also allowed me to peer down the street, the rain lashing down so hard that it stung my eyes, towards one building in particular.

The stinging of my eyes and the biting cold in the tips of my fingers were the least of my concerns, but there was a degree of relief as I tried to reason that fewer soldiers would be out to enforce the curfew.

That said, there had been one or two patrols out

and about, more concerned with the state of their greatcoats than in any figures that lurked down the side streets and alleys of *Tours.* I had avoided the glare of their flashlights, as their beams of light carelessly flickered on the sides of walls and in the puddles that were beginning to form.

As I buried my hands inside my jacket and under my armpits to try and get some feeling back into them, I couldn't help but catch my wristwatch in the faint light that still lingered out in the open, and realised that I had been stood in the dark for a little over an hour.

It was not a great delight to me that I found myself in the position that I was in, but it had become a necessary evil. Mike, whether out of a blatant malice or genuine ignorance, had snuck out of his bed once more and slipped out into the night.

Suzanne's concerns had played on my mind ever since she had raised them and had been heightened the first time that I had followed him. I had not wanted any of it to be true and so I had decided to let things lie for a while.

But, perhaps, that had been the worst course of action, as things had slowly started to deteriorate since then. Not only had my paranoia grown to intolerable levels, but we had encountered more than a few minor mishaps over the last few weeks. And the only connection that I could make, was the way in which one of my closest allies was finding it pertinent to sneak out under the cover of darkness.

I simply had to find out what was going on.

As I ducked my head back behind the wall, to grant myself a brief reprieve from the horizontal rain, I realised that I was just as cold towards Mike now as I was on the outside.

He had disappointed me, frustrated me, to the point where I no longer felt as though he was my friend, merely a man who I had been forced to work with.

The rain seemed to grow louder as my thoughts darkened, as the last few remnants of light were quickly sucked away behind the cover of a rolling cloud.

I felt colder than I ever had done before, so cold in fact that I felt all my energy drain from me, as the shivers took hold and my body began to focus on keeping the slightest bit of warmth in my core.

But then, just as the cold was beginning to turn to pain, I saw a figure emerge from the building, just down the street and off to the left. I craned my neck out further, confident that the darkness that had engulfed the two lone figures in the street, would be sufficient to cover my presence.

I watched him as he emerged coyly from the door, lighting a cigarette as he looked up and down the street, carefully. It gave me a bit more of a boost, to watch him do that, as it meant that he hadn't completely abandoned all of his training.

If he was suddenly set upon by a German patrol, he would simply motion towards the cigarette and say that he couldn't sleep. He had a perfectly reasonable reason for being out on the street so late at night. It would also give him the opportunity to quickly scope out the damp cobbles for any signs that he was about to be followed.

I, on the other hand, had struggled to find any reason for being out, other than the fact that I was following someone else. If it so happened that I was picked up by a German, I would have to simply try my luck at giving him a swift kick in the groin and hoping for the best.

It wasn't a sophisticated plan, nor one that would guarantee me any chance of success, but it was a plan nonetheless, and that went a long way to settling my stomach.

I watched as Mike's featureless face began to grow larger, his footsteps hopelessly loud as they bounced from the walls more boisterous than the golf-ball-sized raindrops that splashed all around him.

My hands, that had been aching with the cold, were now profuse with perspiration, as my fingers moved from the warm clutches of my armpit to the far cooler and sobering touch of the scratched wooden grip of the revolver.

My heart started to pound, as my breaths grew shallower and more excitable, the dull finish to the revolver perfectly suited to the matte sky that loomed above.

My ears were having a difficult time trying to differentiate between the sounds of the raindrops falling and the noise of Mike's footsteps splashing around the cobbled street. There was no other way for me to work out how far away he was than to take a look, but only before I swept the excess rainfall from my forehead, to prevent it from hindering my eyesight any further.

As I stood, clutching a hold of the revolver that was so tight that I thought my knuckles would light up the dim light of *Tours*, I found myself thinking of all the things that could go wrong.

There was a chance that Mike would notice I was there before he got to me and go on the offensive, before I'd even had a chance to show my face. Or, worse still, he might simply run off, convinced that he was about to be snatched.

There was even the possibility that the figure that now was only a matter of yards away from me, was not Mike at all, and that I had gravely misidentified the man approaching. If that was the case, then I may as well have used all my rounds on myself.

That was if I had been in possession of any rounds. I had dispensed of all of them in the graveyard, and we had not had a chance yet to replenish our stores. But Mike didn't know that it was empty, and neither would any man who happened to get in my way.

I waited until it felt like the footsteps were inside my own head, as if they were treading the very beat to my heart.

There was a split second where I told my legs to

move, and they refused. But quickly they got the message, and I stepped out.

I pulled my revolver up nice and high so that I was looking straight down the finned barrel, and aiming square between the eyes of whoever it was that had suddenly become my target.

My grip was firm, my hand steady, so I was unsure as to why I felt utterly petrified. I was in total control of the situation, I had caught my subject completely off guard and I was sure that, had I wanted to, I could have got him to do anything that I wanted.

But there was something that was simultaneously making me feel totally powerless. Maybe it was because the revolver that I held between the man's eyes was empty, or perhaps something to do with the feeling of total inadequacy and vulnerability that I was struggling to shake.

All I knew for certain was that the man who stood in front of me had only seen the barrel of a gun. He was just as scared as I was.

"Bouge toi. Ou je te tire dessus."

Move. Or I'll shoot you.

I wondered for a moment if he knew it was me, but then realised that I had still not been able to positively identify him and so, it was quite possible he had not seen my face clearly enough yet.

The thought crossed my mind about what to do with the man, had it not been Mike, but he soon answered for me.

"What on earth do you think you are doing, old fruit?"

His voice shocked me, not at its coarseness or vague empathy, but by his word choice. He had spoken in English.

I clamped my hand to his mouth, forcing his head into the brickwork with a smack, as I stared into his bulging eyes. What he had done could have been a fatal error.

I could not believe what I had heard, my suspicions reaching a boiling point as I considered what kind of a man would have been confident enough to have spoken in his native tongue. Rapidly, I came to the conclusion that only a traitor, whose handlers already knew his identity, would make such a move.

"What are you doing out here?" I asked, a rasping whisper in the more romantic tones of French.

I felt the humidity clash with the freezing midnight air as I drew my palm away from his lips, slowly, catching his exasperated breath within my clutches.

"You followed me?" His eyes welled as they spoke of the betrayal that he felt deep within his heart.

"Suzanne. She told me about you sneaking out."

He looked away for a brief moment, as if to curse under his breath the woman that he had tried so hard to avoid. I prayed earnestly that he was instead breathing a sigh of relief, one that was so liberated by the thought that I was a friend and not a snooping German.

"And you believed her?" he asked, his voice crackling as if he had just received six of the best from the headmaster.

I couldn't help but scoff.

"I didn't want to believe her. What are you doing out here, *Michel?* I think you owe me an explanation."

"Why?"

"Why?" I repeated, the words sticking in the back of my throat. "Because I thought I could trust you."

"You *can* trust me."

"How do I know that? Things have been going rotten ever since I saw you out here the first time."

His eyes narrowed as we debated which part of my latest statement he would cling to.

"You think I have something to do with our bad luck?"

"It's not luck though, is it? It's been coordinated. Routinely we've hit barriers."

"I don't have anything to do with it."

"Then why don't you tell me why you're out here?"

His lips pursed, his eyes welling quicker than I had ever seen them before, the bags under his eyes swelling too as if they were just as hurt. A gust of wind lashed the rain straight across his face, wincing as it flew into his freezing skin.

He knew that the game was up. Whatever it was that was behind that door, he knew that it had been the last visit.

Eventually, he spoke.

"I don't have to explain why I'm out here," he started, rather defiantly as his chest found a way out of the hiding place somewhere close to his spine. "I can *show* you why I'm here."

He turned towards the building that he had just emerged from, as a sweeping feeling of freedom suddenly leapt across my chest. For a moment, I was able to breathe almost normally.

His eyes glistened as he watched the inner workings of my mind play out on my face. For a minute or two, I debated whether or not I should enter the building with him and what may have met me on the other side of the door.

I pondered whether he was going to have me killed, or maybe turned over to the other side with him but, as I continued to try and read his sunken eyes, his cheekbones sharper than ever, I realised that his eyes were glistening.

This time they did not sparkle out of fear or sadness, but out of an excitement, a happiness almost.

He clung to my every word as I spoke.

"I don't need to come and see what's there, *Michel.* I think I knew the minute that you began to protest Suzanne's suggestion that we leave *Tours.* But I must say I didn't expect it of you."

"Why's that?"

"Because you've never managed to make a girl love you before."

26

As I sat down with Suzanne, I winced, the aches and pains of my muscles really starting to take hold. A large bruise had developed on my thigh, a deep purple that almost shone through my trousers, presumably from the churchyard at some point.

I found myself thinking more about Martin, our informant, who had given himself so that we could get away. I wanted to ask Suzanne more about him, to learn how they had met and nurtured their relationship to the point where he had given her information. How had she known that he, out of all the soldiers in *Tours* would have been the one to hand over intelligence like that?

It continued to bubble away in my head but, as I looked at her feeble and weak frame, I realised that now was probably not the time to probe any further.

"So?"

"Excuse me?" I replied.

"I know that you followed him again last night. And this time you came back together."

"How could you possibly know that?"

She smirked, with a chilling glare that revealed a far darker side to the innocent face that she possessed.

"I know the sound of two bodies on that staircase. It creaks differently."

She smiled, a sweeter smile this time, which filled me with a warmth that I so desperately needed. But, at the same time, there was a fear about what this woman was truly capable of. I could only imagine the way that her mind would work if she had been trained in the same finishing school of the Executive as I had. She could win the war on her own.

"So, what happened? Did he tell you why he has been sneaking out? Can we trust him?"

"I hear Rommel has captured Benghazi."

"I know," she replied, her voice curt and frustrated. I was well aware of the question that she had asked me, but it was one that I was not prepared to answer just yet. There were too many other questions that I would have to work out the answer to, before I could start advising others on who to trust.

"The port there will help their fight in North Africa. It's in all the papers about how much progress they are making."

"You can't believe a word they say."

I looked at her, as I realised that her words could have been applied to almost everything that I was experiencing in my life. From newspapers to best friends, I had to take everything with a handful of salt.

I snorted lightly, causing the corner of the newspaper lying on the table to bend upwards slightly to reveal its bland print on the other side.

"How are you?" I asked, trying to see past the veneer she so often put up and look deep into her soul. But I was too tired.

"I am fine," she replied. "It is just everyone else around me that I am concerned about."

I marvelled at her, as she sat straight-backed and proud in the chair, particularly considering the state that she had found herself in a few weeks' before.

As she had laid at the foot of that tree, a stone's throw from the burning cars, I thought that I was going to lose her. Her face was so smashed and swollen that even if she had survived, I wondered whether I would have been able to look at her again, the memories too painful of what she had once looked like.

But now, there was just the faint tinges of blue and green along her cheekbones, the swelling all but eradicated. Her hands were still scarred, with large chunks missing that would take a lot longer to heal. All in all, though, she looked pretty good for someone who had been blown up and then involved in a high-speed car crash.

"I just want this war to be over and done with now," she exasperated, after leaving a fairly lengthy pause.

"Don't we all," I muttered, feeling a slight guilt creep into my heart. I did want the war to be over and done with, but not for myself, just everyone else.

It was horrific to see ordinary people like Suzanne caught up in the war, and it caused me feelings of utter horror and sickness seeing my wife and child limp and cold in the battered remnants of Richmond.

But it was all I had left in my life; it was the only thing that I could remember. I had been in this war for a little over a year and a half, but the effects on my mind may well have been ten times as long.

I had no idea what I was going to do once this war had ended, if it ever did. I had been trained to kill with the swift chop of a hand, or how to deceive the kindest of friends. I was so petrified of returning to normal life, just in case I inadvertently blew something up.

"Oh, for goodness sake."

I looked towards the voice, already knowing everything I needed to from the loud and gravely tones, that still carried their aristocratic roundness to them. I surveyed Mike's wholly disapproving glare.

"What?"

"Why don't you two just get it over and done with already."

I felt my face flush scarlet, my cheeks roaring warmer than they did when I had stood next to the burning automobiles. Neither of us said anything in response, which Mike took to be a claim of naivety.

"Oh, come off it you two. The little glances? The

hand holds? I've seen it all. We were trained to pick up on this sort of thing, remember? You do remember, don't you? We've been sent here to do a job, not find a replacement wife."

"How dare you?" I seethed, launching upwards from my chair and going to lunge for him, but I stopped halfway across the floor, my shoulder yanked backwards. Suzanne was gripping to my wrist, hard, with more power than I thought possible of a woman her size.

Like a tethered bull, I pulled and tugged, trying earnestly to free myself from her grip and let Mike know what I thought of him.

At the sound of the commotion, Harry came thumping down the stairs.

"What's going on?"

"It doesn't matter," Mike replied, not taking his eyes from me as he pulled his jacket on. "I'm leaving."

"And where do you think you're going?" I squawked, like some incandescent mother figure.

"Do you really need to ask? If you wanted to know that you'd just follow me again, surely."

He spat a vicious scowl towards Suzanne who, for the first time since I had met her, shied away from joining the fight, her shoulders slumped. It was the first time that I had seen her mental state damaged, and I wondered how badly the war had started to affect her, both physically as well as emotionally.

It seemed that everyone was falling apart.

"She was right though, wasn't she?" I hurled back,

finally yanking myself free from Suzanne's anchor but resisting the urge to travel across the ground between Mike and me. There was no point in smashing each other senseless.

"You had absolutely no right! You could have just asked me!"

"I shouldn't have needed to ask, Mike. We were meant to work together, to tell each other everything, and you failed."

"Well, your time hasn't exactly been marked with success, Johnny. Unless you're counting your romantic endeavours. Don't forget what this war has taken from you."

There was a brief silence, as I watched the images playing out in my mind once again. We had run, the two of us, through the bombed-out streets of Richmond, to my own address. There was nothing but flattened rubble and dust lingering in the air.

I held my son shortly after he had slipped into an eternal sleep.

"I'm sorry, son," one of the Home Guard lot had whispered in my ear. "But at least he will know nothing of the horrors of this world."

That had been that. That was the only sympathy I had been shown. The next day, life had carried on as normal for everyone else, their world just kept on spinning. Mine, however, had ceased the second I had seen his lifeless form.

I knew that Mike was replaying the events in his

head too, they had not been without their effects on him either.

In that brief moment, where both sets of eyes transported each other back in time by about a year, maintaining the same gaze as they had done back then, the situation seemed to diffuse incredibly, like the overflowing pan had been removed from the flame.

"Anyway," he eventually spoke, a conscious effort in his voice to curtail its gruffness and volume. "I think it would be best for the two of us if we were to go our separate ways. It is obviously not working. The Executive got it wrong by putting us two together. We've been through too much together, been at one another's side for a little longer than we can both bear."

I tried to muster a look on my face that spoke of shock and surprise, but I could barely conjure up even a flinch. I could hardly say that it had come as an astonishment to me. In fact, I would probably have agreed with him had I had the courage to do so.

The fact was, I found it difficult to think of myself without him, making decisions without his cynicism or aggression.

"Where will you go?" I asked, trying not to sound as hurt as I felt.

Mike looked towards Harry for some guidance.

"You helped him?" I asked, despondency and disbelief flooding my voice.

"He asked me. Besides, I think it would be for the best also."

"Where are you taking him?" I repeated.

"I have a friend. He has agreed to take him in for now. It is quite safe; don't you worry about that. It is probably better if we leave quite soon, my friend," he muttered lowly, as if I couldn't hear him.

Mike nodded, as he retreated upstairs along with Harry.

I buried my head in my hands as I plonked myself back down on the wooden chair, so uncomfortable that it almost pained me.

I breathed slowly and methodically, trying with earnest to think of nothing more than a simple white canvas. But nothing I tried would transport me from the darkness that I felt utterly trapped in.

I felt an arm wrap its way around my neck, a head resting on my shoulder. She squeezed gently.

"It's not like he is disappearing off the face of the earth. Harry will know where he is, we can always get to him if we need to."

There were a few more minutes of silence, which I drank in desperately. It finally started to feel like this was the first time since we had been in France that things were starting to go right.

"Maybe it is for the best," I croaked. "We can get back together once our luck has started to turn."

"Of course," she muttered back into my ear, not believing a single word that I had said. There was no such thing as luck to her, only sheer determination and strong will, neither of which I was displaying.

"There is one thing that you will need to do though," she continued.

"What's that?" I asked, lifting my head from my palms and squinting in the light.

"London ought to know, shouldn't they?"

I thought about it for a moment, knowing that she was right, as she had proved herself to be so often.

"Yes. But I would rather take Harry with me. I don't think you are quite up to it yet."

She offered up no kind of protest or indignation, just a quiet acceptance. I supposed that the argument would come later when I had settled a little more.

"I will go tonight."

27

The attic that we crouched in was nothing more than a few low wooden beams, with some additional planks of wood around our feet to stop us from plummeting through the ceiling. It was difficult to see where the boards had been laid, and so one had to feel around his feet before taking another step, which could be the last taken before a journey to the floor below ensued.

I lit a small paraffin lantern and, as it began to fill the void with its violent hiss, I took a look around, aiming the light into the far corners to chase the bogeyman away. I was careful to dim it to just the right level, lighting just one corner of the attic and not much else.

There was a blackout around these parts that started in the next hour or so, and we could really have done without the unwanted attention that a contraband light would receive.

It was just after six o'clock, the sun falling from its

place in the sky, racing towards the horizon with vigour. We had made the journey to the friendly house during the day, so that we did not have to sneak around during curfew hours, which could end with our premature arrest.

It was a welcome move, especially that since the sun had given up its strength, and the clouds had rolled overhead, that rain had been falling incessantly for the best part of an hour, a lot of it seeming to dribble through various points of the roof and all around us.

The large droplets continued to splash around, each one soaked up into the boards at our feet and weakening them each time.

As I thumped the briefcase into the driest corner that I could find, pulling my coat over my head to try and protect my equipment from destruction, I watched as Harry carefully positioned himself by a small, vulnerable looking window that looked down towards the street below.

We were about three floors up and had one of the best views of *Tours* that could only be beaten by an aircraft of some description. It was perfect for what we would need it for, giving us the ability to see any unwanted visitors in good time, and make haste to escape before they got too close.

But, it also meant that the signal we could receive would be clear and uninterrupted, allowing me an unbroken airwave upon which to inform London of our latest development.

"How long do you reckon we have to transmit, before…"

His voice broke away, but I could still tell what was on his mind. The Germans had sophisticated radio-finding equipment, that would be able to pick up on my signal, and narrow their search to a particular street, or two if we were fortunate.

But they relied heavily on moving closer towards their target in order to get an accurate reading, which meant that we would have time to send and receive before they got too close for comfort. But not much time.

"Ten minutes. Fifteen at most. But if you keep your eyes peeled, then I am sure that we'll have more than enough warning if it comes to it."

It wasn't a case of *if* it came to it, but when. I was confident that I had seen one man carrying a heavy-looking case of wine, a sure sign that a radio direction finder was in transit. But I didn't think that Harry would need to hear that part.

As I spoke, I tried to inject an element of confidence into both him and me, to settle my nerves on more than one count. I was anxious about the fact that I was transmitting with Harry for the first time. He seemed like a decent enough fellow on the surface, but he had not had the extensive training that both Mike and I had benefitted from.

The fact that I was not with Mike came with another problem also. I was good at sending a message back to London, but Mike had always been better at receiving the response. It was something that had played on my mind for the whole afternoon. I would simply have to pray and concentrate as hard as I possibly could, to make sure I understood every single *dit* and *dah.*

I began to carefully unpack the contents of the suitcase, something that I had done many times before, but also not in quite a while. Everything immediately felt familiar to me, as I turned the coils over in my hand and fiddled with the receiver.

I unwound the cord that the telegraph key was attached to, giving it a few taps just to ensure that the spring had not become deformed in transit.

Finally, with the receiver and transmitter the final two things to be slotted into place, I picked up the power supply unit and, clunking it into place, connected all three pieces together. It was only then, as the unit itself was attached to a small six-volt battery, that the thing would become fully operational.

I pulled it all together and let the slight whine begin to sound, the voltage meter leaping slightly and then settling somewhere down low. I let the set warm-up, to the point where I would be able to start transmitting, before shutting off the power completely and standing up, adjusting my coat as I did so.

I noticed that Harry had been watching inquisitively as I had run through the motions of switching the set on before turning it off, double-checking that everything would work exactly when it was meant to. It was pointless in setting everything up just seconds before you needed it to, only to find that something was faulty.

He caught my eye, dragging his gaze lethargically from the set that lay at my feet.

"Quite marvellous, don't you think?" I asked, offering him a cigarette.

"Absolutely."

"To think that some of my folks are out there somewhere and listening in…Doesn't make me feel quite so alone after all."

He snorted gently, the tip of his cigarette dulling slightly as he did so. I took a long drag, watching the nerves appear rapidly on his face. It was not something for me to be overly concerned about, the thought of broadcasting your position to the Germans was not one that anyone took with great pleasure on their first time out.

"Now what?" he asked, rolling the cigarette in between his forefinger and thumb, apprehensively.

"Now we wait," I smirked, inhaling another lungful of warm smoke into my mouth. Whenever I said that, all I could do was to think of Mike. It had, after all, seemed to be one of his favourite sayings.

As I thought of him standing alongside me in that attic, I realised that I was pining for him, yearning for the pointless conversations and unnecessary questions. There was an emptiness to my existence even in the short time that we had parted, as if the breeze that blew over my shoulder was somehow colder without him.

I mulled over what would happen to us over the coming days and weeks. I was hoping for some sort of reunion, one in which we would be able to put our distrust and envy to one side and carry on the way that we had before.

But I knew that, even if a reunion was possible, that things would have to change. Things were getting too hairy around *Tours*, for one thing, we were going to have to move and, in many ways, that would be the best scenario possible.

The worst, apart from being tracked down by the Germans, was the threat of being recalled by London, or simply abandoned by them, thinking that two livewires must simply be struck off. If that was to happen, then we would become just as useful as the butchers and bakers that were in the ranks of Suzanne's local force.

Harry's shoulders flinched, as if he had been squared up to by a much larger man, just as the sound of a bicycle squealing past began to bounce off the walls in the street below. I knew from experience that an innocent bicycle was not always as innocent as one might think but, judging by the fact that it carried on unperturbed, I did not feel like there was much cause for concern.

The main source of my worry lay in the way that Harry had reacted; jumpy and startled. He seemed rather spooked about something, and nothing had happened of any worth as of yet.

I watched his eyes in the dark, the whites burning

a brighter shade in the light of the small lamp, his pupils as wide as possible and darting in every possible direction. He tapped his hand on the side of his thigh and I could see him wipe the sweat away from time to time, in between chewing at his lips or mopping his brow.

I needed to do something to calm him down, otherwise, there was not a chance that he would last the entire time of the transmission.

"Hey," I rasped out to him, in a mock shout but keeping my voice as low as possible. His head turned, surprised by my choice of words.

I held out the carton of cigarettes to him again, lighting it as it hung from his mouth before igniting one my own.

"So," I started, ideas rattling around my mind about what to talk about. "You and Suzanne. You have known each other a while?"

He thought about it for a moment, as if answering would somehow be some sort of betrayal.

"Yes."

"How long?"

"Many years."

I wondered for a moment if he thought I was some sort of Nazi agent, as his body language alone told me that he did not want to talk about her. Still, I persisted, in the hope of drawing more and more out of him.

"Did you know her husband?"

"The Englishman?"

"Yes. The pilot."

"No. But I knew of him. I knew she went up north somewhere and heard that she got married. But I never met him."

I sucked the smoke into my lungs, before breathing it out through gritted teeth, as he finally turned his head from the window and towards me.

"I did."

"You? How?"

"Old comrades. Small world, eh?"

"Yes. Small world."

His head turned to look out towards the inky black sky that had remained unchanged since he had last looked out twenty seconds before. I tried to guess at what was running through his mind, before stopping, aware that I had always fallen far short of anything that resembled a mind-reading ability.

"Do you think she has changed?" He looked at me, puzzled. "Suzanne. Do you think that she has changed?"

"I don't know. Maybe," he muttered, something clearly playing on his mind and threatening to give itself up on the surface of his face. "Yes. I suppose she has," he continued, unprompted.

"She has grown more thoughtful, more…what's the word? Reserved? Yes, reserved. She is closed."

"What do you mean by that?"

"She always used to be so honest. She did not shy away from telling you what she thought. Now she does not. It makes me wonder."

It did me too. I felt the paranoid fibres of my being beginning to twitch into overload, as my mind became awash of suspicions and theories as to why she had changed. I tried to correct my thinking, to straighten out my thoughts, otherwise I could see Suzanne and I heading the same way as my relationship with Mike. And, in many ways, I did not want that relationship to sour more than I had done with Mike.

I took a quick glance at my wristwatch. Somehow, we had managed to while away the hours, as we now had a matter of minutes to go before the agreed transmission time.

"But," Harry began, just as I squatted next to the wireless set, pulling the headphones over my searing ears, "show me a person who hasn't been affected by being blown up, and I'll make you a very rich man."

28

It was time to power up.

Turning away from Harry and pulling the jacket back over my head to protect myself from the falling raindrops, I flicked the switch to the 'On' position. It took a few seconds to respond, before the small dial leapt up in voltage, the working parts slowly warming up like an old man on a winter's morning.

I checked that all the other switches and dials were in exactly the right position, apart from one that I would save until the final moment. Everything seemed perfectly ready, and so, with a sharp exhale, I pulled the headphones over my head, leaving my right ear free from the headset, just in case I could not trust Harry entirely.

It wasn't exactly an assassination of his character, as I knew that Mike had always done the same when I was around. It wasn't really a mistrust of the other person, but three ears were always going to be better than two. Anyone would tell you that.

But still, there was a feeling of cautiousness, not too well hidden, that made me want to withdraw the headset completely, and listen in with Harry. I was feeling enclosed, the damp confines of the attic slowly closing in and pressing down on my chest like heavy brick.

I began to wheeze awfully until I began making an effort to slow my breathing and allow it in through my burning nostrils.

I pulled the jacket back from my head slightly, to stop the humid air of my breath from clinging to the fibres and making me feel even more trapped. It took me all of three seconds to regret my decision, as I observed the look of worry and fear that was etched onto Harry's face.

He was still staring towards me, watching as my hands had danced around the set and got everything whirring, but it wasn't as if he was taking any of it in. He was looking through the case, with the kind of stare that I had seen men return with after watching their best pal shot down. It was a hollow, empty stare, one that told of how a piece of the man's soul had recently died, the rest of it tainted with a gangrenous-like poison.

There was no time to tell Harry to pull himself together, there wasn't even time to call and get him to face the window, so I allowed him his moment of madman meditation, hoping that something would pull him from his stupor soon enough.

As I stared at his pathetic figure, my mouth drying up to a crisp, I realised that I needed Mike, not Harry. Mike would have known exactly what to say, even if it had been one of the bluest words on the planet in an attempt to pull him out of his trance. But, then again, I was convinced that Mike would never have allowed Harry to get into that kind of a state anyway, always more astute than I could ever learn to be.

I had to force myself to look away from him, as the burden of what was upon my shoulders began to worsen, the constriction around my chest squeezing fiercely. For a moment, I felt as though I might have been the most important man in Europe, poised to receive a message that would have earth-shattering consequences. There was a brief second where I thought that what I would hear, through tiny metallic blips, could shorten the war by months, if not altogether.

But then my excitement turned to optimism, even to expectation. Maybe, just maybe, I was about to receive news of the end of the hostilities, and that we would all be able to return home once more, wherever that was.

My thoughts were tinged with a jealousy of those for who that was already a reality, mainly for those who were already dead and would know nothing of the future horrors that this war had in store. But they were also marred by a regrettable feeling of disdain, as if I did not want the war to end after all.

It was, above all else, the only thing that I had found in my life that I had seemed rather good at, having spent months managing to avoid being shot down and killed, when far better pilots than me had lost their lives already. And, so far, I was still alive in *Tours*, something that I thought would come to a rather abrupt halt before too long.

Memories began to rush to the front of my mind, of everything that I had ever achieved. It became apparent, or so it seemed, that everything that I had ever accomplished that was worthy of any note was carried out in this ghastly war. The years preceding had been years spent kicking footballs around, or climbing trees, knees scabbed over and muddied.

I thought of my wife and child, ripped from my side by the cruel trajectory of a floating parachute mine. Suzanne cropped up, as did Alfred and Mike, spectral faces of people who I had come to know and love.

I shook them all away from me, panicking that I was having some sort of vision of my life, just minutes before it was to end.

I looked down at my wristwatch, staring at the second hand and willing it to click by faster and faster with every twitch.

I looked to Harry, just one last time, immediately wishing that I hadn't. But there was no time to feel scared about what was going to happen with him, the second hand had just brushed past twelve.

My hands moved slowly, as if they were thinking for themselves and screaming at me not to do it, but I used all my might to override them.

My fingers ached as I gripped hold of the dial, turning it from its standby position until it clicked into place right next to the embossed 'S' on the raised plate. It was time to send.

As I placed my finger over the telegraph key, a faint tremor developing as I did so, a low and persistent whine began to moan in my ear as the side tone began to burrow further into my mind.

Hello Mother. This is Fortunae. This is Fortunae.

It croaked and quivered as I pressed down on the telegraph key, not too faintly, but not too firmly either, just as I had been taught. The whine in my left ear was so loud that it filled my entire mind, and I thought about looking to Harry to see if he was hearing it too, but decided against it. It would only throw me off what I was sending, in more ways than one.

The *dits* and *dahs* were hardly decipherable, as the soundwaves continued to pitch and roll in my ear, just the faint click of the telegraph underneath my finger all I had to distinguish between the letters that I was sending.

I thought about nothing as I followed my prepared message, scrawled out on a discarded piece of newspaper. I traced over its rough edges as I transmitted, my finger moving at such a pace that I could hardly believe that it was me.

Suddenly, my finger ran from the edge of the piece of paper. It could only have meant one thing. I had finished what I had wanted to say.

Everything had been in it; the security key, the apology for not waiting for a response, the need for urgency and the message itself. I had managed to do it all in a matter of minutes.

I glanced at my wrist and felt my stomach lurch at the thought that I had misread the time. All of that would have been for nothing, nothing apart from allowing the Germans to get a fix on our location and hunt us down.

Carefully, I flicked the dial to 'R' and the side tone wound itself down. I was ready to receive my orders.

But there was nothing. Nothing apart from the most ear-shattering, demoralising silence. For what felt like an age, I heard nothing from London, not so much as an isolated *dit* as the radio operator inadvertently leant on his telegraph key.

It seemed like several minutes passed by, in which time I had convinced myself that we had been set up, completely abandoned by the few people that we thought we could rely on.

I tried to calm myself down, to rationalise my thoughts, closing my eyes and imagining the senior officers all crowded round the operator's shoulder as he deciphered my message. It was not an easy code to have been using, it would take time to unjumble it all, and I wanted him to get it spot on.

So, for that, I forgave the invisible man.

Just as I was about to give up completely, there was a faint noise, that could easily have been mistaken for an over-exuberant mouse scuttling along the floor of the attic. But I had heard it many times before, over very many hours.

It was London.

I resisted the urge to leap up into the air and punch my fist above my head, and tried to stay as cool as I possibly could. It was the first time that I had personally heard from anyone outside of France since we had arrived, and it was liberating.

It felt as though I was no longer on my own, it gave me the confidence and the motivation that I needed to carry on. If an entire garrison of Germans had descended on me in that moment, I was quite certain that I would have been able to take every single one of them on and won.

How could I have lost? I had the might of the British Empire right on the other end of my telegraph key.

My hand began to involuntarily jerk, the nib of my pencil scribbling faster than anything I had ever seen before, trying to guess at letters as they were tapped out, invariably getting it horribly wrong.

As my hand hovered over the paper, expectantly waiting for another sound, nothing came but the silence once more.

Just as quickly as it had all started, the most exciting moment of my war had come to an end. Now all I had to do was work out what it was they were trying to tell me.

First, though, I switched the wireless set off, pulling the battery and power supply unit from its housing, entertaining myself with the thought of some rotund German sitting in the back of his truck, deflated that he had suddenly lost his fix.

I got to work straight away on the message, pulling the jacket further over my head and tugging the paraffin lamp underneath with me. The codes and Morse had been ingrained in me while we had been at Arisaig, so much so that I did not read the words of a newspaper any longer, but imagined it as dots and dashes.

It did not take me long to untangle the jumbled letters, but I went through it all again, letter by letter, just to make sure that I hadn't got what I had received wrong in any way. That could prove to be fatal.

"Well?" Harry asked, his voice surprisingly loud and bold. The eternal stare had disappeared from his eyes, now just the rat-like holes of blackness that he usually possessed.

It was the moment that I needed though, to pull myself from my own trance and realise that the war had not stopped with my little moment of triumph.

All in all, it had seemed overwhelmingly easy to simply spark the set up and talk to London with as little ease as I had done, and it was that ease that immediately began to concern me.

As far as I had been aware, everything had fallen quite still outside the attic, which I had originally put down to my concentration. But the more that I thought about it, the more petrified that I became that it was because the Germans were right outside our door, sneaking up on us.

I said nothing to Harry as I carefully fed the pieces of paper into the paraffin-fuelled flame, waiting for them to turn a golden orange before moving my attention to the suitcase.

Everything started to find its way back into its housing, as Harry appeared over my shoulder to watch.

"Everything alright?" he asked, as I flicked the two catches shut and hoisted the case up.

I pointed to the lamp that was now at his feet, instructing him to put the thing out, which he did dutifully, never taking his eyes off me, even as he bent down. It was an odd move, but one that could be forgiven of a man of his inexperience.

"Fine," I said, clearing my throat. "Everything is absolutely fine."

I normally felt wrong about lying. But, in that attic, it felt like the most natural thing in the world.

29

There was a noticeable spring in my step as we snuck around the blacked-out streets, the shadows that had moments before been our worst enemies, concealing the predators, now shielding us from the very same creatures.

We clung to the darkest corners wherever we could, pressing in close to one another as we stepped in unison, second-guessing the other's next move.

I was surprisingly upbeat, ready to take my message and put the wheels into motion. It was the first time that I felt like I was doing something, no matter how small. I felt in control, a warm blood coursing through me as I realised that I was in charge of this rather small circuit.

It was just Harry and me and, whereas hours before I had felt lonely and vulnerable without Mike's presence, now I felt liberated, as if the shackles that had been cutting into my ankles for so long had finally been released, and that I could make my own decisions. For the first time, I knew that if I was killed or captured on that night, then I would only have myself to blame, and there was something quite emancipating with that thought.

The cooling rain dribbled down the side of my face, my clothes sodden and heavy, but dousing my face, which was still burning on account of the paraffin lamp that I had been sat next to for so long, the excitement sustaining a blazing heat for a good hour or two afterwards.

I stared up to the sky, not expecting to see much, but opening my eyes and allowing the raindrops to fiercely splash into my eyes, causing me great pain yet great enjoyment in equal measure.

Every hundred yards or so, I would stop and repeat the process all over again, the feeling of being cleansed not losing its novelty. For the first time in a while, I found myself grinning, a big, schoolboy-like grin, that would have screamed nothing but mischief to any schoolmaster that had seen it.

I was feeling so weightless and upbeat that the suitcase in my grasp was weighing down even more than it normally did. In fact, it seemed about the only thing that was keeping me from floating up to the heavens in a delirious ecstasy.

It was beginning to take its effect on my aching and exhausted arms, and I could feel myself begin to walk with a limp as I leaned over like some kind of confused hunchback.

The sense of achievement that I carried within that suitcase was just about enough to keep my grasp around it firm and steady, not wanting to lose that feeling of accomplishment that had seemed so long in coming.

It was a feeling akin only to when I shot down my first enemy aircraft, at the ripe old age of twenty-three. It had taken me numerous sorties to finally get my own confirmed kill, but once I saw the jet-black smoke erupt from the port side engine of the Heinkel 111 for the first time, every one that came after became natural to me.

I was hoping that, now that my first radio transmission was in the bag, that each subsequent one would be more successful than the last. Secretly, I was hoping that it would mean I would eventually be able to ditch the need for Harry altogether, and go things alone.

"Left down here," Harry rasped, a few decibels louder than he perhaps should have done.

I nodded, even though his back was turned to me, fully expecting him to turn around and acknowledge me, like he had done the last fifty corners that we had been round. But this time he didn't.

"How do you think it all went?" he asked me, curiously, not lowering his tone at all.

I tried to curb the excitement that was bubbling away inside me, resisting the urge to let out all of my relieved apprehension and sense of accomplishment.

"It went as well as it could have done, I think."

"You think? Well, if my opinion counts for anything, I think it went tremendously well. A very smooth operation. Very concise. Efficient. You must have been very well trained for all this."

I let it linger, hoping that he wasn't expecting some kind of response, but his glancing look over his shoulder told me that he was requiring one.

"Yes. Many months of training."

"And what kind of things did you have to do?"

His voice was growing in excitement and he was struggling to keep his volume down low. Strangely though, whether it was the elation or exhaustion I did not know, but I was not overly concerned by his loud, aggressive whispering. There was a part of me that wanted the entire town, including the Germans, to know what I had done. I wanted them to marvel at me, even if it meant being arrested by them.

"Another time, Harry."

"Of course, of course," he muttered, barely letting another second pass before he launched into his next line of questioning. "So, what was the message? What are your orders?"

He spun around with a mischievous grin and burning glint in his eye that told me he was more excited than I was about the whole affair.

The rain dripped morosely from his fringe, getting in the way of his mouth and nostrils as he somehow seemed to simultaneously breathe through both of them. The rainwater was clearly not irritating him either, his clothes a darker shade than when we had left earlier on and far heavier as the fibres had soaked up as much as possible. Not once had he moaned, nor had he even mentioned it. He simply got on with things in much the same way that I did.

There were a few moments where all I did was look at him, observing the bumps and lines in his peculiar face, and wondering what kind of a man he would have been outside of this war.

He had the air of a university professor, an aloof man who was quite content within his own thoughts, with the occasional foray out into an opinionated lecture to his students. But he also had the traits of a hermit; a man who rarely ventured out into his surrounding area, a widower perhaps.

But, as he stared at me, he seemed like a small child, one glaring at his father for his approval before doing something that he knew that he shouldn't.

All of these thoughts were completely intentional, while I took a few moments to debate whether or not to tell him what London had just told me. It was, of course, all for show, I had made my mind up before he had even asked the question as to whether I was going to tell him or not.

He needed to know.

I gave him a smile, so that he knew my intentions, which was reciprocated in the most exuberant of fashions. He was ecstatic, he was finally being allowed into the club, he had succeeded in becoming one of the key components of our fledgling circuit. For him, the only way from here, was up.

I pulled him over to one side, into a doorway that offered some slight protection from the driving rain, that was beginning to wear thin on my patience.

"What is it?" he rasped, specks of spittle landing on the bridge of my nose.

"Lower your voice," I breathed back, only just starting to worry that someone might hear. He obliged, only nodding his reply, his eyes widening as he prepared himself for what might come next.

I lowered the suitcase to the floor, before placing both hands inside my jacket pocket to shield them from the cold. My right hand, however, was chilled further, as it moved its way along the barrel of the revolver, searching for the grip.

My hand settled around it and, ever so carefully, I curled my finger around the trigger and gave it the softest of squeezes, readying myself physically and mentally for what might be just around the corner.

"We have three nights."

"For what?" he replied, his voice so low that it was drowned out by the pounding rain that crashed all around us. It worried me slightly, at the thought that someone would easily be able to sneak up without us being able to hear their approach, even if they were on a motorcycle.

I peered my head out of the doorway and adjusted myself, so that I could at least look down one direction of the side street and hope that one who hunted me appeared in my eyeline.

"Another agent. To replace Mike. He's dropping in in three nights."

"Where?"

"*Cinq-Mars-la-Pile.*"

"It is a large area, my friend."

"One of the farms."

"There are many farms."

"Then we will just have to work it out on the night. It's better that way."

His face was agitated, but excited, as we stepped back out into the rain, the chilled droplets taking on a more ferocious guise as we continued our journey back to the safehouse.

I began to muse as to why I had felt the need to tell him straight away, instead of forcing him to wait until we made it back to a relative safety. But there was an urgency to my life now, one that had grown especially over the last two weeks, that told me that I shouldn't waste any time in telling him what was going to happen.

Besides, if I was to die between now and the night of the drop, then at least our new agent would have half a chance of being picked up by the right people.

After a few minutes of splashing our way through the rapidly forming puddles, Harry sidled up to me, his louder, hasher whisper replacing the dulcet tones that he had possessed before.

"They would just replace someone like *Michel*, just like that?"

"He is no good to us now, is he?"

"But he is still alive."

"For now. But how much longer will he have if he is on his own?"

He muttered something under his breath which sounded like some sort of agreement with me. But I never quite got the opportunity to ask him to repeat himself.

He guided me down another street, that looked exactly like the last one and the thirteen or so before that. But this one was different, not at first, but within a split second it was.

As the beam of light exploded and hit me straight in the face, I could feel its warmth begin to pierce my skin. Immediately, I knew that none of this could have been good news.

I clamped my eyes shut, screwing them as tight as possible to avoid the blinding glare of the headlights, simultaneously trying to wish myself away to some far-flung land. But the burning heat on the other side of my eyelids told me that I hadn't been successful.

At first, I could hear nothing; nothing whatsoever. And I took that as a good sign. But then, quite distinct from the noise of falling rain, was a voice, a croaky, quivering one, but a voice that spoke with such authority that I felt compelled to obey.

I was instantly petrified, still refusing to open my eyes and face the reality of what was happening around me. I knew the sight that would meet my eyes had I been courageous enough to open them. There would have been men with guns, probably an entire platoon, complete with machine gun and twitchy trigger fingers. I couldn't believe it.

All those months of training, all those hours of reconnaissance and making sure that we knew the area like the backs of our hands, and I had been caught clutching the very suitcase that had minutes before been in contact with London.

"Halt!"

Thankfully for me, it did not seem to Harry that it was a voice that commanded such obedience.

"*Jean!* Run! Go! Get away from here!"

30

My knees felt as though they were dislocated as I spun around on the spot, everyone as surprised as I was that I was trying to make a quick getaway. I had still not seen a single German soldier, as my eyes were still struggling to adjust to the sudden beam of light, but I knew that they had been lurking there, the spectral outlines of rifles and submachine guns silhouetted against the brilliant white.

I was quickly out of breath, but in that moment, I did not need oxygen to see me through. All I needed was the surge of adrenaline that pulsated through me, and the desperate, pathetic, willingness to want to survive just one more day.

I could have no thoughts of anything past the next few seconds, each of which could well have been my last. There were no thoughts as to what might happen now that a platoon of enemy soldiers had seen my face, some of them maybe even able to recognise me from my time in and around *Tours.*

All that possessed my thoughts was the impulsive footsteps that I took, my legs striding wider and further with every pace that I took. Soon, I would have to stop running away from the scene of the crime, and instead focus on where it was that I was actually heading.

I slipped on the wet cobble-stoned path and, as I fell to the floor, I took in a large mouthful of rainwater, the first bit of air that I had managed to take in quite a considerable time. My knees smashed into the ground, and I felt one of them open up like a sodden piece of paper, blood beginning to gush from the open wound at my joint.

Sucking in air through gritted teeth, I had no other option but to get back up, hoisting the suitcase back up to my side and hobbling my way further away from where we had been confronted. As I used the suitcase as a support to hoist myself up, I realised that the street was empty.

The dimmed streetlights were still chucking out little light, the only advantage that I felt like I had, and the rain was still cascading from sloped roofs and onto the pathways below.

The whole street seemed to bask in an odd kind of light, one that was merely more than a reflection of the darkness, mirrored in the pond-like puddles that had now well and truly taken hold.

But I was on my own, which took what little breath I had away from me immediately.

I began to flick my head around as I ran, growing more and more concerned by the fact it was just me. Harry was nowhere to be seen.

Even if he had tried to give me a head start then I would have at least been able to see him, several yards behind, but he should have been there by rights.

I gave even less thought to where it was that I was heading as I began to fill my mind with all sorts of scenarios as to what had happened to him. Maybe he had simply given himself up, tired of the deception and avoidance that had overtaken his life. But that didn't seem to be his style.

The thought popped into my head that there was a chance that he had made off in a different direction, giving us both a better chance at survival than if we had stayed together. But, somehow, I didn't think that his mind would have worked like that. But, then again, maybe I was doing him a discredit. Just because he hadn't had all the training that I had done, it didn't mean that he could not think on his feet.

My feet slipped again as I rounded another corner, which somehow seemed more familiar than all the others, but I could not discern why. As I tried my utmost to stay on my two feet, the suitcase slammed into the ground and I heard an unmistakable crack as something gave way to the force.

A stripe of red-streaked over the leather of the

case, my own personal contribution to its decoration and, as I looked down, the front of my trousers were hanging open like a pair of curtains, the chill of the night finally reaching my senses as it hit the exposed skin. Blood gushed down from my knee faster than it would have done had it not been raining, the pale mixture running towards the ground with a speed that I was envious of.

With loose pieces now throwing themselves all around the inside of the suitcase, it began to take on a more manageable form, more lightweight. The pain and discomfort that had gripped my shoulder and arms as I had lugged it around had all but vanished, replaced with a buoyancy that made it feel like a feather.

So much so was the ease with which I now carried the case, I swapped the hands that clamped around the handle, to ensure that I had not, in fact, let go of it somewhere.

I had no way of telling just how far I had managed to run until I made out two faint noises, that seemed close enough to be relevant to me, but far away enough to not present much of a threat.

Two gunshots.

Instead of stopping, straining my ears and trying to work out if I had heard correctly, I found myself opening my legs up further, heaving at my chest to help carry me away to a much greater distance.

Whatever the reason for the gunshots, I had to ignore them. They had to become irrelevant to me.

But the more stoic I strove to become, the more I found my thoughts encompassed by their existence.

Particularly when a rapport of a couple more rifle shots reverberated off every roof tile in *Tours*.

31

It was difficult not to think of Harry in every spare moment that I had. He had, after all, become a more reliable accomplice than some of the others that I had alongside me recently. It did not take me long to miss seeing his odd, bespectacled face, waxy-like in appearance and pointed in his demeanour. His direct and unashamed observations had been noticeably lacking as I had tried to move on, as I began to yearn for just one of his quips to reach my ears again.

I had no contact with him whatsoever in the seventy-two hours or so since I had last seen him, rain dripping from his nose, as his cavernous mouth opened wide to bellow at me to get away. The gunshots had echoed around inside my mind every time that I had returned to that rain-ridden evening.

The rainfall had stopped, reluctantly, but, even days after it had ceased, the effects were still visible across the landscape. As I had made my way across several furrowed fields, the ground sucked at my soles and threatened to take them down to the core of the earth, making it an incredibly laborious and long-winded journey to my laying-up point.

The chill of the water that was reaching up over the balls of my ankles had subsided after twenty minutes or so, the initial numbness finally giving way to a sense of familiarity with the icy-cold liquid. It was not the most glamourous of places to hide myself away, a shallow irrigation ditch, but it would do exactly what I would need it to.

I needed to stay hidden, the darkness simply wasn't enough tonight, and I knew that making use of the farmer's barns and outbuildings, no matter how much warmer and comfortable they looked, would be too dangerous to fathom.

But, then again, since being caught out in the side street by the blinding light, the invisible faces glaring at me intently, danger had become a fixation of mine, seeing it lurking around every corner. I had not left the safehouse since that night, until I had to, and even making my way downstairs for food had seemed fraught with risk.

Had it not been for Suzanne's presence in the house, I was sure that I would have gone quite mad.

I had learned a valuable lesson, however. I was not a good agent. I had allowed myself to become cloaked in a feeling of security, built on a fragile foundation of one good transmission. I did not know what I had done to assist the Germans in working out where we were, and our subsequent route home, but I had become resolute in my determination not to give them the same opportunity again.

For many, mistakes like the one that I had made had already cost them their lives. For me, I was lucky, taking away only a great sense of humility and more than a touch of sheer embarrassment.

My new-found meekness was complemented by the long wooden barrel of a well-thumbed rifle that rested itself on my shoulders like a weary child. The *Lebel* rifle was old, from the last war, and had been the possession of a portly farmer who had surrendered it over to me, his liberator.

It was an odd design, and not one that I particularly relished in utilising, its bolt-action stiff and sticky, the bolt itself sticking out to one side as if dislocated from the main body of the rifle. Its eight-round capacity magazine should have been a source of confidence for me, but it wasn't, owing to the fact that the farmer had surrendered the weapon with just six in the breech. Two had been used on vermin shortly before the German invasion.

I hoped that I would be able to return the weapon to him with the same number of rounds in it. It felt good to have a little more firepower behind me as I lay in the darkness, compared to the puny revolvers and sidearms that I had become used to. But, I knew with a certainty, that my little escapade out into the darkened French countryside would either go so well that I would not have to even pick the rifle up, or I would need to use every single round that the fat farmer had supplied me with.

There would be no in between.

Either way, whatever was going to happen, the outcome would not be one that I would be able to take comfort from. My stomach churned again as I began to think too deeply, and how I was sure that things were about to be exposed that my conscience would rather keep hidden.

I shuffled around in the water, making an awful noise but doing just about enough to mask the gurgles of my stomach, bile and vomit burning away at my insides causing me to wince.

None of this was doing me any good at all. If I carried on like I was doing, I was sure that my nerves would be shot in a matter of weeks. I needed to get away. Above all else, I needed some sleep.

Ever since I had received news of my new assignment, as I had laid stretched out on my back in a Cornish stream, I had known that my days were numbered. But, normally, that thought had been accompanied by a tremendous amount of adrenaline and excitement, a rush that prevented me from thinking through the inevitable.

But, it was in that irrigation ditch at the side of a French field, near *Cinq-Mars-la-Pile* that I acknowledged that my days were coming to an end, without the rush of blood that made my heart leap. If anything, my blood thickened, chilled, my heart slowing and becoming despondent.

I desperately needed the bolt of electricity to fly through my body like a lightning strike, otherwise I was going to die a slow and rather miserable death in the depression of ground that I clung to for dear life.

And I got it.

It was feeble and indistinct to begin with, so much so that I cleaned my ears out with my index fingers, ensuring that it wasn't just the internal mush of confused thoughts that I could hear. But, as I waited for it to subside, it grew stronger, more defined.

I couldn't make out what kind of engine it was, it seemed muffled by the clouds that decorated the sky, hiding the radiant stars that I knew existed somewhere. I had always struggled to differentiate between the different tones of aircraft engines, even struggling to identify a Rolls-Royce Merlin as I sat in the cockpit of my very own Hurricane.

But I took a guess, as I crept up the side of the ditch, excited that I had friends close by. It was certainly twin-engined, maybe even four-engined, but I could not quite tell. There was definitely more than one, its deep, throaty roar beginning to shake the water in which I stood, all the while allowing me to become infuriated by my inability to determine what aircraft loomed somewhere in the sky.

I lifted my eyes to the heavens, trying to trace its movements through the blackened sky, every now and then convincing myself that I could make out an outline, just skidding through the clouds. But I knew that it had all been the working of my imagination.

The voice of the engine continued to peak and trough, as it was manipulated to match the movement that it took part in.

I followed its assumed path as it began to bank round in a wide arc, taking in a vast area of nothing but fields and trees. Eventually, it began to circle one area in particular, its engine pitch quivering slightly as the speed was brought right down.

The pilot possessed either great confidence or a near-fatal stupidity, as I was sure I heard the engine cough and splutter as it tried to avoid stalling. He must have been going so slow that even I would have been able to run and catch up with it, even with the huge scab that had formed over the stitches that Suzanne had etched into my knee.

I stayed where I was, daring not to move and give myself away needlessly. If everything went according to plan, everyone else would be doing the work for me tonight.

Instead, I entertained myself with the thought of what the pilots were like; whether they had volunteered for this kind of work or been coerced into it. I thought about what they might be thinking of themselves. If they had been anything like me, then they would have been thinking of home, the coffee and bacon that would be awaiting them in the mess once they made it back.

What I would have done to have swapped places with them on that night.

It was the first time that I had seriously started to

miss home. I guessed that was what came with facing the perils of death at the hands of a cruel enemy. It was never something that I had to think about whilst flying over the patchwork quilt of south-east England's fields.

I began to feel excited for them, hoping that they make it back and go on to do all kinds of damage to the *Reich*. My heart rate began to increase, as I felt the rush of excitement begin to reach the tips of my frosty fingers, and my knees beginning to ache with a desire to start running towards the danger.

My agitation and enthusiasm began to swell in my stomach, as the engines, however many of them there were, began to ebb away into the distance, the bellow quickly tuning into a purr as they reached a much faster speed than before. Whoever was piloting that aircraft, was desperate to get away, climbing to such a height that he would almost be able to touch the stars hidden from my gaze.

My thoughts quickly turned to the subject of what the aircraft delivered, the reminiscent feeling of falling as I recalled my first jump into enemy territory.

There had been a brief moment of panic as I fell through the frigid air, the wind buffeting my face and making my eyes water. I had reached for the emergency cord that would have initiated my reserve chute but, just as I had got my fingers around it, there had been a swift tug, and my rapid descent towards the ground had slowed greatly.

I had been fearful of it for so many months, the

endless training and stories that we had heard of it all going wrong. But, in the main, my first jump had been nothing but a rousing success. The only thing that I had come to regret about the whole affair was that I hadn't been given the opportunity to do it again. The thought was melancholic and not one that was going to be particularly helpful to me, so it was ejected quicker than I had free-fallen through the sky.

Instead, I thought about the exhilaration that would be going through the mind of the parachutist, as they descended towards the ground in much the same way I had done. I hoped that they were fresh from training, but with a head screwed on so tight that it almost hurt. The fresh ones were always the most enthusiastic and being of sound mind would be good to counteract my own insanity.

I waited for a few moments more, until I pictured the landing, ankles rolled, and knees cracked, as the soft silk slowly slumped to the floor. The ground around would be perfectly still for a minute or two, as the mind slowly tuned into the new surroundings and began to pick up on the novel sounds around, hopefully nothing more than a whistle through the trees and not the readying of weapons.

With my heart sitting in the back of my throat, thumping with a reassuring vigour, I pulled myself out of the water, my feet itching and shrivelled, and began to limp my way towards the landing site.

32

My feet were engulfed into the quagmire of sucking mud as I lumbered my way towards the drop point. I was so consumed by the effort not to lose my boots, that I kept my head down, staring into the abyss that seemed far darker than that of the sky.

My legs began to belch with pain as I felt as though I was fighting my way through quicksand, to the point where, if I was to stop completely, I would disappear into the very centre of the earth.

The fibres of my sodden socks began to attack the nerve endings in my toes, which were already burning spitefully with pins and needles as the blood quickly rushed back into them. The contrasting temperature of freezing water and perspiring soles was quickly causing me great anguish.

Without any warning at all, I found myself flat on my face, taking in a mouthful of muddied rainwater and caking myself in a thick layer of dirt as I did so. Immediately, I began trying to hoist myself up, fighting with the drowning muck which had a less than welcoming stench to it.

As I did so, I found myself oddly comforted. It hadn't been a misplaced foot that had caused me to stumble, but a distant dog bark, followed by a succession of others. It seemed as though my unconscious mind was not as dormant as I had thought it was.

I waited a few minutes longer, as the dogs continued to scream at the tops of their lungs, as I tried to work out whether they were barking at the strange figure limbering through the fields or not. There was a chance that they were the farmer's dogs, out in the yard late at night and there to scare away the vermin from the fields.

But it became quickly apparent that these beasts were no belonging of a local farmer. Their barks were vicious and clear, louder than any other bark that I had heard before, even though I was still quite some distance away. I could imagine their snarling teeth, combined with an imposing stature, that could only come with an Alsatian.

They were a creature that I would rather not have entangled myself with on any occasion, but especially not as I made my way to the drop zone.

Shortly after, I rapidly began to make out the telltale signs of a compromised drop zone. The lights that shone out, in a complete contradiction to the blackout laws, were bold and a brilliant white, beaming down on a handful of trucks and other motor vehicles.

I could not see anyone from such a distance, but I knew that they would have been there, milling around and waiting for their moment. This was an easy night out for the occupiers; I was even sure that one or two would be lighting cigarettes and flippantly holding their weapons, focussed completely on a nice warm bed, as opposed to rounding up newly-dropped agents.

I knew that I should have withdrawn there and then, but the curiosity got the better of me and, confident that I had not been spotted by the riled-up hounds, I began to edge my way forward once more, this time taking even more care over where I put my feet.

I kept my head up, however, scanning both the edges of the fields and where, on a slight rise in the terrain, I could see the headlights, intermittently interrupted as a figure or two staggered through their path.

Surprisingly, I failed to involuntarily hit the ground as the bullets suddenly let fly, instead having to force myself down into the ground with a slight splash. By now my clothes were completely ruined, my face blacker than the soul of Hitler himself. It would take me a great deal of effort to rid myself of the evidence that I had been out but, on account of not a single clean bit being about my person, I was well camouflaged at least.

A few tracer rounds had flown in my direction and, not wanting to greet them as they continued on their path, I had collapsed back down into the ground once more. Warily, and mindful of the fact that more than one weapon had started firing, I moved my face out of the bath of mud and craned my neck to look up.

The small incline in the land had suddenly lit up further, rounds of tracer firing in every direction imaginable, with others flying in towards the centre of the group.

I could now make out silhouetted figures throwing themselves around, and a great array of sparks suddenly flit upwards as a round smashed into the headlights of one of the trucks.

There seemed to be far more tracer than there was gunfire, but still the noise was terrific, my ears bleeding with the onslaught of the pandemonium that was occurring up ahead. The lights seemed to criss-cross in such a fashion that I was sure that rounds were hitting rounds, a great wall of ammunition so thick that it would never make it to its targets.

I could not tell who was firing at who, but I took little time to concern myself with that. In the end, it did not matter all that much to me about who was firing what and at who. All that mattered to me in that moment was that the firing was going on. It meant that my plan was beginning to work.

The big guns, that had been sleeping until now, suddenly sparked up, sending huge fireballs of tracer from right to left, as someone finally managed to get onto the German's machine gun.

I was sure that there was a mortar somewhere in the mix, firing slowly, methodically, as if the operators were careful to select their targets each time.

I tried to guess at who was firing the mortar, as I was confident that it could not have been a German. They were well prepared, well-armed, but even they did not take a mortar out onto a routine pick up like this. It had to be whoever it was that had joined in the ambush.

Just as I had imagined, the ambushed had come up with a contingency plan. A third cluster of rifle and automatic gunfire erupted, further up the incline, pouring fire and fury down on the group that were ambushing the Germans.

It did not take long for the Germans to begin to get their foothold back, with only sporadic firing occurring as one brave man, on either side, would break from cover and make for a new position.

In between the eruption of noise, I could make out the voices as they shouted to one another, a few anguished groans here and there as men refused to die, mixed with the commands of officers and NCOs as they tried to regroup.

I considered joining in with all the fun, the *Lemel* rifle still strapped faithfully to my back, a coating of mud probably not helping the sticking bolt action. Even if I did have a fully working yet inferior weapon, I still did not really fancy my chances in amongst the heat of the skirmish.

Grenades had started to detonate one by one, as the fighting became bitter. Before too long it would be hand to hand, where revolvers would do more damage than a mortar could.

It was not because I was a coward that I did not want to be in amongst the quilt-like tracer fire, but because I was convinced that I would have done more harm than good.

If the fighters were to stop now, and make a run for it, then there was a chance, however slim, that they might get away. And, even if they did not make it back to their safehouses, then they might end up simply being arrested. If I was to throw into the mix a defiant resurgence in the battle, then those men would be as good as dead. The Germans would not take too kindly to a few men raising their hands while one other fought back.

Besides, I told myself, my body simply wasn't up to it. The stitches that Suzanne had come up with to hold the two flaps of skin in place were seething, threatening to fall apart and hinder me from moving much further. It had taken me an age to walk across half a field, and I would still have another one to go after it if I had wanted to join in the fun.

As well as all that, my vision had begun to haze

over, and I could feel the pressure in my head beginning to build, as if my own brain was too large for the skull that housed it.

There was a part of me, perhaps a younger, naïve version of myself, that screamed out about being gutless and timid, but for now self-preservation would have to come first. Whether I liked it or not, I had to put myself above those that needed my help in the battle.

It was not because I was better than they or even more informed, but because I had been given a different role to them, orders which did not coincide with their own.

I had no other choice but to leave them to it and, with a heavy heart, I pulled myself up and out of the ground for a second time, but this time began to retrace my own steps back towards the irrigation ditch.

I did not intend on sitting in there like I had done for so long before, but it would help me get my bearings back, as the excitement of the tracer and gunfire had left my sense of direction all but useless.

As the pockets of resistance began to die down, hopefully as the ambushers retreated to safety, I wondered which side would try and claim the victory.

If I knew anything about the plucky resistors that resisted the German occupation in any way they could, they would claim the triumph for themselves. Even if they had failed to hit a single German soldier with their rounds, then even something as small as a smashed headlight would be enough to cheer about. Anything, it seemed, that would hinder the Germans in some way.

On the flip side though, I worried about how many of their number they had lost. They were not plentiful in supply nor were they invincible in spirit. But we had committed a large number of them that night, and to lose so many could have been a fatal error. If things did not pan out as I had envisaged them, then the resistance in *Tours* could have been all but over for the foreseeable future.

If the Germans had claimed the small scrap that had broken out in the middle of *Cinq-Mars-la-Pile*, then they were welcome to take their spoils of war, including whatever it was that the unidentifiable aircraft had dropped a few minutes before.

I hoped to the highest heaven that whatever London had discerned from my message, that they had sent something of little value to them. A crate of chocolate perhaps, or even a small dog to keep the Alsatians entertained. But, knowing their love of placing their people in great danger, it would not have surprised me all that much if they had dropped a fully trained, well-equipped agent.

Whatever the cargo had been, I would need to forget all about it. The night had been a success, everything had gone to plan.

All I had to do was to sink back into the innocuous shadows and exchange the rifle on my back for something more familiar, something that I felt far more at home with. I looked forward to the moment when I would take hold of my revolver again. But until then, I tried to stay focused, as I wanted nothing more than to give the rifle back to my farmer friend, with all six of his vermin-hunting rounds intact.

33

By the time that I had made it back to the house, it was almost dawn, the sky just paling as it prepared to host yet another beautiful sunrise. I was tired, but the excitement that was surging through my whole body would have kept me awake for weeks on end.

I did not bother with washing, allowing the dried-out bits of mud to fall from my body, letting the rest settle where it had started to harden. The aroma that oozed out of me was inconsequential to me, I had started to get so used to it that I almost forgot that everyone else would turn their noses up at the stench. But it would have to do, for now, I wasn't there to meet the Queen after all. I had a job to do.

I threw my clothes into the corner of the room, ripping at new ones and almost breaking a bone here and there as I pulled them on. I growled as a jumper got caught as I tried to force my head through an armhole, before I composed myself, and found my way around the maze of wool.

I exhaled sharply, as I tried to calm my thoughts and slow my reactions down. My heart was thumping so hard that I thought it would soon give up under the strain, and my blood felt so thick that I could almost feel it congealing in my veins. I needed to relax. If I was this wound up then mistakes would be made, and it was not a time to be doing that at all.

I leapt for the revolver that lay on my bed, as I heard the soft sound of knocking coming from downstairs. I resisted the urge to peer out of the window, as I thought that seeing an arresting officer and his men would do my heart no favours whatsoever. Whoever it was at the door would find their way into the house whether I liked it or not. I would just have to face the consequences.

As expected, the weight of the revolver, which felt a far superior build quality to the ageing *Lemel*, gave me a warmth, one that was both welcomed and feared. I embraced the feeling of security that it gave me, that it was down to me and my trigger finger, whilst also running scared of the excitement that I was feeling at holding such a life-altering weapon.

I felt uncomfortable with the excitement of taking a life, but that was all it was, excitement, it did not mean that I had to enjoy it.

As I carefully crept over the floor of the bedroom, avoiding the two floorboards that I knew would creak the loudest, I could make out movement down below.

It was a non-threatening movement, accompanied by a silence. Not what one would expect if the *Gestapo* had been kicking down the door.

Carefully, feeling awfully vulnerable and open to attack, I edged down the stairs, one by one, revolver drawn and fully loaded up.

He had his back to me, as Suzanne began to give him a quick briefing, but I knew who it was immediately. He must have sensed me and, as he spun on his heel, he startled me, so that the first thing that he saw was the barrel of an inky-black revolver.

"Well, you can put that ruddy thing down for starters," he said, peering over the weapon and into my eyes. "Hello, old fruit."

It had been a number of days since I had seen his face, quite how many I could not recall, but enough for me to have missed it. His eyes were as sunken back in the caves of his skull as they had ever been before, but this time there was a fire behind them that seemed to give the rest of his skin a warm glow.

"Hullo, Mike."

We shook hands, patting each other fondly on the forearm, stopping short of the full embrace that I felt I needed.

I took a step back and observed his face properly. It was dirty, not as dirty as mine had been, but it had a noticeable layer of grime to it, as well as a few days stubble beginning to peek out from under the surface. He looked ragged, but perhaps better looking than he had ever done before, his dark, thick hair, that was normally slicked all the way to the rear, hanging at funny angles and left to droop over his forehead.

"It's good to see you," I said, feeling something catch me at the back of my throat.

He gave me a good slap on my arm, making me wobble slightly.

"It's good to see you too. What's the matter? Had a little too much to drink?" he asked, looking down at my dancing feet, as I re-found my balance.

"I wish. Remember those pints down at the Rose and Crown?"

"Remember them? I'm still suffering hangovers from the blasted things."

"Yeah, well I could murder one right about now."

My leg burned agonisingly as I finally managed to steady myself, as Suzanne grew irritated at the pair of us.

"I hate to break up this loving reunion and everything," she muttered, with a clear helping of indignance. "But a week ago you two were at each other's throats. You seemed to have made up pretty quickly."

I looked sideways at Mike and got the same chipper feeling that I had got when we had been hauled in front of our CO, for too many misdemeanours around the Squadron. He gave me the all-familiar side smirk that I had so missed as he struggled to keep his eyes away from mine.

"We haven't made up quickly, Suzanne," Mike quipped.

"Because we never fell out," I finished, as we both

snorted and screwed our faces up, as I held back the tears that cried of insanity. We giggled like the school-boys we were, finding a situation so helpless infinitely funny. Once we had begun to let our chuckles subside, wiping the tears from our eyes, we were met with the stern gaze of Suzanne, who began muttering under her breath.

"*Je ne comprends pas vous Anglais.*"

I do not understand you Englishmen.

Mike and I snorted as we took a great delight from her frustration, before taking a few deep, long breaths to finally bring ourselves back into the room.

"How could we fall out?" Mike asked her, her face becoming more baffled and perplexed as the seconds wore on.

"We've been through far too much to fall out over the fact that Mike is in love."

Mike smacked me on the arm, as if I had just revealed one of the most embarrassing secrets of his entire life.

"In love?" she quizzed.

"Yes, well, there will be time for that story, later on, I'm sure."

Mike blushed, eager to move the conversation along.

"It was a façade all along. It was part of our plan."

"What kind of a plan has two grown men fighting with each other like petulant little boys?"

"One of *our* plans," Mike quipped with a beaming

grin, his warm breath almost visible in the air.

"We had to. Things haven't been going smoothly for us recently, have they? First, you go and get yourself blown up, then we're chasing trains that aren't there and to top it all off there's that episode in the churchyard."

Her face dropped at the thought of her friend, Martin, being executed by his own comrades. I still did not know what the connection had been between the two of them, but there was enough emotion in Suzanne's face to tell me that it was anything but malice. It almost made me feel quite jealous.

She tilted her head slightly, as if waiting for the great revelation.

Mike joined in the fun, "Someone, somewhere along the line was talking to the Germans. They were letting us roam around freely, but the minute one of their assets was at risk, something magically appeared that prevented us. No one is that unlucky."

"Except you with the ladies."

"Shove off."

"So, we came up with something. Split up and come up with a fake drop that only three people would know about. That way, if it all went belly up then we would have a pretty good idea about who was our leak."

I was certain that the cogs had all clicked into place and she knew where we were going, but she wanted clarification all the same.

"Harry?"

We both nodded in unison. She did not even seem all that surprised.

"So, you let him lead you on in thinking that Michel was the leak, so that you could smoke him out?"

"I think we did it pretty well, don't you?"

She didn't answer.

"So, what do you propose we do next, then?"

She seemed more than a little agitated that she had been left out of what appeared to be one of the most exciting plans that she had ever heard of. But I wouldn't have changed a thing had we done it all over again.

We needed everyone to believe that we had fallen out, otherwise, it increased the risk of being found out. I had even tried my hardest to convince myself that Mike had been a traitor, inserting malicious and harmful thoughts into my mind, to the point where I had felt real anger whilst shouting at him.

It had needed to appear genuine, so I had to have real thoughts of malevolence towards him.

"Do you have any idea where Harry would be now?"

"He is probably at home, getting his bits together before leaving, if I know him at all."

"Well then," Mike announced, baring his teeth and allowing his eyes to widen and burn brighter than before. "I propose that we go and kill him. What do you say?"

Neither of us agreed with him, but there were no

movements towards a disagreement either. In our silence, our plans were confirmed.

Letting Suzanne come to terms with the treachery of someone that she thought she could trust, I turned to Mike.

"Did you get the other bits then?"

"Oh, yes," he said with a flourish, slamming a large suitcase down on the table before us. "I knew it was a good idea to have that emergency drop zone set up with them on our first transmission."

"And there was me thinking you were just being overly pessimistic," I said with a grin, but also a genuine sense of consolation. The emergency drop zone had been agreed with London within our first month of being in France so that we could get anything; from new identities to specialist explosives that we couldn't trust other people to know about.

But we had used it for something different entirely.

"Almost exactly where we had agreed. Long live those bomber boys."

"If only they could drop a bomb on Hitler's house with that accuracy."

With exuberance and a delighted smile on his face, Mike dramatically flicked the two catches on the new, but battered leather suitcase, that was suffering the same fate as I was, courtesy of the sucking mud. If it had skin, then I was sure it would have been itching all over.

Mike waited a moment, building as much

suspense as he dared, before spinning the case on the tabletop and flicking the lid open.

Inside was an array of brightly coloured pieces of paper, each one bent and turned up at the corner and a few with a rip or two in their sides. Each piece of paper bore a different colour and an associated number, in an array of denominations.

On the top row alone, there was a one hundred, fifty and five franc notes, all hastily bundled together and stuffed into the case.

"How much is there?" I asked.

"Twelve thousand francs," Mike replied, with triumph oozing from everywhere in his body.

"I've never seen so much money in one place," Suzanne said, stunned. She seemed almost in tears as she stared at it, but I knew the inevitable questions would come once she had calmed down.

Why was London letting her live in such poverty if they could help her in her cause so easily?

But that was a question for another day.

"There's enough here to keep us going for a while," Mike said, running his fingers through the notes affectionately. "Might even buy myself something nice."

"Well, we've got to make sure that we live long enough to use it first," I said, despondently.

"Agreed," Mike announced defiantly, slamming the lid shut and breaking the trance that we were all in.

"Let's go hunt ourselves a Frenchman, shall we?"

34

"You are absolutely certain that he is in there, *Madame*?" Mike's tone was courteous and polite, truly masking what our intentions really were. We had entered the old lady's house under the guise of returning friends, wanting to surprise our companion that had saved our lives not too long ago.

Madame Joie had been most accommodating, her lack of eyesight and awareness meaning that with any luck she would not remember our visit for too much longer.

"Nothing happens in *Charsay* without my knowing," she said with a wry smile. She was old, but maybe she hadn't been as docile and unaware as she had appeared. In fact, I wondered if all this went wrong, and we weren't able to apprehend Harry today, then we could recruit her into our little circuit, as one of the most hidden agents in the whole of the Executive.

Her house was full of antiquities and quirks that came with any elderly person's residence, and I wondered how many invaluable items were hidden under the layers of dust that had accumulated over the years. I felt like offering to help her clean up, as my chest became constricted by the dirt that hung in the air, no doubt contributing to the rough tones of the old lady's voice.

But, instead, I found my eyes staring intently at a house that I had been in myself only a few weeks before.

From the outside, it seemed as battered and worn as ever, and I wondered how much more filth and dirt had been dragged in on the soles of German soldiers, and other men who had a vested interest in Harry Landes.

I had many wild thoughts about Harry since the night of the transmission, a lot of them circulating around how he had managed to escape the German roadblock that we had encountered, if he had managed to escape at all.

Unsolicited thoughts of a heroic battle against the odds had floated through my mind, as well as images of torture and interrogation that awaited every captured resistance fighter.

Whatever he had done, he had allowed me to get away, which was why I was still alive, and able to stare at his home with eyes that were completely unwavering.

But I had started to question his motives for letting

me live, an unhealthy, or perhaps necessary, side effect of the level of paranoia that plagued my mind.

I had run as fast as I could, only once turning back to see if he had been following, by which time it was probably too late. I had not been able to see what had happened next. I had not been able to see the handshakes as familiar faces greeted each other or overhear the conversations about what was to take place at *Cinq-Mars-le-Pile.*

The gunshots, I presumed, had been timed to perfection, to let me get far enough away so that I could not turn back and see what had happened, but also timed so that I could hear them perfectly.

"There. Top window. Something just moved."

"Are you sure?" I asked Suzanne, looking over at her still badly bruised face. Her eyes were firm and steady, unblinking, to the point where tears had formed up to clear her eyesight instead.

I had worried about her for a long time, but the way that she had started to conduct herself in regard to Harry had concerned me a great deal. She had taken the death of her German friend Martin very personally, and if Harry had anything to do with it at all, then she was determined to see him dead for it.

"Absolutely."

I peered towards Mike, who looked back at me with a similar expression on his face. He had seen no movement. Suzanne was wanting to see something so hard that her mind was beginning to play tricks on her.

I looked toward the weathered wooden frame, the glass sitting at a jaunted angle compared to the rest of its border, and where Suzanne's finger was now pointing.

I could see nothing, except the faint outlines of bedroom furniture, that were, unsurprisingly, standing as still as an inanimate object could.

Suzanne gave her head a quick rub, as if that would get rid of the headache that was thumping inside her skull. I wondered how much of a lasting effect the blast had on her, and whether she was fit enough to carry out this kind of work anymore.

She was, in my eyes, damaged goods now.

After this was over, I had decided, we would cut ties with her, at least while she got some good, decent rest. And, if we were lucky, hopefully by the time we would need her again the war would be coming to an end.

The silence that forced itself upon us began to clamp its teeth into me as hard as it could, like a dog refusing to surrender a fresh bone. My ears were close to bleeding point, as the faint ringing in them grew louder and stronger, driving me to near insanity.

I desperately needed some other kind of stimulus, before I went completely doolally.

I broke off from the monotony, turning around from the window and taking up a seat in the old woman's sitting room. It was worn and well-used, but comfortable enough to almost send me to sleep.

I was completely exhausted. The pain that had

festered in my muscles and the stitches in my knee had given up inducing the agonising burning feeling, as I simply could not muster up the energy any longer.

"Would anybody like some refreshment? I have tea, or some food if you would prefer..."

I looked at the old woman, who had entered the room humbly bowing her head as if such esteemed guests had never been in her presence.

I tried to smile but could only conjure up a weak twitching of the lips which I hoped she took as a symbol of gratitude.

"No, thank you for your kind offer, *Madame* Joie."

I yanked my lips up into a smile, just enough so that my teeth could be seen, which were quickly withdrawn on account of my warm, rancid breath.

"Do you think we are doing the right thing?" Suzanne asked, taking me by surprise as she turned her head from the window to look at me.

I sighed, rubbing my face with my palms and taking a few more flakes of dried mud with me, scattering itself all over the floor. A few months ago, I would have been horrified and would have tried my best to hide the mess, or even offer to clear it up for my host. But now, I did not care in the slightest, there was a war on after all, and it did not appear to me that the woman was all that fond of a clean residence anyway.

"I think we should just go in. If he is in there, why wouldn't we?"

Her face was burning with a passion so strong that I thought she might burst into a ball of flames, without warning.

"This man needs to die. The quicker it happens the better in my opinion."

Her voice was cold, dangerous, and as the hairs on my arms began to prick upwards to the sky, I quite quickly became concerned. She had only one thing on her mind, which was exactly the thing that we had been taught to resist.

She wanted revenge.

"We don't know if he *is* in there, Suzanne," Mike said, soothingly, rebalancing the aggression that loitered in the room.

"I saw him."

"Yes, but no one else has. Besides, there is no telling whether that was Harry, or someone else."

"Why would it be someone else?"

"If he is working for the Germans, there is a possibility that he has some sort of an escort. That could have been a well-armed German soldier that you saw in the window for all we know."

"Well, it wasn't," she replied, indignantly.

Mike took a few moments to drink in the silence, as Suzanne turned her gaze back to the house.

"For what it's worth," Mike suggested, looking over his shoulder at me, "I think we should wait. There are too many risks that we would have to take if we were to go in now."

I looked around the room, as the two inquisitive faces stared at me, waiting for an answer.

"What?"

"You have the casting vote, *Jean*," Mike breathed, as I looked to the old woman for some sort of guidance. I was hoping that she would be standing beside me, ready to whisper some advice in my ear that she had garnered over many years on this planet.

But she was nowhere to be seen.

"I'm not sure," I started, not hitting the right chords with either of them. "But I can see the argument for both sides. The quicker we can dispatch of Harry the quicker we can all move on. But," I said as a victorious smile began to appear on Suzanne's face, "*Michel* is right. We don't know if he is alone in there. It isn't worth the risk."

"So, we wait?" Mike asked.

"I think it would be best to wait and see what happens, yes. Something might happen that would make our decision for us, either way."

"Alright then," Mike said conclusively, as all three of us returned back to our respective posts. "For now, we wait."

I worried about what kind of harm we would do if we were to barge in there and put as many bullets as we could into Harry. There was a strong possibility that he was not alone and, even if he was, it did not mean that he would be unable to do us some serious damage.

There was the third possibility that Madame Joie

had got it wrong, and it wasn't even Harry that she had seen enter the house, but a total stranger, a stooge maybe employed by Harry to get himself killed for him. Harry might even have been watching from afar.

I gave myself a mental slapping as I tried to push the paranoia to one side. It was helpful to have a degree of it, but when it began to take over all your thoughts and decision making, it could become quite dangerous indeed.

"Wait a second," Mike muttered, shuffling closer to the window, whilst simultaneously ducking his head lower. "Look who it is."

I waited for the suspected "I told you so" from Suzanne, but nothing came, although I could sense her feeling of elation in the silence.

I rushed to the window, crouching down as low as the others while still being able to peer through the murky and dirtied windows.

Everything had suddenly changed.

Our decision had been made for us.

He looked as odd as ever, wearing a sand-coloured suit that would have looked more at home in the South African colonies than on the continent. His face appeared like it had always done, waxy and rat-like, however a little more weathered and tired than before.

His shoulders twitched as he took a quick look around the smattering of houses that surrounded his, before he turned to lock his door and pick up the suitcase that he had at his feet.

There was a moment of uneasiness between the three of us, as if no one wanted to be the one to suggest that now was the time to act.

He had stepped out of the house alone and, unless he had something concealed in his jacket, he didn't appear to be carrying any kind of a weapon.

In the end, it fell to me to make the decision.

I looked at them both in turn.

"Are you ready for this?"

Both faces stared back at me, unchanging. I took it as a yes.

"Well, now's a good a time as any. Let's go."

35

My legs felt unsteady as I reached the front door of the old woman's house. I was vulnerable and fragile, and I could feel the perspiration begin to form in great swathes on my palms, as I tried to relieve myself of some of the pressure by thinking of happier times.

With all my might, I attempted to think of a happy memory, one where I felt safe and warm, a place where I felt that love could trump anything and everything. But there was nothing. I had no happy memories; they had been eradicated or at least superseded by the ones of fear and depression.

I was blinded for a second by the brilliant change in light as the front door was opened and, as one weary body, the three of us stumbled from the house.

I pushed the barrel of the revolver back into its housing with a satisfying click, as I checked that all the rounds that I had put in the weapon earlier on had not disappeared by magic, or my memory had deceived me. Pulling the hammer back, I knew that I was ready to go and that, the second an adequate amount of pressure was applied to the trigger, the thing would buck as it expelled a round.

It was an exciting thing for a young man to use, but in that moment, I was terrified about what it had symbolised that I had become. I could see myself as no better than a common criminal, who killed on command and felt little for the victim that I had disposed of.

Mike led the way, with me following closely behind, my eyes looking anywhere but in the direction of Harry.

I scanned the windows of the other houses, hoping that I would see something that would comfort me greatly. But I knew that nothing, short of seeing an allied army cooped up in one of the windows, would bring me any comfort whatsoever.

In fact, it wasn't an ally that I was looking for, but an enemy. It had not crossed my mind until then that we were being watched by enemy rifles, each one of them waiting until we stopped moving to put something through our skulls.

I could see nothing, however, not even any of the locals checking their windows at the strangers who lingered around their street. Not even the old woman whose house we had just been in had wanted to watch what was about to unfold.

I kept myself alert, however, as I knew that just because I had taken a cursory glance around at my surroundings, it did not mean that we were in the clear. I was sure that a professional soldier would not have simply been dallying around in one of the windows, in the hope that we would appear.

I developed a great itch in my side, as the paranoia that bubbled my blood began to take hold of my other physical senses, my heart thumping harder than ever and causing a lump in my throat. I was almost finding it quite difficult to breathe.

It was only then that Harry looked up from his feet, to see the three figures striding towards him. His face was not one of joy, nor was it one that seemed overly concerned to see us, but merely one of a placid acceptance that we were there.

He did, however, look paler than he had done before, as if an illness had recently got the better of him and he was only just beginning to recover. Maybe it was the treachery and disloyalty that he harboured in his heart.

We continued to silently move towards him, with nothing at all to acknowledge one another's existence.

But, as we strode forwards, I felt like stopping on the spot and allowing the other two to continue my job for me.

I had been trained in fierce hand to hand combat, the best ways in which you blow up a train or building to cause maximum loss of life and how to poison someone who loved to gnaw a bit of French bread. In short, I had been transformed from a fearful, nervous fighter pilot, into a deadly weapon of war.

But, as I forced one leg in front of the other, I realised that I had not been taught one thing in particular. One that was making my heartache as it pounded and forced me further forward.

No one had taught me what it would feel like to kill someone who had, until very recently, been considered a friend.

I watched as Harry placed his hand on the top of his crooked gate, but stopped short from swinging it open, in the hope that it might buy him some time if he was to need it.

We were still some distance away, but I could already make out the dirt under his long, curling fingernails, and the grime that still sat on the backs of his hands.

My own hands had been far dirtier, but there was no way that he would have got that kind of dirt on himself if he had been in all night. He had been in that field. I was sure of it.

We reached him, but no one seemed willing to say anything. Instead, we just let our breath mingle with each other in the shared air between us, as Harry looked at us one by one.

Had it not been for the silent animosity that was clearly prevalent between us, then our little gathering could have been just like old times. I had spent many hours in the company of these three other people, mostly when we had our backs to the wall and were in a serious predicament. But it was in those times that I had felt closest to them, as if we could each draw our courage from one another and fight for the person stood next to you.

But things had changed since then.

"I wondered when I might be seeing you lot again."

Neither of us responded to him for a while, as his hand retreated back from the fence, ready to make a run for it.

His voice was withered and frail, quite like the old woman's when she had offered us some tea. He seemed tired, frustrated, as if he was annoyed with himself for not second-guessing our arrival there.

The temples at the side of his head bulged, the veins almost bursting as the cogs began to churn in his head. He was under an immense amount of pressure, and he was trying to work out what his best chances of survival were right now.

If Suzanne had much say over the matter, then he needn't have bothered to think things through all that much.

"I'm surprised you were even giving us some thought," Mike replied, placing his hand on the gate in Harry's place. "I bet you had hoped us dead by now."

Harry stood firm in where he stood, allowing Mike to lean over the gate and whisper threateningly in his direction. His stoicism and defiance were what worried me, as he refused to be concerned by Mike's aggressive stance.

"No, not at all," he tried to utter, as the words stumbled and tripped from his mouth.

"No?" Mike said, almost mockingly. "Not even when you went to your friends about our little delivery that we had planned?"

All of a sudden, and as if he had been quite unaware of the circumstances until that point, his face drooped pathetically, as the penny simultaneously dropped.

It was only at that moment that he realised that the three people stood at his garden fence were not there as friends, but enemies. I thought for a fleeting second that he would turn and run immediately, but to his credit, he didn't. He stood and awaited his punishment like a crook at the gallows.

"Out of interest," Mike started, "What did London actually send the Germans? I was hoping for a booby-trapped container of some description. *Jean's* money was on a dog of some kind."

Suddenly, he seemed quite smug, as if he had gained the upper hand somehow.

"Oh no," he replied. "They sent something far more valuable than a dog."

"Then what?"

"They sent another agent, just as you said," he mumbled, nodding towards me.

My face paled, as I felt the vomit lurch around in my throat. Mike staggered on the spot for a moment, using the fence as a support for the legs that had suddenly lost balance.

I tried to reason with myself that what we had done had been the right thing, and that it had been the Executive that had made the mistake. They must have decoded my message incorrectly, or simply not cared enough about the lives of their agents to have taken my consideration into account.

The thought suddenly hit me that that was why Harry had been so careless in his attempt to hide, going back to his own house and not somebody else's. He thought he had won. He wasn't to suspect that anything was amiss.

An ambush by resistors at the site of a drop zone would have been expected, and not a sign that something was up.

"Look," he said, interrupting my imaginings of what had become of the compromised agent. "If you are going to kill me, I'd rather you just get it over and done with. I don't think we have all that much left to say to one another."

I felt Suzanne immediately bring her arm up to do as he had wished, but I gripped it just in time and forced it back down by her side.

"Let's go back inside," I suggested. "I still think we have plenty to say to each other. And maybe you can still be of some use."

It went against everything that I was feeling for the man in that moment, but I knew that I had to overcome those emotions and do what would benefit the resistance as a whole, and not something that would just make me feel better.

As if frustrated with the whole episode, Harry sighed, and began to turn back towards his house once more. The contempt that he was showing us told me all that I needed to know about the future of this man, he needed to be disposed of. He could never be trusted again.

But there were still things inside his head that would be of use to us, and I intended to extract as much of it as I possibly could. I could only hope that the elderly lady, as well as the rest of her neighbours in the near vicinity, had lost as much of their hearing as possible.

We had only made it a matter of paces down the cracked garden path when the sound of an engine began to reach my ears. It was not something that was particularly out of the ordinary for a small village, but something told me that it simply was not good news for us.

This vehicle was making its way towards the street that we now stood in, and specifically towards Harry's house.

The engine roared louder as the gears crunched down, as it whined its way around the corner and into the street.

Its big, black bonnet swung into view, its grill snarling at us as it came closer.

The snarl was accompanied by a smirking Harry. He was clearly proud to have been back in his commanding position once more. It somehow suited him.

"It would appear that my lift is here. I'm sorry that we won't be able to have that little chat that I was so looking forward to."

I looked across at Mike, the dejection written across his face, tears beginning to form in his eyes.

"I don't believe it," he muttered under his breath. "I've always hated those Renaults."

36

The car, taunting us, drew to a halt about thirty yards from where we stood, just inside the perimeter fence of Harry's garden, with nothing but a small picket fence and a few garden ornaments between us. It was severely lacking the ten-feet high concrete wall that I was so desperate for, but I would have to make do with what I had.

The brakes squealed gently as the wheels finally stopped turning, the engine idling for a few seconds before shutting down completely. It was a strange move, I thought, a confident one. It was as if they already knew the outcome, and that they did not need to worry about getting away at speed.

In unison and as if they had practiced their movements several hundred times before, the doors swung open and two men, in near-identical clothing, hoisted themselves out.

One was far taller than the other, the shorter one

also possessing a slight frame that screamed of weakness rather than authority. Their long, cloak-like coats looked warm and comfortable, but it was what might be concealed beneath that drew most of my attention.

The peaked hats, that I had often seen on these men pulled forward over their eyes, were set back on their heads slightly, so as to get a better field of vision of the surrounding area.

They were, in the main, near-perfect copies of the two men who had chased us and ended up burning bodies in their automobile, albeit that one was a Mercedes-Benz.

There was a brief moment of perfect calm, where I thought that maybe these men weren't who we had all suspected them to be. Maybe they had been travelling salesmen and it had just been at that particular time that they had chosen to visit *Charsay.* But unless they were selling crooked window frames then I was sure that the residents of *Charsay* did not want to know.

But as they both reached into their coats, pulling out identical pistols from identical pockets, my worst fears were confirmed that they were not travelling salesmen, but were, in fact, part of the *Reich.*

No one, not even the agents of Hitler, seemed like they wanted any bloodshed, at least not at first. Nobody seemed willing to make the first move, to shout the first word or indeed to fire the first shot.

It was an almost surreal moment of total calm, a peace that I had not experienced since the summer of

1939. It was almost as if everything had been forgotten, apart from the five weapons that were now all drawn, and that time had frozen completely still, not so much as a bird flying gracefully in the sky to break the tension.

"Come on, come on. Do something. Do something."

I wasn't sure if Mike's mutterings were meant to be aloud, but the gentle encouragement for someone else to make the first move was something that I welcomed. But the two men continued to stare silently, as if weighing up their chances of three guns up against their two.

If I was them, then I would have fancied my chances, particularly if they were to make the first move and render one of the weapons obsolete immediately.

From then on, things seemed to move along in a blur, but still at a pace that could be considered sedentary.

Harry, sensing that no one would make the first move, cleared his throat, as if to make some grand announcement. Instead, he slowly raised one leg, placing it carefully in front of the other one, and began to make his way towards the two men and the Renault.

His shoes clipped loudly on the gravel around him, confident that he was about to be delivered by his two guardian angels.

He had got no further than a few paces when

Suzanne lunged at him, wrapping her arm around his neck and dragging him back towards her. The movement was so sudden and unexpected, that Harry immediately relinquished the grip on his suitcase, which proceeded to spill its contents over his feet.

Books and clothes flapped about in the breeze, much like his hands as they grappled with Suzanne's firm grasp around his neck. She was not suffocating him but giving a firm enough indication of what might await him if he was to try and do anything stupid.

The revolver in Suzanne's right hand made its way to the side of Harry's head, pressing so firmly into his skin that his temple bulged brilliantly. One squeeze of her trigger and the temple would burst, spraying scarlet matter over all three of us. Which I decided I would prefer over the mud right now.

The two men barely flinched, as if they had been there a hundred times before, but instead slowly and gracefully raised the arms up, so that they could look down the top of their pistols and line up a shot.

Both, from what I could make out, were aimed in Harry's direction, presumably hoping that they would be able to hit Suzanne if Harry was to duck.

From what I could tell through my hazy vision, neither of them seemed to be pointed at me. Which would buy me half a second to decide on how best to continue the fight.

"Woah. Woah, alright then everybody. Let's just take this a little bit easier, shall we?"

He turned to Mike and me, no hint of fear in his eyes but pure exhilaration.

"Come on. Let me go, you'll be able to walk away from all this. They won't shoot as long as you let me get to them. Let me go."

"I think you're forgetting," my unrecognisable voice croaked, "we aren't the ones who have their arms wrapped around your throat."

Suzanne gave a little squeeze to hammer home the point, his eyes bulging as his Adam's apple began to bob up and down in the crook of her arm.

"Su-Suzanne. L-Let me go. I will make it worth your while. T-they won't shoot if you hand me over."

She squeezed all the more, "I think you value yourself too much, Harry. They don't care for you anymore than we do."

She relaxed her grip slightly and allowed him a bit of space to begin rasping and get his breath back again. Sweat was now pouring down his neck and dripping nicely into the collar of his freshly pressed shirt. He looked so dapper that it was as if he was about to board a luxury airship and make his way across the Atlantic Ocean. Maybe that was what the deal had been. Us for a lifetime of freedom and money.

"She's right, Harry," Mike suddenly chimed in. "To them, you are nothing more than an asset. Something by which they can get to their reward. If you have to die, then I don't think they will even bat an eyelid."

I watched as the perspiration increased and the scarlet pigment in his cheeks began to flush vibrantly. It was only then that he had started to panic, realising that he wasn't in as much control as he had hoped.

He tried to bluff his way through, blindly.

"You don't know how much I mean to them. The rewards that I will get for being part of the group that caught you. I will get so much glory."

"Is that what you were after, all this time? Glory?" Suzanne spat.

"That and the money. They pay well you know, I'm sure they could even make you an offer if you would like."

Suzanne squeezed.

"Harry, you don't realise that once they have achieved their aim you will be nothing to them. You will be worthless. Especially after they kill us. What do you have to give them anymore? You'll be nothing but a hindrance that they will want to get rid of."

He was silent for a few moments as he got his breath back from the latest constriction around his throat, his eyes now beginning to stream as he fought hard to stay conscious. He was sweating so much that I thought the waxy-like skin was beginning to melt, and that before long we would have nothing more than a skeleton on our hands.

I wasn't entirely sure who it was that fired the first shot, but suddenly two rounds exploded simultaneously, each one ripping into something close by on either side. A wooden slat in the fence suddenly splintered and disintegrated, as a round pinged off the bodywork of the automobile.

Trust Mike to have fired at the Renault, before the two armed men.

I fired my revolver twice, as Suzanne pulled Harry with her as some sort of shield and behind any cover that we could find. There was little, and I was barely comforted by the display of the wooden fence panel, as I found myself cowering behind one of its cousins.

I watched as the two men, loosely firing off a few rounds in our direction, retreated slightly, taking cover behind the outstretched doors of their car. One of the men had lost his hat in the retreat, revealing a thick head of dark, floppy hair that stuck up at various angles.

A few more rounds sailed high over our heads, as I caught sight of the old woman pulling her curtains shut as if that would shield her from what was going on outside.

The Germans kept on firing, keeping up a steady stream of rounds so that we felt adequately suppressed that we could not move. I began to count the number of rounds that sailed a little too close to my head, waiting for the number thirteen that I was convinced would find its way into my flesh.

Mike suddenly peered up and over the fence, firing three rounds as well as he could.

"Don't let them reach the boot of that car!" he screamed at the top of his lungs, as the two men began to move round to the rear of the vehicle.

I recalled what we had seen in the trunk of the Mercedes-Benz that we had disposed of some weeks ago; stuffed full of petrol and other supplies that they would need for their operation.

If they had even anticipated coming up against some resistance, then I knew for certain what would be in there.

I shuddered as I failed to fire a single round at the car, the risk of not hitting one of the men far too great to waste a valuable round. But it meant that they had got to the boot and that we had reacted far too late.

The air suddenly took on a very different form, as the small, but deadly rounds suddenly started to fly through the air at a much quicker rate than a pistol would ever allow.

The sub-machine guns began to spray anything and everything that they could, to try and diminish our inadequate cover, as I watched Suzanne attempting to drag Harry somewhere else that would afford them a little more security.

"Do we go back inside the house?" I screamed as loud as I could above the noise. "It might give us a bit of time to work out what to do next!"

"Well I definitely don't want to kick the bucket in this garden!"

"That's decided then!"

Just as I looked back towards the house, I watched as Harry, with all the might that was left in his body, threw his head back as far and as hard as he possibly could, smashing into Suzanne's nose with such a force that I saw it begin to crumple.

With an anguished cry, and a smattering of blood, she relinquished her steadfast grip on Harry, and he lunged away from her with a great shout of victory, a band of sweat on his neck reddened by the force.

Within a matter of seconds, Harry had broken free.

37

I looked on in disbelief and dejection as Harry strode across the open ground towards his freedom. I hated the feeling of injustice that this man was not going to get what he deserved, and that instead, he would get a life of luxury and security, everything that I would never have in my life.

The muzzles of the submachine guns traced everyone's movements as Harry continued to arrogantly stride towards them, nervously twitching through the wound down windows of the car.

I could just about make out their feet from underneath the car doors, shuffling about apprehensively, as if readying for a starting pistol in the one-hundred-yard dash. Everyone was on edge, not able to trust even themselves as the seconds wore on.

The Germans grew bolder now that their subject was apparently free, as both faces appeared at the bottom of the windows, peering out towards us and trying to second guess what we might do next.

Their guess was as good as ours. Never for a single second had I thought we would end up in this situation, so even I did not know what we were going to do.

"Do we still make for the house?" Mike shouted over to the two of us, Suzanne still reeling from the crumpled nose that she now possessed.

"No…" she mumbled pathetically, as the blood rushed into her mouth as well as out of her nose, as she shuffled back to her feet.

"I agree, let's –"

The world around me suddenly sped up and, as if the Germans had somehow read our minds, the front door of the house was peppered with bullets, acting as a warning that if we were to try and find an escape route that way, all that would meet us would be a grisly end to our lives.

"That settles that then!" Mike hollered, as he checked how many rounds he had left in his revolver. "Three left! Eight more in my pocket."

"I have four, plus the eight as well!"

Suzanne seemed unable to speak, but I guessed that her number would be just inadequate as ours. Between the three of us, we would have just enough rounds as one magazine of the submachine guns that were now spitting towards us.

The bullets began to slow, to the point where I could almost watch as they sailed over my head and buried themselves into something solid. The panic, on the other hand, continued to grow in my stomach, to the point where I could barely think straight.

My mind flew around faster than it ever had done before, as I scanned around my surroundings to look for something as a way out, anything at all. But the only thing that I could fix my eyes on were the two Germans, poking their weapons out towards us and occasionally forcing my head into the ground, splinters of wood, brick and anything else that they could find, showering all over my back.

After one such flurry of activity, I risked poking my head above the parapet, in the hope that a stray round had caught Harry somewhere along the line. To my great dismay, he was still standing, not only that, he was still walking, towards the Germans.

He had, however, only made it four or five paces away from us, which was causing him great discomfort. He was shouting something, towards the Germans, which was indistinguishable from where I was crouched.

I thought for a second that maybe he was calling for calm, in an attempt to grant us a reprieve and an opportunity to escape alive. But then supposed that it was far more likely that he was calling for an end to the shooting so that he could have a safe passage to his guardians.

The fence above my head suddenly erupted into a thousand pieces, and I had already started spitting bits of wood from my mouth as I pressed my face back into the grass, burying myself deep so as to avoid my inevitable fate for as long as possible.

As the shattered wood subsided, I watched Suzanne as she got up, blood pouring from her face at an alarming rate, as if she had bitten into the flesh of a wild animal.

Without any warning whatsoever, she leapt over the small fence in pursuit of Harry, enraged that he would have broken free from her grip.

This time she didn't reintroduce her grasp around his neck, but instead raised her revolver up, so that it was perfectly in line with his body, and squeezed, twice.

Harry's back exploded terrifically, and a geyser of bloodshot from his mouth as he fell to the ground. He flapped around on the floor like a fish for a second, as I looked at him, before I turned my attention to Suzanne.

There was no time for her to bask in the glory of disposing of Harry, as the chatter of the submachine guns suddenly replied, ripping into her flesh as she collapsed into a heap on the floor.

She gave off a pathetic whimper as she fell to the floor, in a crumpled mess not five yards away from Harry. I thought for a second that she was going to try and finish him off, but the revolver that had pointed towards him suddenly fell down by her side, as did the defiant arm that had held the weapon.

Harry continued to squirm around next to her, as if he was still fully aware of what was going on and he was trying to drag himself closer towards the Renault. Loud grunts could be heard over the top of the gunfire, as he succeeded in pulling his body closer to the finish line, inch by inch. At the rate that he was going, he would still be there in several hours' time.

A part of me hated myself for it, but I was glad that he was suffering.

My eyes were drawn away from him as I sensed movement up ahead, and I watched as one of the men, his hat flying from his head as he ran, broke cover. There was only really one possibility about where he was going, but it surprised me.

It turned out the Germans really did value Harry after all.

He moved as if his joints had started to seize up, an abrasive ointment rubbed into his knees perhaps, as he found it difficult to stand up straight, instead hunched over and using his submachine gun to try and cover his face as much as he could.

He moved slowly at first, before the wind started to flicker at the ankles of his trousers and he managed to build up some speed, growing in confidence with every step that he took.

It was only as he jogged towards Harry, his coat flailing in the breeze and his shins momentarily becoming visible, that I realised how foolish he had been.

There must have been a great deal of panic commanding his actions, as if he needed to desperately have some French companionship. I could not think of any other explanation as to why he would have broken cover in the way that he had.

He had a twenty-yard sprint over to the injured Frenchman, and then goodness knows how long exposed to us as he tried to drag his body backwards.

I exhaled sharply, saliva flying everywhere, as my face dug into the ground once again, just as the German depressed the trigger and held it there until the magazine was empty. Twenty rounds or so manically dithered in the sky, some coming far closer to me than others, with one or two being blasted into the atmosphere.

Once I heard his weapon fall silent, I knew that I had to act.

He would have to change magazines now to respond which, if he was well trained, could take him anything between seven to fifteen seconds. His chum was still quaking behind the car door and I was hoping that by the time he had reacted, my job would be complete.

I got up. Not just crouching or hunched but standing. Proud, determined, victorious.

I pulled the revolver up to my eye, settling the blade at the end of the barrel at just above the man's belly button. I knew that as I kept firing, my grouping would slowly move upwards and so I hoped that the second or third round would be straight through the heart.

The figure grew no larger as he continued to run towards Harry, and he seemed to find it difficult at all to run, but realised that nothing was moving, not even a hair on his head.

I squeezed. The revolver kicked back and up. I squeezed again.

By the time that I had managed to line up a third shot, the man was already on the ground, the first two rounds more than sufficient in doing the job that I had needed it to. He did not writhe around on the floor like Harry, he did not moan and whimper like Suzanne had started to, but he lay quite still, his chest frozen, his wounds gushing blood.

There was suddenly a flurry of excitement as I was bundled to the ground, the unmistakable aroma of Mike's breath clashing with my nose as he rugby tackled me to the floor.

Moments later and the old wooden fence posts were obliterated, as the German's friend suddenly began furiously seeking revenge.

No sooner had I realised that I was face down in the dirt again, then Mike had taken his turn to be the brave one.

I looked up, as he began walking confidently towards the vehicle, revolver already bucking and viciously trying to break free from his grasp. The rounds made an impressive sound as they struck the bodywork of the car, sounding far more deadly than they perhaps were.

But he ran out of rounds earlier than he had hoped, and I watched as he lobbed the revolver towards the car, aiming for the German's head.

He sprinted, skidding to a halt by the dead German, hoisting his submachine gun into his shoulder and slotting home a magazine.

I watched the fear in the German's eyes as he realised that the fight was coming to a close, and he was losing. He began to flap around, dropping his weapon at one point before floundering to bring it to bear again. But he decided against firing off his rounds, instead choosing to clamber through the car and towards the steering wheel, just as a round penetrated the windscreen, before burrowing into his head.

The glass seemed to take an age to tinker around his body and it was still falling as Mike hoisted his body from the inside of the car. There was remarkably little blood.

Mike fumbled around for a moment, picking up magazines and turning the engine over. I left him to it, as I skidded to a halt next to Suzanne, ripping the stitches in my knee and adding my own blood into the mix.

She was not looking her best. The pigment of her skin was pale and clammy, as her body fought to keep up with the blood loss in her thigh.

I was stunned for a second, as I became quickly soaked in Suzanne's scarlet river. As I stared at the tinged blood on my hands, I became aware of the roar of an engine.

Looking up, I was surprised to see that Mike was able to stop in time before bundling over the three bodies that lay in his path.

"Come on, get her in!" he screamed.

"What about Harry?" I found myself asking, completely understanding the look of bewilderment on Mike's face.

"Just get in the car, now! We need to get away from here, this thing should be able to do the trick!"

"I thought you didn't like Renaults?"

"I thought now would be a good time to change my mind!"

38

My head pounded as Mike pushed his foot as far as the pedal would go, crunching his way through the gears and grimacing each and every time the engine called upon him to do it. He still did not seem like much of a convert, but the old Renault was better than anything else we would have been able to get our hands-on.

As the car was thrown side to side, my leg burned all the more, as my brain seemed to disconnect itself and rattle around inside my skull. My limbs were heavy and loose, as if all the excitement had rendered them completely useless. I prayed that Mike's did not end up going the same way.

I cracked my head on the window as we slammed into another uneven patch of road, as I twisted my body to try and look to our rear.

The rear window was completely intact, except for a small, perfectly round hole in the top of the left of the glass, which looked as though it had been put there deliberately. But, the small nine-millimetre round of a German submachine gun was undeniable, and I began to notice various other strike marks and burns where Mike had truly peppered the Renault with all his might.

I kept my gaze on the horizon that seemed to be getting farther and farther away, hoping desperately that another similar dark vehicle did not come screaming over the crest of the road, weapons blazing.

But to my utter astonishment, nothing was forthcoming. Not even so much as a bicycle. It seemed like we were in the clear.

"Mike, no one's on our tail. No one's on our tail…"

I was abruptly overcome with pain and discomfort, so I did not hear Mike's response, if there was one at all. But as I had thoroughly checked our rear, I decided it was probably best if I checked that I was in as good condition.

My knee had opened up even further than it had done when I first injured it, blood pouring all over the cloth interior and seeping into the stitching and fabric of the car for years to come.

Like a fool, I began to run my hands all over my body, pressing down here and there to work out whether or not there was any pain. But, apart from my leg, there was none. I hadn't been hit; I was pretty much fine. I couldn't believe it.

I began to chuckle, a pathetic, crackled attempt, but the relief made none of it seem to matter.

"Mike," I said, like a child that was reporting everything to his mother, "I'm alright. I'm not hit."

"Good," he grunted, his eyes fixed on the road, if you could call it that, ahead.

"Are you alright?"

"Yeah…Little niggle on the back of my right foot, but other than that…"

"There's blood, Mike."

"Don't keep going on about me, old fruit. How's the girl holding up?"

I had, for some reason, avoided looking at her thus far, too scared of what might be expected of me when I did. Half of me was hoping that she was already dead. Any other person probably would have been.

I know that if I had been blown up, shot at and wounded as much as she had been in the last few weeks, then I would have wanted it all to be over as quickly as possible.

But she was stubborn, resolute. Her breathing was weak, but still strong enough to notice her petite frame quivering up and down as she drew in oxygen.

I started doing everything that I felt I was meant to. I felt for her pulse. I checked her breathing, even though I knew that it was weak. I began to wipe away some of the blood.

"There's too much blood."

"Here, use this," Mike said, tossing a piece of fabric into the back of the car. It was an expensive, tender scarf, that I presumed had been owned by one of the previous occupants of the car. Whosever it was, they wouldn't be in the need of a scarf such as this for a long time.

"I'm sorry," I muttered as I tore at her clothing to get a better look at her wounds. I wasn't sure if she could hear me or not, but it made me feel better to reassure her. Her eyes were half-closed, but all I could see was the pale whiteness of her eyeball, even the tiny veins having evaporated as her whole body joined the fight to stay alive.

I pressed down hard on a near-perfect circle that had torn into her flesh, as I felt around the other side of her leg to find an exit wound. There wasn't one. That was good news and bad news.

"No exit wound," I called to Mike.

"Should I be happy about that?"

"Not sure."

Yanking her around like a sack of spuds, I pushed her legs into the side window and lifted them up gently. Manoeuvring myself beneath them I was able to prop her foot on my shoulder, whilst also pulling tight on the scarf to keep the pressure on.

I was trying my utmost to stop the blood from pouring from her body, but the liquid was defiant as it seeped through the tiny fibres of the scarf.

At first, I thought that her moving lips were just an attempt to try and draw some air in, but as a few grunts and groans passed out of her, I realised she was trying to talk.

I bent down towards her, an agonising contortion of my body, trying to work out what she was saying, if anything at all. But my grip slipped on the scarf, causing her face to screw up and a torrent of blood to pour out.

"Save it, Suzanne. Don't say anything."

"What's she saying?"

"I don't know. I can't work it out."

"Well, if she's trying to tell us to get to one of her chums, she can forget it."

"Agreed."

It wasn't so long ago that we were in a startlingly similar predicament, with Suzanne gravely injured while Mike and I tried to figure out a way to keep her, and ourselves alive and safe. That had ended with Suzanne managing to tell us to get to *Charsay*, and to find her now-infamous friend Harry Landes. And if he was the sort of calibre of friend that she had, then her enemies must have been unthinkable.

I tried not to think of Harry, hoping to the highest heaven that he had died before anyone could have reached him. But he was a cockroach, a rodent of the lowest order, and it was always within their beings to survive anything that was thrown at them. They thrived on the hatred of others.

"Hey, Mike."

"Yes?"

"Where are we going?"

He spun the wheel back around, piling his foot to the floor again, as he finished his left-hand turn. It seemed to me that he had some idea of where he was headed, some sort of purpose, but had no idea how he knew these roads so well.

"I don't know. I'm still piecing that bit together. I just don't want it to look like we don't know where we're headed."

"Fair enough," I replied, my heart sinking. I had hoped that he was taking us to some secret rendezvous with the other resistance fighters, but instead, he was coolly working his way through everything that we had been taught in the Highlands.

"Never," the old Scottish voice bellowed, despite only having a handful of students, "dilly-dally. Do not fanny around working out whether to go left or right. Even if you don't know, pretend you do. Look at maps before a meeting, know your route like you know your own mind. You will be locals. Act like them."

It was as I was picturing the old, skinny major that a thought suddenly came to me, a thrill shooting up my spine at my own genius.

"Mike, might I make a suggestion."

"I'm all ears, old fruit."

"Your girl. Reckon she would take us in?"

He chewed it over, annoyed that I had come up with the same idea as him, but not one that was welcome.

"I don't want her embroiled in all of this, Johnny."

He crunched down a gear as he took another turn, cursing the gears as he tried to appear like he knew what he was doing, but I knew the anger was more directed towards me.

I had to press it home.

"She has to be, Mike. What other choice do we have? I'm sorry. But she would at least be able to get a doctor for Suzanne."

"She doesn't need a doctor. She needs a priest."

I looked down at her ashen face, worried that his words had permeated into her mind. If they had, then she showed no outward signs of it, her eyes were gently flickering like the wings of a butterfly.

Her face was peaceful, albeit covered in a smattering of bruises that gave the only bit of colour to her face. Her lips had begun to crack and flake and the areas where her lips still appeared intact, were beginning to tinge with a slight blue colour.

I picked up her hand, intending to hold onto it firmly to let her know that I was still with her, but her fingers seemed weak, as if I was able to simply crush them with the gentlest of touches. Her fingernails were beginning to match her bruises, a deep purple gradually expanding from thumb to little finger.

Her mouth though, refused to stop moving, the groans having grown weaker so that they were nothing more than whispers. But then, I noticed that her tongue was active, slowly, but moving as if trying to form words.

This time, I encouraged her, even a traitorous friend would be able to help us out right now.

"Before I...go," her frail, almost inaudible voice croaked. She breathed in deeply, a rattle in the back of her throat and one that seemed like she would never be able to clear. It took a few moments more before she had conjured up the energy to speak again, by which time the car was beginning to approach another bend.

"My pocket. Left pocket. There is something that...you two should have..."

Her voice, however weak it was, seemed to echo around my mind, as it took far too long for me to realise what it was that she had said.

I burrowed my hand into her pocket, and pulled out a now bloodstained handkerchief, but had once upon a time been a pristine white.

I held it in my palm, letting the fabric separate and reveal what was inside. It was then that I noticed the embroidery on one of the corners of the handkerchief.

AS.

The handkerchief, which now sat sprawled out in my palm, had bundled up a few things together and I wondered how long Suzanne had kept them on her person.

There were two pieces of card, one that seemed quite familiar to me, the other not so much.

One was a small map of Europe, like the one that I had seen Suzanne hurriedly bundling away a few days before, the other a faint sepia-toned picture of what appeared to be the most glorious mountains.

I turned it over. There, in a sprawling hand were four words, that stretched from one side of the card to the other.

The skiing is wonderful.

I looked back at Suzanne, whose flickering eyes still fluttered, but this time with a blood-stained grin to accompany it.

"Alfred. He is alive. He has made it to Switzerland."

My heart gave a little leap, as I looked towards Mike with tears in my eyes. I repeated the words under my breath, over and over, and I felt the car lurch with a sudden renewed purpose as Mike shouted above the elation.

"Well, it's about time you went and joined him, Suzanne!"

The End

Johnny Parker returns in 'Close Quarters' the third book in the Circuit Fortunae series.

Available on Amazon now!

ALSO BY THOMAS WOOD

Gliders over Normandy:

The Silent Invader

All Men are Casualties

As If They Were My Own

The Trench Raiders:

Slaughter Fields

Wavering Warrior

Invisible Frontline

Take Aim

Clouded Judgement

Long Forgotten

Alfie Lewis Thrillers:

The Evader

The Executioner

The Betrayed

Circuit Fortunae:

Don't Look Back

Playing with Fire

Close Quarters

www.ingramcontent.com/pod-product-compliance
Lightning Source LLC
Chambersburg PA
CBHW030558310726
48979CB00003B/481

* 9 7 8 1 9 1 6 4 1 3 8 6 3 *